Melissa Koslin

THE LOST
LIBRARY

The Lost Library
Copyright © 2024 Melissa Koslin
All rights reserved.

ISBN (ebook) 978-1-964636-07-8
(print) 978-1-964636-08-5

Inkspell Publishing
207 Moonglow Circle #101
Murrells Inlet, SC 29576

Edited by Audrey Bobek
Cover Art by Emily's World of Design

I give them eternal life, and they will never perish, and no one will snatch them out of my hand. My Father, who has given them to me, is greater than all, and no one is able to snatch them out of the Father's hand. I and the Father are one.
John 10:28-30

For Ellie.
You will inherit my library someday. I hope it serves you well.

THE LOST LIBRARY

CHAPTER 1

"He asked for you specifically."

"Mr. Cross?" Cali asked. "Why?"

"I don't know, but I'm not risking his wrath." Josephine, Cali's supervisor, motioned for her to follow.

Cali glanced around, as if she could find answers from her tidy desk or the spreadsheets on her computer monitors. Then she stood and followed. Up the elevator to the fiftieth floor and down the hall to the fanciest conference room Cali had ever seen. She'd been working at Cross Enterprises for two years but had never been up to the executive floor before—it was not an area where lowly bookkeepers usually traversed.

Cali had expected more people, but when Mr. Cross' assistant showed them into the room, it was just her and Josephine. They waited for a couple of minutes. Cali assumed the Chief Financial Officer, or maybe someone just beneath him, would be the one to meet with them.

Then Mr. Cross himself walked into the room. He stood on the other side of the conference table from where they were seated.

Cali had seen him in passing, but never up close. His scars looked much worse when he stood there in front of her, not just walking across the lobby. The side of his face was gnarled like an ancient tree. Scars traveled from his eyebrow down his cheek and neck.

His neat dark hair and polished suit seemed to contrast with the stubble on his face. Though she understood why he wouldn't shave every day. It had to be hard with all the gnarled skin. The worst of the scarring obviously didn't grow a beard anymore, but the edges were splotchy and were probably difficult to shave without slicing his skin.

If she looked at the other side of his face, she could see why he'd been such a heartthrob when he'd played in the NFL. He had a strong jawline and angular features. Then he'd joined the Navy SEALs and gone to war. The youthful glow had been replaced by a hard, rough exterior.

He passed a file folder across the table to Josephine. He didn't take a seat, and Cali wondered if she should stand. She followed Josephine's lead and remained seated. Josephine opened the file and read.

Cali had no idea why she was here.

Josephine's eyebrows shot up and disappeared into her curly, graying hair. "You suspect Bob Walsh of stealing?"

"The information I have appears to indicate such," Mr. Cross said.

"That's horrible."

Mr. Cross gave no response, just kept looking at her with that dead stare of his. Pretty much everyone was terrified of Mr. Cross. Cali could understand why, certainly, but she also saw that his eyes weren't full of anger but just kind of nothing. Like something inside him had died. Maybe the lack of anger, the lack of all emotion, was what scared people.

"I'm sorry," Josephine stammered. "Is there something you want my department to do about this? I'm not sure how Property Accounting can help."

Cali was just as confused as Josephine, but she figured they had to be missing something. She'd been here long enough to know Mr. Cross always had a plan and was rarely wrong.

"I know your department has forensic accounting capabilities, Ms. Banks." His gaze flickered to Cali then back to Josephine. "I expect a preliminary report back tomorrow." He turned and walked out of the room.

Cali stared as he walked out.

Could Mr. Cross possibly know about her background, her education? She purposefully kept that to herself. She didn't want to be anything more than a bookkeeper. She was safer that way, less likely to be found.

If Mr. Cross—somehow—knew her background and abilities and wanted her help with something this important, why hadn't he spoken to her? He'd barely acknowledged her existence.

Josephine stood. "Looks like we've been volunteered."

Cali stood as well. "Why me?"

"Who knows. He's famous for doing things his own way. I can *usually* follow his train of thought, but I'm not sure about this one." She gave Cali a weak smile. "Maybe he reads performance reviews and sees you're one of the best team members in my department." She headed for the door.

Cali followed. Alone together in the elevator, Josephine said, "No one hears about this. I'll do what I can to dig into the records and will try to keep you out of it."

"I'd like to help. Try anyway."

Josephine pressed her thin lips together. "I guess you'd better at least take a look, just to make sure we're following his directions." She handed the file folder to Cali, but before letting go of it, she added, "No one else hears anything about this."

Cali nodded. "Yes, ma'am."

After getting off the elevator, Cali went straight to her cubicle and looked through the file. She didn't have a background specifically in forensic accounting, but she understood accounting in general, and that along with her other skills should be enough to make some kind of headway.

But then she paused. She wanted to dig in and get to work. She'd always loved the challenge of numbers, patterns, and deciphering what others had hidden. But *should* she? She couldn't risk being found. The smaller the life she led, the less chance they'd find her.

***

Cali heard heavy footsteps coming down the hall from the elevator. She looked up just in time to see two police officers walking by.

Everyone in the office was peeking over tops of cubicles and out office doors, watching and whispering to each other about what was happening.

Cali knew exactly what was happening.

Josephine had gone upstairs this morning to speak to Mr. Cross. She'd found all the breadcrumbs Cali had left for her to find yesterday—all the evidence that Bob Walsh was stealing from Cross Enterprises.

From across the office, over in the Accounts Payable section, there came a commotion—yelling and sounds of a scuffle.

"They're arresting Bob Walsh," Christine in the cubicle across the aisle from Cali whispered not quietly. "Mary just texted me."

Cali feigned shock. "Wow."

A few minutes later, Bob Walsh was led out in handcuffs.

Josephine came out of her office and got everyone back to work, but the whispers continued all afternoon. Cali was thankful when five o'clock came.

What kept bothering her as she walked home was how in the world had Mr. Cross known she would be helpful in tracking down Bob Walsh's treachery. What did he know about her and how? And most importantly, why?

She walked into her sparse apartment, dumped her

purse on her small kitchen table, and turned on her computer. She typed *Asher Cross* into the internet search bar. The top results were all about his NFL career and Cross Enterprises. She sorted through the NFL stuff first. He'd been a quarterback recruited straight out of high school. Multiple MVP awards and championships, and plenty of records. She also read an article about a time he'd played defense when the first-string defensive end player had been injured. They'd won the game because he was able to stop several plays. She saw the word *legend* many times.

Then she read about how he'd been adored by women. She saw several pictures of how beautiful he'd been. She didn't think his mangled skin was what really changed his appearance so dramatically. It was that look in his eyes, the dead stare. What'd happened to him?

She tried to look up his military record but couldn't find anything. Literally nothing. He was so well known, wouldn't someone want to write *something* about his military career?

Eventually, she gave up and stood to make something for dinner. But she didn't get past opening the refrigerator. Instead, she picked up her purse and headed out the door. Once she started on a puzzle, she'd never been able to let it go.

They weren't expecting her tonight, but she was sure the Gray Hats wouldn't mind her showing up.

It was dark by the time she walked down to the basement apartment. As usual, she carefully watched her surroundings. The neighborhood wasn't the best, and her appearance had always made people think she was an easy target—dainty and innocent, though she did what she could to dispel that assumption. She didn't ever wear makeup and always kept her long, blonde, loosely curly hair in a ponytail. She'd tried to convince herself to chop her hair off many times but had never been able to do it. And she never wore fitted or flashy clothes. Her father had called her a porcelain doll all her life, and she hated it.

She knocked on the door.

A few seconds later, a man opened it. "Fancy what the cat dragged in."

She shifted to come inside.

He didn't move. "What's the password? We gotta be careful not to let the riffraff in."

She pushed Floyd's bony frame out of the way.

He laughed and closed and locked the door. "To what do we owe this pleasure, lovely Lady Lavender?" They'd given her a handle like hackers used. Well, Floyd had given her the handle—due to her pale lavender eyes.

Bl@ze and Mt Dew looked up from their computers set up on tables formed into a square in the middle of what was supposed to be the living room. Floyd was the only one who had told her his real name. At least she was pretty sure it was his real name. But who knew with these guys?

Before she could answer Floyd, he said, "You've come to finally accept my proposal, haven't you? We can elope to Las Vegas and go on a whirlwind tour of the world. Just give me five minutes to pack!"

Mt Dew said, "You're lucky a girly that pretty will even look upon a weed like you."

Floyd held his hand to his slightly concave chest. "I'm wounded."

Bl@ze smiled at Cali. "Anything wrong?"

"No. I actually wanted to see if you could help me with something."

Bl@ze raised his black brows, almost invisible against his very dark skin.

Floyd moved to her side with a flourish. "You've come to the right place, milady."

Mt Dew waved his hand in mock disgust and went to the kitchen.

"What can we help with?" Bl@ze asked.

How to say it without giving too much away? She

trusted these men a lot, but she didn't trust anyone with her past. It was partially to protect them—if they knew too much, they could be targeted. "I need more information about Asher Cross. I'm not asking for anything truly personal, just a little more than what's online."

Mt Dew walked back into the room with another bottle of his favorite soda. He had seven empty bottles on his table already. "*Everything* is online."

Not everything. Cali kept certain information in her head that no one else in the world knew. "Okay, more than what's readily available to normal humans."

"Normal is boring." Mt Dew took a long swig from his green bottle.

Floyd slid into his chair and rolled to his station. He wiggled his fingers in the air and then held them over his keyboard like a great composer about to begin a symphony. "Anything in particular you want to know?"

"Nothing personal," she said again. "Can you find his military records?"

"Pshah. Child's play." Floyd hunkered down in front of his middle screen, and his fingers roamed the keyboard like scuttling bugs.

Mt Dew and Bl@ze also began typing and working their mouses.

"Are you going to ask me why I want to know?" she asked them.

"Nope." Floyd didn't even pause.

Mt Dew took another swig and kept typing.

Bl@ze glanced up at her. "You trust our intentions and motivations when we ask you to decipher things. We trust you in return." He turned back to his keyboard.

Cali sat in the one other chair in the room, the one positioned at the only table with no computer equipment. The chair was a rolling desk chair like theirs, but purple rather than black. Floyd had picked it out, of course.

A few minutes later, they started blurting out information as they read.

"Joined the Navy at twenty-five," Floyd said. "I've heard gossip that he got in the SEALs because of who he is, a publicity stunt by the Navy to get positive press, but nope—he got in on his own."

"Active duty for six years," Bl@ze said. "Deployed a bunch of times. Honorable discharge. Most of his mission details are classified."

"I don't want anything classified," she said. "No national security stuff."

Bl@ze nodded and kept typing.

"Purple Heart, three silver stars, and a Navy Cross." Mt Dew cursed under his breath. "Do you have any idea what you'd have to do to get all of those?"

"Purple Heart is for being wounded in combat, right? What are the others for?"

Bl@ze answered as he read from his screen, "Bravery and exceptional service under fire, bravery in combat."

"Does it say what exactly he did?"

"Not unless you want to dig into classified," Floyd said.

She shook her head. She didn't need to know, but she was dying of curiosity. She worked for an actual, undeniable hero. Then she asked, "So, why doesn't he let anyone know any of this? Everyone is scared of him or hates him."

"The Beast," Floyd said, "has earned his name in other ways, so I've heard."

"Don't call him that." *The Beast* was what the gossip rags called Mr. Cross.

Floyd held his hands up in surrender. "As the lady likes."

"Any indication as to why he left the NFL and joined the Navy?" she asked. "Was his football career waning?"

Mt Dew finally stopped and looked up. "Are you kidding? He's a freaking legend. I think every single fan of football, whether they cheered for his team or not, cried themselves to sleep the day he broke his contract and signed with the Navy. The man could literally play any position on the field. And not just decently, but exceptionally."

"That's impressive?"

Mt Dew stared at her and blinked once slowly.

Floyd laughed. "You've done the impossible. You've made him speechless."

Mt Dew turned to Floyd. "A miracle would be to make you speechless."

Floyd grinned. "God himself would have to clamp a hand over my mouth."

"You'd probably learn how to speak through your nose."

"When did he start his company?" she asked.

They all resumed typing.

"Filed the corporation back when he was twenty, still in the NFL. Started buying properties." Bl@ze raised his brows. "Looks like he spent most of his football earnings on investments—properties, various types of businesses. No wonder he's so rich."

"And powerful," Floyd added. "No one makes a move in real estate in this region without him having a hand in it, one way or another."

"His sister ran the company while he was deployed," Mt Dew said.

"I didn't know he has a sister," she said.

"Had," Floyd said. "She died shortly after he was discharged, several years ago."

Her posture slackened. "What was her name?"

"Rose Watson."

"Not Cross?"

"Different father, apparently." Bl@ze looked up. "Want more on that?"

She shook her head. "I don't want to inhibit anyone's privacy." Although, she really was inhibiting his privacy, wasn't she? He obviously didn't want anyone to know any of this for some reason. But why?

And more importantly, how did he know she had more

skills than she admitted to on her résumé or on the job? Why? And why didn't he speak to her directly about it? She sighed and slumped back in her chair.

"Not getting what you need?" Bl@ze asked.

"I don't think I can get the information I need from a computer."

"Nonsense," Floyd said.

She smiled at his aghast expression. Then she stood. "Thank you guys so much for the help. I better get home."

"Want me to drive you?" Floyd asked.

"No, I'm good." She started for the door. "I need to think, and walking is good for that."

"Sure?"

She paused at the door. "Let me know when you need help decrypting again." She headed out to the hall, up the stairs, and outside to the sidewalk.

She made it several blocks and still no theories came to her. The one thing she was confident about was that Mr. Cross wasn't involved with anyone in her past. If he were, he'd have alerted them long ago. So, how did he know she could do more than the average bookkeeper?

At the sound of someone yelling obscenities, she focused her attention better on her surroundings. A little farther down the block, there was an alley. She jogged in that direction.

Just inside the alley, a man raised his fist and smashed it across a woman's face.

"Hey!" Cali yelled. "Stop."

CHAPTER 2

The man looked back at her. He raised his scruffy brows and grinned.

The raggedy woman he'd been beating ran.

He glanced back at that woman but then turned toward Cali. "Why don't you come on over here?"

"I don't think so." She backed away, keeping her gaze on him and peripherally watching everything else around her.

He lunged and grabbed her purse.

Cali glared. "Back off."

He yanked at her purse, but she had it slung across her body—exactly for this type of circumstance. As he yanked, he pulled her off balance, but she took a step and strengthened her stance, all while continuing to glare at him.

He raised a hand to slap her, but she blocked it. Then she used both hands to shove him away.

A curse slurred from his lips.

He shifted, and she thought he was going to leave, but he came at her.

She blocked a punch and threw a kick at his groin. But she didn't quite connect the kick—his legs were too close together.

As she was pulling her leg back to the ground, he swung his fist again. This time, it connected with her cheek.

Rage filled her like boiling water. She attacked with an elbow across his chin. And then the other elbow, and a kick to the groin. This time, her foot connected.

He stumbled back and fell.

She ran.

She felt guilty for not calling the police and pressing charges, making sure he didn't try mugging someone else. But she couldn't take the risk. Invisibility was her best defense.

She ran the rest of the way home.

When she finally plopped down at her table, she had to focus on calming down. She was usually a calm person, had been a rather placid child. But occasionally, rage would fill her. All the things she was furious about in her life boiled to the surface. The hatred.

Bob Walsh stealing from a good employer, a man beating a defenseless woman, the terrorism the Gray Hats uncovered. Her father, her mother.

She closed her eyes to try to calm down.

Then she slid from the chair down to her knees and bowed her head. *Please.* She rarely prayed in actual sentences. God knew exactly what she meant.

She stayed there for a long time, sending her thoughts and fears and anger up to God. Asking him to help her do better.

Eventually, she started to feel better, more herself. As much herself as she ever felt anymore.

In the morning, she looked in the mirror and realized her face was puffy and bruised from where the mugger had punched her. She was still angry she hadn't defended as effectively as she expected of herself. She'd taken many self-defense classes and had felt comfortable in her skill level. Now she doubted. She tried to remind herself that anyone was likely to get hit in a physical altercation, no matter how well-trained. What mattered was that she'd helped that woman get away and she'd defended herself effectively.

But what if someone more skilled attacked her? Or multiple people attacked at once?

She didn't own makeup, so she stopped at a drug store on the way to work to buy some concealer and powder. Considering she wasn't accustomed to applying it, she felt she did a decent job with just the little mirror on the powder compact. Thankfully, the bruising didn't look to be too bad—it would probably clear up in a couple of days.

At the big office tower owned by Cross Enterprises downtown, she slid into the chair at her cubicle and started working. She hoped to avoid any fuss, but that hope was futile.

"Oh my gosh," Christine said. "What happened?"

Cali sighed inwardly and forced a smile. "Ran into the bathroom doorway in the dark. I am such a klutz."

Christine looked like she wanted to say more, but Cali asked, "Do you need help with your reconciliations?"

Christine hated doing reconciliations, so Cali was able to distract her by agreeing to do some of hers. It also gave Cali a reason to stay at her desk and work through lunch. She just needed to make it through a day or so until the swelling went down.

In the afternoon, she was forced to leave her cubicle to use the restroom. She took a route that avoided the main halls as much as possible.

She was slipping down a row of cubicles when Mr. Cross turned the corner ahead of her.

She paused.

His presence was imposing—his height, his broad shoulders, the way he held himself, but mostly the way his eyes had no expression at all.

His gaze flickered to her, the briefest second, and she

thought she saw something in his eyes, something other than that dead stare. But then he walked past her, didn't speak to her or even acknowledge her existence. Just like the other day.

She continued on to the bathroom and was back at her desk in a few minutes.

At the end of the day, she stayed a little longer than everyone else in order to avoid as much interaction as possible.

The next day was the same, but without any sightings of Mr. Cross. She still felt the need to finish deciphering him but tried to control that urge.

She came home to find her neighbor, Clarence, standing out in the hall directing men going in and out of his apartment.

"Are you moving?" she asked. He'd been there at least ten years, and she'd thought he'd planned to stay indefinitely. He'd retired a few years ago, and the place was decent and affordable.

He smiled brightly. "That house my daughter was hoping to buy, she got it. A real good deal, much better than we thought she'd be able to get. Now she has a room for me."

"That's awesome." Then she added, "But I'll miss you. And your butterscotch cookies."

"You won't miss me. They already have someone moving in, as I hear it. I'm sure it'll be someone much more interesting than an old man who likes to watch Bonanza up so loud all hours of the day." He looked over at the movers. "Careful with that."

She left him to it and went into her apartment.

He was right—someone else moved in the next morning. A younger man. He didn't talk much, but he seemed all right. Military type—he had that kind of haircut and demeanor.

Then her neighbor on the other side moved out two days later. She'd been more of a party girl, so Cali didn't mind her leaving. And someone else moved in the next day, another young woman but much quieter.

Both neighbors moving abruptly like that set her on edge. But then maybe the party girl had planned to move? Cali had never spoken much with her, so she didn't know. It could be just a coincidence, right? But Cali didn't believe in coincidences. Every pattern was explainable. If you just looked hard enough.

She paid close attention to everything around her. Even contemplated picking up and leaving. But if her past were catching up with her, this wasn't how it would go down. It wouldn't be slow and methodical like this.

She usually jogged a few days a week, but now she started doing it daily. She needed to be and feel more prepared, on top of things.

And then lights were installed along the jogging path. It could be the city making improvements, but this didn't seem to fit with the kinds of projects the city usually did. The path wasn't even all that well-used, not enough to warrant much attention and budget dollars.

She asked the Gray Hats to look into it. It was simple for them to find.

The city had not paid to have the lights installed.

So, who had?

She supposed it could possibly be some do-gooder who lived in the area, but it still seemed odd to spend that kind of money on something few people used.

She felt on edge, watching for something else to happen, for any kind of pattern, some indication that any of it was connected.

When Floyd texted one day, she was relieved to have something else to focus on. She went straight there after work.

She sat in her spot in the purple chair and took the drink Mt Dew offered. "What've you got?"

"I think I found something in a chat room." Bl@ze handed her some printouts. They knew she liked to work on paper, not on a screen, and were kind enough to print things out.

She took the papers, pulled out her pencil and dug in.

She went through the chat room conversation over and over. She agreed with Bl@ze that it was probably something more than it seemed on the surface. She just needed to figure out exactly what that was.

Hours passed.

Floyd went to bed, but she stayed. They weren't regular in the hours they kept. Sometimes they worked all night and slept all day, and sometimes, their hours were almost normal. But they never cared how any of the rest of them worked. If they were tired, they slept. If they were hungry, they ate.

Bl@ze and Mt Dew stayed up and chatted about some Bug Bounty work they were doing. That was how they made legitimate money. There were sites that laid out rules of engagement and invited white hat hackers—or gray hat hackers, as the case may be—to dig into certain systems and try to find weaknesses.

"Do you need to work in the morning?"

She vaguely realized Bl@ze was talking to her, but her mind was too deep into the puzzle.

He left her alone. She liked that about them—they understood she wasn't being rude. She couldn't just flit in and out of a cypher.

And finally, she found the pattern.

She decrypted the messages and handed them to Mt Dew—Bl@ze had gone to sleep, his head laid down on the table next to his keyboard. "It's a new type of code," she said. "Might be a new cell forming."

He started reading what she'd written.

She stood and grabbed her purse. Before he could push her to let him walk her home, like he often did, she was out the door.

Maybe it was stupid to walk home alone this late—almost midnight—but she felt the need to prove that she was independent, that she could take care of herself. She *had* to be able to take care of herself. If she occasionally had to fend off a mugger, it would just make her feel all that more prepared if her past ever caught up to her. Plus, she'd been working with the Gray Hats for over a year and hadn't had any trouble before.

But she was still careful. She watched her surroundings and took a different route than usual.

She walked several blocks.

Footsteps behind her.

She glanced back to see a man several yards back, face obscured by a hood.

She kept going.

It could be nothing, just another person out late.

Then another man stepped out from behind a van parked along the curb, the same man as last time. His face was darkly bruised from where she'd struck him with her elbow.

She ignored him and shifted to cross the street.

He jumped into her path. "No, no."

"You should have a doctor look at that bruise," she said. "Looks pretty bad."

He sneered. "You're going to look *pretty bad* here in a few minutes." He called her a derogatory name.

The footsteps behind her moved closer. She'd vaguely hoped that man was not connected to this man, but that hope evaporated when she heard his footsteps stop just behind her.

She evaluated the men, her surroundings, and plotted the best method of escape.

The man behind her spoke. "She might be more valuable if we keep her looking pretty."

And then there was a scuffle from behind her.

She turned to see a third man, bigger than the other two, wearing all black clothes, punch the man with the hood and then slam him to the ground.

She shuffled back, away, still watching, determining

who her enemies were.

The scruffy man from the other night lunged at the new man. The new man's face was in shadow, and he moved so quickly. He barreled a shoulder into the scruffy man's gut and took him down to the sidewalk. The scruffy man struggled, but the other man landed a punch across his cheek. His head lolled, and his body went limp.

The larger man stood, and light from the nearest streetlamp caught his face. His mangled skin.

Mr. Cross.

CHAPTER 3

Mr. Cross barely glanced in her direction, and then he walked across the street and up the sidewalk, hands in the pockets of his black hoodie.

She stared.

She wanted to doubt what she'd seen, that it'd been him. But she knew she'd seen right.

What in the world was going on?

She crossed the street and ran after him.

Up ahead, he turned a corner. By the time she got there, he was gone.

She paused and looked around, but she knew better than to push her luck. She'd avoided being assaulted. Best to count her blessings and hurry home. But she wasn't letting this little incident go.

The next morning, she went straight up to the fiftieth floor.

"Can I get a meeting with Mr. Cross?" Cali asked his secretary, Ruth.

"Name and department please?" The middle-aged woman scrutinized Cali through her red-framed glasses.

"Callista Lebeau. Property Accounting."

"And your position?"

"Bookkeeper."

Ruth blinked once and didn't write anything down. "And what is the purpose of the meeting?"

Cali paused. "I just have something important to discuss with him."

"I'm afraid you'll need to be more specific. Unless Mr. Cross requests the meeting, I can't put something on his schedule unless it needs his specific attention."

In other words, what did a bookkeeper need to speak to the owner of the whole freaking company for? It was a fair question. One Cali couldn't answer. While she was very good at spotting deception, specifically, finding inconsistencies, she was not great at lying herself. After watching what a mess her father had made of his life, she'd decided to be honest at all times. It was a rule she'd had to break over the years, but mostly through omission, not directly lying.

"Can I just leave a message for him?" Cali asked.

"Of course." Ruth picked up her pencil.

"Please just tell him I have something I urgently need to speak to him about."

Ruth looked up at her over her glasses. "That's it?"

"Yes, ma'am. Thank you." Cali headed back downstairs to her cubicle.

She waited the rest of the day, not sure if maybe he'd call her desk phone, summon her upstairs, or maybe send an email. He had to respond in some form, right?

But the end of the day came, and nothing.

On the way out of the building, she spotted him from across the lobby. He was in his usual simple but polished suit. He didn't appear to have been meeting with anyone and walked alone across the expansive black granite lobby.

She jogged to try to catch up with him.

She accidentally bumped a young man in the shoulder. "Sorry," she said and kept going. Thankfully, she always wore ballet flats to work and didn't have to stumble over high heels.

She could have sworn he glanced at her out of the corner of his eye, but he kept going.

She got stuck filtering through a crowd just getting off an elevator. As she finally got through, he disappeared through a door behind the security desk.

One of the guards stood. "May I help you, ma'am?"

She forced a smile. "No, thank you." The guards were notoriously strict—no way would they let some random person into a secure area. She headed outside.

Over the next several days, she caught glimpses of him but always from a distance. And he never responded to her request to speak with him.

As she sat at her desk Friday afternoon, she added up how many times she'd seen him around the building recently and realized the frequency had increased significantly from before. And she didn't think she was just being more alert and noticing him more easily. She tended to notice the people around her as a general rule, and the owner of the whole company tended to be more noticeable and memorable than the average cubicle rider.

Finally, she lost patience and went to see the Gray Hats. They were a little surprised at her request but got her the information she requested.

On Saturday morning, she borrowed Floyd's car and headed outside the city to the address they'd found for her.

She pulled off on the side of a rural highway. Could this be right? There was a drive where her GPS said there would be, but it was just a narrow gravel drive buried in trees. She hadn't been exactly sure what to expect—maybe a gated community or some fancy country house—but certainly not a drive with weeds sprouting through it that looked like it hadn't seen a car in ten years.

But the Gray Hats had never been wrong or led her astray. It took a lot to gain her trust—it was an almost-impossible task—but once a person had it, the trust didn't easily waver.

She turned down the gravel drive.

The lane was narrow and twisted and turned like a serpent. Trees hung low and even brushed the car a few times.

Several minutes passed as she drove deeper and deeper into the woods.

Just as she was about to give up and put the car in reverse, hoping she could navigate back out in reverse, the trees parted. A large house sat in the middle of a clearing barely large enough for the house and circular drive in front of it.

There was no actual yard to speak of. The area in the middle of the circular drive was filled with wildflowers. Trees and various types of vegetation came right up to the house and partially obscured how massive it was. It didn't feel unkempt so much as wild, like the house belonged to the forest.

The house was entirely made of stone that looked like it'd been taken from some European castle. The architecture reminded her of the late 1800s, something a Vanderbilt would've lived in—a steep and complicated roof line, leaded glass windows, and multiple chimneys. At the center of the façade were massive wooden double doors, and to the left of that was a turret that rose three stories to a pointed roof.

She pulled to a stop and stared up at the house. To the left side of the property was a four-bay garage made from similar but slightly different stone than the house. Other than that modern amenity, the place looked like it'd been lost in time.

She got out of the car, almost wondering if she'd fallen into the pages of a fairytale, and walked slowly up to the massive doors. The gravel crunched under her feet, and the breeze ruffled leaves all around. Other than that, there was nothing but silence. She tried to spy any evidence that someone lived here. Over by the garage, she noticed tire tracks in the gravel, but how old were they? There was no wreath or other decoration on the doors, no potted plants on the wide steps, nothing.

To the side of the door, she was surprised to see a modern doorbell. She'd almost expected an old-fashioned pull. Then she realized the doorbell also had a camera in it. She stepped back and glanced around the house again. Hidden inside a rock at the base of the steps was another camera, so tiny, it wasn't noticeable unless you were looking for it. Tucked into second-story window ledges on either side of the door were more cameras. And she spotted security lights hidden in the trees.

Yes, this had to be the right place.

She walked back up the steps, pressed the doorbell, and listened to it clang through the house.

She waited.

Nothing.

She rang the doorbell again, and as the chime bounced around the house, she stepped back and tried to get a look in the nearest window. It was hard to see from this angle, especially since the curtains were only partially open, but it looked unfurnished, or at least sparsely. She started to doubt again if she was at the right place.

As she glanced around, the garage caught her attention, the windows set high in the doors. She walked across the drive. She had to jump but caught a glimpse inside. There was a black sedan and a black sport utility. There were no vehicles in the other bays, but there looked to be a workbench and tools, so maybe cars were never parked there. Or maybe there was, and he simply wasn't home.

One more time, she walked up to the door and rang the bell.

Again, nothing.

She was annoyed. The trouble of borrowing a car and driving out here had been a waste. But mostly, she was annoyed to—again—get no answers. Next time she saw him at work, she may not be so professional. Her general rule in life was to be as invisible as possible, but there was a limit to how much patience she had.

She walked back down the steps to the drive.

Then she caught movement out of the corner of her eye and looked out into the woods to the right of the house. There was something, but it was moving too quickly to get a good look.

Should I get in the car and get out of here?

No, she'd come to get answers, and she would do everything possible to get them.

She watched whatever was out there as it made its way through the woods. And not on a path, but through thick brush, under and around trees, and even sliding down slopes. And not jogging, but full-on running. It wasn't until he was about twenty yards away that she got a good look.

Mr. Cross.

He was wearing nothing but jogging pants and tennis shoes. No shirt.

The scarring traveled down his chest and arm, his side, part of his stomach, and down his hip. He was well-built—she could see he was solid muscle by how flexed everything was as he ran. But it wasn't a model's body. He had a thin layer of chest hair, no waxing or shaving. He was in shape from work, not for vanity's sake.

As he emerged from the trees and through the brush to the gravel drive, he slowed to a walk. His shoulders and chest were broad and thighs strong, but his waist was narrow. He was somehow lanky yet still thick and solid.

For the first time, he looked directly at her. With that dead stare of his.

But there was something else too. He wasn't completely dead inside; there was something there. But she had no idea what it was.

Then he walked past her up the steps.

"Mr. Cross, I need to talk to you."

No response.

"I'm sorry to intrude like this, but it's really important." *Let's see how far nice gets me.* That was usually the best way to approach most people.

He opened the door.

"Mr. Cross."

He walked inside and closed the door with a quiet click.

She jogged up the steps and slammed her hand against the door. "Mr. Cross!"

No response.

She pounded her fist on the door.

The only sound was a bird taking flight from a tree nearby.

She felt the rage rising inside and closed her eyes to calm herself. *Please.*

Then she opened her eyes, took a breath, and opened the door.

Just inside was a two-story entry hall, lined with wood paneling up to a coffered ceiling. Just off that was what was probably supposed to be some kind of grand parlor, but it was unfurnished. To the left, the turret held a massive staircase that spiraled up to an open landing. Across from that was a large room with a crystal chandelier hanging from the ceiling. Again no, furniture, not even a rug covering the old but shiny wood floors.

At the next room, she paused. A library. It was an octagonal room, two stories high with a catwalk around the second story, accessed by a spiral staircase made of intricate wrought iron. Bookshelves covered every wall except where windows stretched across the outside wall. This room was furnished. There was a desk and a few wingback chairs. And books. Everywhere books. Every single shelf was full, and several also lay on tables and on the desk. She'd never seen a more beautiful room.

The sound of Mr. Cross' voice drew her attention away. It was quiet, sounding to come from just down the hall. She couldn't hear what he said, but it was definitely his deep voice.

She continued down the hall and came to a kitchen. It was an interesting combination of old and new. The cabinets looked to have been hewn from the same old, polished wood as the walls and the bookshelves, but the countertops and backsplash were white quartz, clean and glistening smooth.

Standing at the island, Mr. Cross was petting a cat.

His rough hand was gentle on the cat's fluffy fur. It had stripes like a tabby but was fluffy like a Persian. The cat purred as it strutted back and forth in front of him.

"Mr. Cross." She expected some kind of answer this time, probably anger.

He gave no reaction.

She moved farther into the room and stood at the other side of the island, facing him. "Why were you there the other night? In that neighborhood when I was walking home."

No response.

"I'm not going away."

He turned, took a bowl from the cabinet, and filled it with water from the battered farmhouse sink in the island. Then he set it down in front of the cat. The cat started lapping up the fresh water.

"You're hiding, correct?"

It took Cali a second to realize he was speaking to her, not the cat.

He finally looked at her. "I'm not stopping you. You're welcome to stay at the company." His tone was level and manner direct, but not unkind. As if he'd had many conversations with her, as if he hadn't completely ignored her at every turn.

She paused. She needed answers, and she finally had his attention, however fleeting it might be. She had to handle this just right. "Do you know why I'm hiding?"

"No."

"Is that the truth?"

"I won't lie to you."

"But you'll ignore my existence."

He made direct eye contact. "No." His gaze seemed to bore into her, but not in an aggressive way. As if he knew all her secrets.

Then he turned and walked up the stairs at the back of the kitchen.

The cat jumped down and scurried across the room to follow, still purring.

CHAPTER 4

"What were you thinking?" Mr. Cross' voice roared down the hall. Cali guessed he was in the executive conference room, but the entire floor could hear him.

Cali paused. She'd come upstairs to try to force him to talk to her. On Saturday, she hadn't followed him up the stairs, and he hadn't come back down. She hadn't been quite brave enough to not only enter his house uninvited but also follow him up the stairs. She could be brazen, and even flat-out rude if needed, but even she had her limits. The man was her boss, after all.

She veered over to a nearby cubicle and asked the occupant, a young woman with very curly red hair, "What's going on?"

She pursed her lips with attitude. "Who knows? It's Mr. Cross."

"Does he yell like that a lot?" Maybe if she understood a little more about the man, that would help.

"Sometimes."

"About what?"

She shrugged. "Above my paygrade."

The young man in the cubicle behind her pushed his chair closer. "I heard someone put in an offer on a property on behalf of the company without consulting Mr. Cross first."

Cali sucked in a breath. "That doesn't seem smart. Was it at least a reasonable offer on a property that would be good for the company?"

"About a hundred thousand over market value."

The redhead had turned back to her computer, but said in a sing-song voice, "Someone's gettin' fired."

Cali asked, "Does he fire people a lot? I'm down in Property Accounting—I haven't seen a lot of terminations."

"I haven't seen a lot either," the young man said.

"Does he yell a lot?"

He shook his head. "It's when it gets really quiet that you need to worry."

"What do you mean?"

"Every time it gets really quiet in a meeting with Mr. Cross, the people come out looking all drained of color. They don't talk or even look at anyone on the way by, just get out of there."

"What do you think is happening when it gets quiet?" Like it was right now all of a sudden.

"Ritual sacrifices." The redhead still faced her computer screen.

"I don't think he's all that bad," the young man said. "Pay is fair, and the benefits are really good."

The redhead looked over her shoulder. "HR decides all that, not Mr. Cross."

"But you know he approves everything that happens in this company."

She pursed her lips and turned back to her computer.

"You don't like him?" Cali asked her quietly.

"You see what everyone says. *The Beast*. There's always at least some truth mixed in."

Cali wasn't sure if she agreed with there *always* being truth mixed in. "Why do they call him that, anyway?"

She raised her brows. "Have you never seen him?"

"His scars, you mean? Didn't he serve in the military?"

"I heard he didn't do a lot of *serving*. Well, more like serving himself. You don't get that rich from being in the Navy."

"What do you mean?"

The young man jumped in. "That's all just gossip rag stuff."

"He's a billionaire—with a big ol' capital B. Truth to everythiiiing." She finished in the same sing-song voice, then swung back around in her chair to face her computer.

Cali decided chatting with people might be more helpful than trying, yet again, to get Mr. Cross to tell her what was going on, so she headed to the breakroom for the fiftieth floor. A few people who'd probably taken a late lunch were still lingering. Cali grabbed a drink from the soda fountain, struck up a casual conversation, and waited for an opening.

A pudgy middle-aged man in slacks and a short-sleeve button-down was saying, "My time off got approved. The wife's happy."

"So, do you like working here?" Cali asked.

"Depends on what day you ask."

She smiled a little and waited for him to clarify.

A woman with long gray hair pulled back in a braid sat down at the table. "Policies and pay are fair. That's enough for me."

"That's because you don't have to have meetings with Mr. Cross."

"You go in with your team. You don't even have to talk. What could be so bad?"

"You don't have to sit there with the pressure of his stare on you."

Cali could understand that. She'd seen enough in her life that his demeanor, that harsh gaze and the way he held himself like a brick wall, didn't get to her. But she saw how it might make the average person excessively nervous.

"I always feel like he's about to punch me in the face if

I use the wrong word," the man said.

"He's not going to punch anyone in the face," the woman scoffed. "That'd be an HR and legal nightmare. He's *way* too smart for that. If he wants you scared, he'll whisper real quiet, so no one but you can hear."

Cali swore the man shuddered.

"You think he's smart, then?" Cali asked.

"I think he's a whole lot smarter than anyone on the outside gives him credit for," the woman said. "A lot of people think he's just some dumb football player with too much money from getting his head bashed in."

"Getting his head bashed in?" the man said. "He did the bashing, not the other way around."

"Even so, people seem to think he's not that smart."

"But you disagree," Cali said.

"Let's just say I've been watching how he directs this company for years, and he's *never* made a bad turn. Got us through a recession leaps and bounds ahead of the competition. This place is in solid hands. And that means my job is solid as long as I perform well."

"Yeah, he's smart," the man said. "But ruthless. Did you hear about the Baker deal? The seller didn't give him the price he wanted, so he had his construction group jack up pricing on all their projects until they complied."

"I heard the price Baker wanted was outrageous. Maybe he's a little aggressive, but he's also not a doormat."

The man leaned closer, elbow on the table. "So why all the security? This place is Fort Knox. What's up with that?"

Cali had noticed that as well. There were two armed guards in the lobby and a guard at each floor, as well as cameras and a sophisticated badge system. It was something that had drawn her to this particular job—she felt safe inside this building and could properly focus.

"He's a celebrity," the woman said. "I, for one, appreciate that we don't have to deal with a media circus every time we come to work."

"Maybe if he stayed out of the headlines, he wouldn't have to worry about any of that."

"Maybe if the gossip vultures left the poor man in peace, it wouldn't be an issue."

"Are you really defending him like he's an innocent?"

Cali jumped in. "What kind of gossip?"

"Anything and everything," the woman said.

"First of all, he sleeps around," the man said.

"No one has ever won a paternity suit."

"I have one word as a response: *Billionaire*."

"Not every woman is so easily paid off."

"Apparently, he chooses wisely."

Cali wasn't so sure about any of that. He didn't live like a playboy—or at least his house certainly wasn't set up for the life of a playboy. Almost no furniture, and the room that did have furniture was filled to the ceiling with books. She'd guess Unabomber before she'd guess playboy.

She needed to get back to work, so she told them goodbye and headed down the hall.

On the way to the elevator, she caught a glimpse of Mr. Cross. She almost turned and walked toward him, but he disappeared around a corner.

After getting off the elevator, she walked to her desk.

Maybe she needed to look at things more like that man in the breakroom. Maybe Mr. Cross suspected her of something—like stealing. But the way he did business, from what she'd seen, was direct. And she wasn't high up like Bob Walsh had been. She was so low that if he suspected something nefarious on her part, it would be easier just to let her go and hire another of a thousand bookkeepers. And he definitely wouldn't have brought her in with Josephine on that Bob Walsh meeting if he thought she wasn't trustworthy.

She got to work but kept rolling everything around in the back of her head.

When she walked to the Gray Hats that evening, she watched for Mr. Cross, half-expecting him to be standing around every corner.

But she didn't see anything. Fewer people than usual, actually.

The Gray Hats had more deciphering for her—it appeared to be from the same group as last time. The code they used was similar, so she was able to crack it much more quickly—a bunch of chatting about shipping methods. They said the last bit she'd decrypted they'd sent to the NSA, but no action was being taken—she didn't ask *how* they knew no action was being taken inside the NSA. She suspected the group might be dangerous, so it annoyed her the NSA wasn't acting. But there was nothing she could do about it and so started her walk home.

She continued to watch her surroundings extra closely.

She paused when she spotted a Latino man sitting on a bus stop bench. He didn't look out of place, quite the contrary—he wore simple jeans and a jacket similar to most of the neighborhood inhabitants. But she'd seen him earlier, on her way to see the Gray Hats. Maybe he lived in the area? But then she remembered the buses didn't run past six o'clock in this neighborhood. It was now past seven. If he lived in the area, he'd know that.

He glanced over at her and then away.

Something wasn't right.

She kept walking, rather than tip him off.

Maybe someone was watching the Gray Hats? That idea made her nervous. She knew a lot of what they did wasn't totally legal, but they'd stopped at least two terrorist attacks that she knew of. And they were good people. She would not let them be hurt.

Determination burned.

The next evening, she borrowed Floyd's car again and headed back out to Mr. Cross' house buried in the woods.

The sun was fading by the time she pulled to a stop in his drive. The place was just as peaceful as it'd been last time, like it was a world unto itself.

She rang the doorbell.

No response. As she'd expected.

She tried the door handle, an intricate piece of black hardware. It was unlocked.

She cracked the door and called out, "Hello?"

Nothing.

She opened the door a few inches more. "Hello?"

The same cat as last time turned the corner and walked up to the door. It stared up at Cali and then looked past her outside. Rather than let the cat out, Cali slipped inside and closed the door.

The cat sat down and stared up at her with annoyed amber eyes. Cali wasn't sure if the cat was waiting to be pet or to attack her if she moved any farther.

She called out, "Mr. Cross?"

Her voice echoed, and then silence filled the house once again.

"The door was unlocked," she called, "I know you're home." Both of his cars were in the garage.

Several more seconds of silence.

And then his voice: "Willow."

The cat stood and ran down the hall. Apparently, the cat's name was Willow, though he hadn't sounded like he was calling a cat. He'd used the same level tone he used with everyone else.

He obviously wasn't far away so he had to have heard her calling him. On the plus side, he wasn't yelling at her like she'd heard him yelling in the office yesterday. That had to be positive, right?

Or maybe he was calmly calling the police.

She walked down the hall, the same direction Willow had run.

She found him in the massive library. He was sitting at the desk reading a very thick document. Willow lay sprawled out on the corner of the desk purring and lazily curling her fluffy tail.

"Mr. Cross?" She tried for a polite tone, tried to mask her frustration and annoyance.

He flipped a page on the document and continued reading.

She walked into the room and stood in front of the desk. "Okay, I'm just gonna lay it all out. No more treading lightly. You know more than you're letting on. You knew I'd be able to help with the Bob Walsh thing, although there's nothing on my résumé or in my work that would indicate that. Not even Josephine had any idea I'd be able to help. I've seen you more at the office recently, about a seventy-five percent increase. And I need to know what you were doing in that neighborhood the other night. How did you—of all people—just happen across one of your employees in some random neighborhood? A neighborhood that is definitely not stomping grounds for billionaires. And why in the world do you refuse to speak to me?"

He continued to look at the document, though his gaze was no longer focused on it and he'd stopped turning pages.

Finally, he looked up at her with that dead stare of his. She braced herself to be deafened by his booming roar. And to be fired—definitely fired.

He sat back in his chair and crossed his arms over his broad chest. He was wearing a plain gray t-shirt, and as he crossed his arms, his biceps flexed and stretched the fabric. He had a few days of dark beard growth as usual, and his hair was ruffled, as if he'd pulled his hand through it several times. The dying sun streamed through the windows and highlighted the gnarled skin on the side of his face and down his neck and arm. She noticed for the first time how mangled his right hand was—it looked even worse than the rest of him. She wondered if he could even move all of his fingers.

But at the same time, she found his scarring oddly beautiful. Like an ancient gnarled tree. She assumed whatever had happened to him had been during combat, and that was how he'd gotten his Purple Heart. She really wanted to dislike him, but she respected him too much.

Finally, he said, "You do realize I employ over a thousand people. I do run into employees outside of the office from time to time."

"But what were you doing in *that* neighborhood?"

"I fail to see how that's your business."

She wanted to growl. He was just as infuriating when he talked as he was when he ignored her. "What about the rest?"

"I also fail to see how my comings and goings around the office, in a building I own, is any of your business."

"How did you know I'd be able to help with the Bob Walsh thing?"

He hesitated. "I didn't. I thought Ms. Banks might like to have some assistance, and you seem to be her top performer."

"She told me you'd asked for my input specifically."

"She must have been confused."

"You and I both know Josephine is not the confused type."

He raised his chin and seemed to pin her in place with his assessing gaze. Several seconds passed. "Josephine Banks is exceptional."

"I agree. But you and I also both know she's not a forensic accountant."

"She admitted as much."

"Are we going to keep turning in circles, or are you going to actually answer questions?"

"What have I been doing the last few minutes?" Then he added, "In my private home. Uninvited."

She took a slow breath and silently said goodbye to her job. "I'm not stupid, and I'm not crazy."

"I would certainly never insinuate you're anything less than highly intelligent."

"Then you must think I'm crazy if you think I'm going to quietly accept any of this bull. I've quietly accepted far more than my fair share in my life, and I'm done."

He uncrossed his arms and sat straight.

This is it—I'm fired.

But instead of yelling, he shifted his gaze to the side, toward the windows. "I'm sorry, Cali."

She felt like she might melt to the floor. Maybe from shock, maybe from relief he wasn't screaming at her. Or maybe from how he said her name. His tone was just as strong as usual, but there was a gentleness in the way he quieted slightly.

Her hand shook, and she clenched her fist to get it to stop, so it wouldn't betray her.

His gaze flickered to her fist. He stood and walked across the room. At the door, he paused and turned his head only halfway, didn't look at her. "Please don't come back." He walked away.

Willow jumped down off the desk and followed.

Cali stared after him. She had no idea what had just happened.

***

Asher stood at the window of his bedroom, watching the front drive below.

Willow rubbed at his legs. She always seemed to know when something wasn't right. Nothing was right.

It took a few minutes, but Cali finally walked out and across the drive to the car she'd driven.

Then she sat in the car for several more minutes. Surely furious.

And he didn't blame her.

He knew he'd gotten too close. But he certainly wasn't about to back off.

CHAPTER 5

Cali reviewed everything over and over and over. Usually, she could eventually find the solution. But it was not coming clear this time. Asher Cross may just be the enigma to finally stump her.

She didn't think he had anything to do with those trying to find her—too many details didn't align. He was rude to her, but he'd also saved her from those men the other night. She felt comfortable concluding that he was a good man, underneath it all.

But that was about it—the rest was a garbled mess.

She managed to get a decent amount of work done and left just after five o'clock. She walked down the sidewalk. Sometimes, she wished she had a car, but she lived as small and lean as possible, kept money fluid and her options open.

She took a breath, and her shoulders sagged. She was tired. Usually, she could focus on the here and now, on living a good life. But sometimes she really wanted a future, to be able to make plans, do something more with her life than merely survive.

She straightened her back and tried to push those thoughts away.

When she came to a window display, she paused to look inside. It was a fancy department store. Sometimes there were beautiful clothes in the window, sometimes jewelry, sometimes handbags. She'd never gone into the store, but she liked to look at the displays. Today, a female mannequin donned a long white trench coat made of fabric that looked like milk and a necklace with a pearl teardrop pendant.

Someone walked up beside her. "Hello, Callista."

She didn't turn. She knew exactly who it was. Michael Dinetti. Her mind sped into overdrive—how to handle him, and also how to get away. She continued to remain facing the window display, but she used the reflection of the glass to survey her surroundings. No police within view, though she would never go to the police anyway. This man had blackmailed officers before by threatening their families, had even killed those family members when the officer didn't comply. She would not do that to anyone again; she had enough blood on her hands. She'd accepted long ago that she was alone.

There were plenty of people walking by on the sidewalk, so he probably wouldn't snatch her up right here. Probably. She posited that he didn't know where she lived, or else he would have waited for her there, a more private and controlled environment. The probability that he knew where she worked, less than a block away from this spot, was high. Had Mr. Cross been involved in revealing her location? He'd figured out she was hiding from someone—perhaps it'd taken him time to find who that was and strike a deal to provide her location.

But he had her home address in her employee file. No, if he'd been involved, he would have provided that address. He wouldn't have wanted one of his employees attacked so close to his building—the press could be bad for the company and for him. He was smarter than that.

Behind her at the curb, a black Mercedes sedan pulled to a stop, and a man stood from the front passenger side and stood by the back passenger door.

"What was it your father always calls you?" Michael said. "A porcelain doll." He touched his fingertip to her chin. "I can see why."

She lifted her chin away but kept her gaze focused on the window in front of her. "I'm not his, which means he had no right to barter me away. I don't belong to anyone."

"The money your father owes tells a different story."

"In case you missed that history lesson, slavery was outlawed over a hundred and fifty years ago."

She watched in the window's reflection as he scrunched his face. "We'll just call it indentured servitude."

"That would involve standards of behavior and a preset ending to the contract." She looked at him with a cold gaze. "Are you saying you've agreed to anything like that?"

"It's an agreement among friends. We don't need so many rules." He grinned, and his pearly teeth gleamed against his tan skin. His dark hair was perfect as usual, his shave fresh, and his long black trench opened to a pressed white dress shirt and black slacks. He looked like a polished businessman, rather than the sociopath he was.

"Funny how sometimes you like rules and other times they're not needed." If the rules benefited him, then he was suddenly a man of honor just looking to uphold integrity and fairness. If the rules didn't benefit him, they were antiquated and he was a trailblazer.

"Funny how things work out, isn't it?" Then he added, "Why don't we go get a bite to eat and catch up?"

She simply glared at him—still calculating options.

He smiled that pretty smile. When they'd first met, he'd tried to charm her with his good looks, but she wasn't one of the flighty, idiotic women he usually preferred to surround himself with.

She determined her best option at this moment was to continue to stand right here. If he wanted her to go anywhere, he'd have to force her. But she had limited time. The people coming and going would thin out as all the nearby offices emptied.

He and his men could force her to get in that Mercedes. She'd trained in self-defense and kept herself in good shape, but she was intelligent enough to realize these three capable men could overpower her. Unless she did something to tip the scales.

She kept a handgun in her purse, but she would not draw it with all these innocent people around, and she knew Michael and his thugs were armed as well.

Some kind of distraction had the best possibility of helping her get the desired outcome. But it had to be done right. If she simply started swinging, Michael would grab her and stuff her in the Mercedes. He would surely prefer to keep this lowkey, but he was not afraid to do whatever he needed to do to get what he wanted. She needed a distraction that would create some distance between her and him, give her a chance to run. She knew the area well, knew several places where she could disappear quickly. She just had to get to them.

Peripherally, she noticed another black sedan pull up to the curb directly in front of the Mercedes, this one a Lincoln Continental.

No, it couldn't be...

Mr. Cross stood from the driver's seat and calmly walked toward her.

Michael glanced at him and then at his man standing by his car. Mr. Cross had parked so closely to the Mercedes that it was blocked in.

Mr. Cross stood directly in front of Michael, so close the difference in their heights was accentuated. Michael wasn't short, but everyone seemed smaller when standing that close to Mr. Cross.

In his usual, direct tone, Mr. Cross said to Michael, "I'll be escorting her from here. Thank you for making sure she was *safe*." He emphasized the last word, as if to say she was now *safe* from the likes of him.

She wasn't sure what was going on. This could be the

means of escape she needed, but she did not want to get Mr. Cross involved.

Michael lifted his chin. "Ah, *The Beast* who employs my friend here."

If he expected a reaction from the use of that name, he didn't get it. Mr. Cross did nothing but keep his dead stare leveled at him.

To his credit, Michael met his gaze, not the easiest thing to do. But then his eyes flickered over to his car and his men.

Mr. Cross kept his gaze pinned on Michael, but also held his hand out to Cali.

Cali hesitated. A part of her would rather die a brave death right here on this sidewalk than involve Mr. Cross. A truly good man.

"I will not be stopped." Mr. Cross said it to Michael. But he also slightly moved his fingers, and Cali understood—he wouldn't leave her here.

She set her fingers in his palm. The smooth and yet rumpled texture of his hand was oddly comforting. He gripped her hand, and she felt the difference in pressure. His index finger and thumb felt stronger, and the other fingers barely gripped. As she suspected, he had limited use of this hand.

Michael glanced at their hands and then smiled up at Mr. Cross, though the pretty smile was now tight at the corners. "Why don't you come along? We were just about to grab a bite to eat and catch up. It's been ages since I've seen my dear friend Callista."

Mr. Cross leaned closer. His voice was low, barely audible, but the rough growl of it definitely conveyed the threat. "Do not follow." He started toward his car, holding her hand, and she followed.

He opened the passenger door of his Lincoln and murmured to her, "Don't look back."

There wasn't much choice but to trust him at this point. She sat, he closed the car door, and she looked out the windshield as he walked around the front of the car. Without moving her head, she glanced at the side mirror— she saw Michael's thug standing by the Mercedes, staring at Mr. Cross.

Mr. Cross sat in the driver's seat, started the car, and pulled out into traffic. He watched the rearview mirror almost more than he watched the road in front of him.

Cali watched the side mirror. Michael returned to the Mercedes, but they didn't chase Mr. Cross' Lincoln.

"Why did you do that?" Cali demanded.

No response.

"He knows who you are," she said. "He's going to come after you."

He made a turn.

"Answer me."

Finally, he said, "The answer is obvious."

She let out an annoyed breath. He was a good man who had the ability to help someone. Of course, he'd stepped in. She was so furious that her past had reached out and snagged someone else.

Rage burned through her.

She rested her head back on the seat and closed her eyes, tried to send all her anger up to God. God could handle it, knew what to do with it.

She didn't feel the usual calm start to ease over her.

Barely a whisper, she said, "Please."

Her thoughts started to clear. She could push the anger away enough to be able to think properly. Her best asset was her mind—she had to keep it clear.

She kept her eyes closed a little longer, making sure her head was straight.

Then she opened her eyes and glanced around. "Where are we?"

"Almost there."

"Where is 'there'?"

"The safest place in the city."

"For a man who is usually extremely direct—downright

harsh, a lot of people would say—you don't ever give me very clear answers."

No response.

She calmed her voice. "Please."

His lips parted slightly, and he took a slow breath. His voice wasn't as hard as usual. "I'm taking you to my house. You'll be safe there until we figure out how to handle this."

"But he recognized you. He'll know where to look."

"I own thousands of houses, all through various corporations. I don't even receive mail there—it all goes to the office. I've purposely made it so no one knows where I live."

Which made sense given how famous he was. And how disliked. And having worked for him, she understood the corporate structures he used—not the easiest to dig through. She was impressed the Gray Hats had found the address somehow.

She looked out the side window. She could not draw him into this any further, but he'd already gotten Michael's attention. How was she going to keep him out of it? While he drove, she formulated possible plans of action.

He turned off the road onto his secluded gravel drive, and a few minutes later, he pulled into his garage.

She got out of the car and walked out onto the driveway but did not move toward the house.

He stood in front of her, but several feet away, unlike how he'd faced down Michael.

"I have to leave," she said. She'd come to the conclusion that the best, the only, thing she could do to protect him was to leave. Michael would hesitate to attack someone as powerful as Mr. Cross, so once he found that Mr. Cross didn't know where she'd gone, Michael would leave him alone.

"And where do you plan to go?" He was back to his usual direct tone.

"I'll pick a random city and disappear. Like I always

do."

He paused. "How long have you been hiding?"

"A long time." She didn't like to put an actual number to it. She didn't like to put numbers to unpleasant things in general if she could help it. Numbers were too beautiful to be tarnished like that.

"Who were those men? Organized crime by the looks of them, but who exactly?"

She started walking around him and toward the long drive. Away from him.

CHAPTER 6

Cali passed Mr. Cross and started up the long drive. She needed to get to an ATM and pull cash—she tried to think of where the closest ATM was. Then she needed to decide on some kind of transportation. As for the city she would go to next, it didn't really matter.

Mr. Cross walked ahead and stood in her path. "You're safer here."

"I'm safer away from Michael Dinetti."

"You do realize who I am." Then he added more quietly, "You're safer with me."

She didn't doubt that she was safe with him. She was always fighting back fear. She made herself do things that scared her to try to desensitize herself, but it never fully worked. She was still afraid most of the time. It had been nice to work at Cross Enterprises—it was the first place she'd ever felt safe. And it wasn't only because of the building security. She knew Mr. Cross was powerful, and even though he didn't know her from Adam, it had always been comforting to be in his circle, even being on the very outer band of that circle. She took a breath. "I already have blood on my hands. I won't tolerate anyone being in danger because of me."

He moved closer. "I have resources. Connections."

She shook her head.

He moved even closer, now just in front of her, though he didn't feel so intimidating, domineering, as when he'd stood so close to Michael. He met her gaze. "Let me help you."

She started to shake her head.

"I'll go after him myself. Michael Dinetti, you said. I'll dig into him, find weaknesses, exploit them. I'll destroy him." He added in a low, dangerous voice, "You have no idea what I'm capable of."

"Please don't." Mr. Cross was the first person she'd ever met whom she thought had a chance of taking on Michael Dinetti. But even if he succeeded, he would not get out unscathed.

"Stay, and we'll figure it out together."

"No."

"I'll go after him anyway. And I'll be distracted watching for you."

She hesitated.

"You deserve to live your life, Cali."

She felt her expression strain. Maybe from the stress, or maybe from how he said her name. But she didn't cry. She hadn't allowed herself to cry in years.

He took her hand in his, and she didn't fight as he led her to the front door of his house. His hand was warm, strong. Comforting. She wanted to grip tighter but restrained herself.

He pulled keys from his pocket, unlocked the door, and led her inside.

"You should eat, and we'll talk." He led her down the hall to the kitchen.

Willow was sitting on the counter, as if waiting for him.

He let go of her hand, and she squeezed her fist, trying to hold onto the warmth and comfort. She sat on one of the stools at the island.

After he draped his suit jacket on the back of one of

the chairs that surrounded the table on the side of the room, he came over and looked in the refrigerator and then a cabinet.

"You're not used to having guests." She'd tried to say it in a teasing tone, but it didn't quite come out that way.

He looked over at her. "No one else has ever even seen the inside of this house since I've owned it."

She was thankful he was speaking to her. She didn't have the strength to try to force him to communicate. "Just you and Willow." Then she thought about it—no cleaning service or maintenance service of any kind? He did everything himself?

He opened a different cabinet. She liked the slight creaking sound the antique and solid cabinet doors made. This house had a soul.

"I don't have much," he said.

"I spied some oatmeal in that cabinet."

"I intended to provide you something better than that."

"You don't know me very well—most of my meals aren't even hot. Oatmeal sounds great."

He pulled out a couple of packets of oatmeal and took bowls out of another cabinet. Since the cabinets were obviously original to the house and the house was definitely older than microwave technology, there was no built-in microwave. It sat on the expansive countertop. He put the first bowl in, and about a minute later, he set it in front of her along with a spoon.

"I didn't think today would end with Mr. Cross serving me dinner in his kitchen."

He put the next bowl in the microwave. "How did you think it would end?"

She shrugged. "Read for a while. Go to sleep." She scooped a spoon of oatmeal and lightly blew on it.

"Sounds like most of my evenings." He faced the microwave and waited for the timer to count down.

Willow lay sprawled out on the end of the counter. Cali had always wanted a pet. As a child, she hadn't been good with people; animals were always easier. Her father had never allowed pets, and now, she thought it unfair to subject an animal to her life.

She swallowed a bite of oatmeal—it was nice to have a hot meal. "I didn't see you as a cat person."

He stayed facing the microwave. Or maybe he was looking out the window to the front drive. After a few seconds, Cali assumed he was done responding. *Back to being ignored.* She took another bite.

Then, still turned away, he said, "She came with the house."

"How does a cat come with a house?"

"The previous owner had lived here something like seventy years. She had no children, so distant relatives inherited and then sold the house. As I understand it, they sold everything in the house that they could and then dumped the cat outside to let her fend for herself."

"That's horrible. How'd you figure out the cat was the old woman's?"

"They'd left a bunch of photographs in the house—not valuable enough to sell, I assume—and Willow was in a few of the pictures. One of them was marked with her name, and when she responded to the name, I realized it was the same cat that kept skulking around outside."

"And you let her come back inside and live with you."

He was still turned away. "It seemed like the right thing." He paused for several seconds. "I like to think it makes the old woman happy to see Willow taken care of."

"I believe it does." This whole conversation was surreal. But she felt calmer.

The microwave dinged, and he took the bowl out. He remained facing the window as he ate. She could see his limited dexterity in how he held his spoon.

Several minutes passed. He remained turned away, even when he finished his meal.

Cali sat there. She should feel awkward, or maybe even annoyed at the silence. But it was oddly nice. She didn't feel like he was ignoring her existence anymore, more like he was used to silence at home. She understood that.

Then Willow got up and cautiously came over to her. She hesitated to move closer than arm's length and sniffed.

Cali held her hand out, palm up, and let Willow smell her.

It took a little time, but then Willow moved slowly closer. Cali lightly stroked her fluffy coat.

But then she stopped and set her hands in her lap. She didn't like to let herself get attached to anyone too much, even animals. All relationships were temporary—she had to remember that.

Finally, Mr. Cross turned around. "Now that you've had a few minutes, will you tell me what's going on?"

She'd known this was coming, but it was still hard. She made it through each day by pretending she was normal. That was the only way she could blend in. It was nice sometimes. If she pretended hard enough to be happy, she could almost believe she was.

"Start with one detail at a time," Mr. Cross said. "I know there's a lot."

She tilted her head.

"You look a little overwhelmed. Cali Lebeau does not get overwhelmed."

How would he know that?

"Who is Michael Dinetti?" he asked.

Focus on one thing at a time, she told herself. "He's the leader of an organized crime family in Chicago."

"You're from Chicago?"

She nodded. Then she took a deep breath and dove in. "I grew up with my father."

"No mother?"

"No. My father owned a shipping company at one point, but that was a long time ago. He's had a gambling problem since I was a small child."

Mr. Cross lifted his chin in understanding.

"Exactly," she said. "My father got into debt with

Michael Dinetti. It'd been a cycle for years. He'd get massively in debt. Get out. And get right back in."

"How'd he get out of debt?"

She sighed, and her posture slouched.

"You helped him? Based on your skills… Figuring odds? Counting cards?"

She lowered her brows. "How'd you figure that out?" And how did he know about her particular skillset?

"Why is Michael after you?"

She paused, deciding how much to push. But then she decided to answer his questions. She'd get her answers eventually. Right now, she owed him this much for what he'd done for her. She'd be a prisoner right now if not for him. "Several years ago, I stopped helping my father. I tried to convince him to get treatment for gambling addiction and told him I would not help him again. I finally realized I wasn't really helping him. I was simply enabling destructive behavior."

Mr. Cross waited, no sympathy on his face, but not quite that dead stare either.

"He got into massive debt again. Of course," she said.

"And you refused to help him?"

"He was angry. He said the most horrible things…" She pushed those memories to the back of her head. "I thought if he finally hit rock bottom, maybe that would wake him up."

"He wasn't ready to change?"

"I've accepted he'll never be ready to change."

"What did he do?"

This part was the hardest to admit. She'd always felt her father did truly love her, no matter what he'd done in the past. But she'd had to finally accept who he was. Perhaps he'd once been a good man, and she knew he could be redeemed if he ever found God, but she had to accept that he loved gambling more than her. Probably always had.

"Cali, what did he do?"

"He sold me."

"What do you mean he *sold* you?"

"He explained to Michael what I'd done so many times to get him out of debt. That was valuable enough to get him out of debt and then some."

Mr. Cross straightened to his full height, well over six feet. He seemed to tower over her. His voice lowered, more of a growl. "Michael Dinetti thinks he *owns* you?"

She nodded. She wondered if this would be too much. Would he regret getting involved? If she sensed that in him, she would leave.

"Are your skills with numbers the only thing he wants from you?"

"If he owns something, he believes he can do anything he wants with it."

His jaw, his neck, his shoulders, all of him, tightened so much she wondered if he might turn to stone.

His voice was low, deadly. "Has he hurt you?"

"He's beaten me. But, no, he's never hurt me like that."

"But he's touched you inappropriately."

Barely a movement, she nodded. Then she said, "I've taken a ton of self-defense classes, and I always carry a weapon. If he tries to touch me again, he'll pull back a bloody stump."

Something in his eyes… Was that a hint of a smile? He glanced to the side, perhaps looking at the clock on the wall. Then he turned back to her. "What if I paid off the debt?"

"It's way too much."

"Try me."

"I think it's almost two million."

"That's doable. Do you think he'd honor it and leave you alone?"

Doable? Was he insane? Then she said, "No, I don't think he'd honor it."

"You're too valuable."

He didn't phrase it like a question, so she didn't answer. She'd proven over and over again how good she was with numbers, calculating variables and determining incredibly accurate odds, counting cards. She wished she'd never helped her father that first time. She'd just wanted to protect him. But participating in gambling and cheating had only made things worse and worse. She'd asked God's forgiveness a thousand times.

"What about the police?" he asked.

She shook her head. "I won't do that again."

"What happened?"

Her throat tightened, and she turned her gaze down to the countertop.

He moved closer, just on the other side of the island. "Cali."

If he was going to try to help, he needed to know everything. But this may very well be the detail that made him change his mind. "I went to the police once." She looked up at him. "A couple of detectives were working with me to put together enough to prosecute Michael and several of his top men. They were making good progress. Or I thought they were."

"Did he buy the detectives?"

She shook her head.

"He threatened their families," he surmised.

"They refused to comply. They sent their families away and kept working the case. But..."

"Michael found their families."

"The next time Michael caught me, he showed me pictures." She closed her eyes. "The children..."

She shook from the memory. She clasped her hands in her lap so hard she started to lose feeling in her fingers.

"Cali," he murmured. "It wasn't your fault."

Tears pricked the backs of her eyes, but she didn't let herself cry. Then she met his gaze. "I won't do that again."

He nodded. "I understand."

"Mr. Cross, I can't do this."

He gave her that dead stare. "You don't have a choice in the matter." Then he added, "Besides, I don't have family, no friends, no one to threaten. And I have a reputation for being brutal and heartless. And I have limitless resources. I am the only person who can help you."

"Why are you doing this?"

He stepped back and leaned against the opposite counter.

"I've figured enough out about you to know you're a good man," she said. "But why would you do this for someone you don't even know?"

He crossed his arms.

She waited for him to answer.

CHAPTER 7

Finally, Mr. Cross answered, "I won't turn away when I can help someone. Especially someone deserving." Then he added, "And I would prefer it if you stop calling me Mr. Cross."

Her gut told her there was something more. But then she didn't know him; surely, his past was just as complicated as hers. "Why do you care what I call you?"

"Please call me Asher."

She considered if she should call him out for not answering her question, but then she nodded. She'd be selective about what she pushed him on.

"May I call you Cali?" he asked.

"Sure."

He turned and looked out the window again.

"No one knows where you live? Not even a roofer or plumber or something?" she asked.

"No." Then he added, "Which begs the question, how did you find it?"

"I had help," she admitted. Then she braced herself for an interrogation.

All he did was nod, still looking out the window.

She allowed his silence for a minute or so.

Then she said, "I saw the cameras, at least some of them, and the security lights in the trees."

"There are motion sensors around the house. We'll be alerted if anyone approaches."

"You installed all of that yourself?" When he didn't answer, she added, "Why does *no one* know where you live?" It seemed odd for a billionaire in this big house not to have ever had any cleaning or repair companies here.

"I prefer privacy. And I meant it when I said I don't have friends."

She risked being rude. "Why?"

No response.

She hadn't really expected him to answer that. He was talking to her more, but only out of necessity. She could feel the wall around him, almost as if she could press a hand to it.

Another minute or so later, he turned. "You're probably tired."

She shrugged.

"Give me a few minutes. I'll make up a room." He headed for the stairs at the back of the kitchen.

Willow sat up and watched him. Then she turned her amber eyes on Cali. The cat probably wondered what in the world Cali was doing here. Willow was used to having him all to herself.

Cali looked around the room. For an older house, the kitchen was large. There wasn't much on the countertops, but at least there was some furniture in this room—the stools at the island and the round table with six chairs tucked in a big bay window. But there wasn't any décor at all—no curtains on the windows, not a single vase anywhere to be seen, not even a tablecloth. He was a single man, so she understood he wouldn't be into decorating, but single men usually had conveniences, maybe a big recliner and some clutter on the countertops, in the least. Why did a billionaire—with a big, old B—live like this?

***

Asher climbed up the steep back steps. They'd originally been intended for servant use. He rarely used the front stairs.

He found a spare set of sheets in the linen closet and put together the bed.

The events of the last hour had upended his simple life, but he steadily moved forward with each task that needed his attention next. He didn't have the luxury of allowing himself to stop and think too much. To question his own motivations.

After setting up the bed and checking the rest of the room, he headed back down the back stairs.

But he paused halfway down.

"You seem to like him, Willow. Tell me your thoughts." Her voice was quiet, gentle.

Willow meowed, which was a little surprising. She wasn't a particularly shy cat, but she didn't talk much in general.

"I think you might be biased," Cali said. "But you have to admit he's a little odd."

He had good reason—just nothing he would ever share.

A few seconds of quiet.

Then Cali said, "I must be insane."

Insane to allow him to help her or insane to trust him? Perhaps both. He accepted there wasn't much he could do to dispel her doubts about him. Her doubts were perfectly valid, and he would not try to convince her otherwise.

However, Cali must be kept in the dark about certain things.

***

Cali heard a floorboard creak and looked up. Mr. Cross turned the corner into the kitchen. His steps were much quieter than she'd anticipated. She had to remember he wasn't the loud, out-of-control "beast" everyone thought he was. No, he was much more cold and methodical. Perhaps he didn't fight back against the moniker because it allowed him to hide behind it, conceal who he really was.

"Would you like to select a book to read from the library?" he asked.

"I don't know if I can concentrate on a story right now."

He nodded.

She felt like he was either trying to get rid of her or perhaps he just had no idea how to entertain a guest. She made it easier on him and stood and pointed toward the stairs. "Lead the way."

He turned, and she followed him up.

"What are your thoughts on what to do next?" she asked. If he'd pushed so hard to help, he had to have some ideas. Her only idea was to run. She worried he didn't understand the situation well enough to realize running was the only option she had.

He continued climbing the steep stairs. The walls here were white plaster, unlike the wood paneling at the front stairs and entry hall. "I have some thoughts."

"And those thoughts would be?"

"Things I'm not sure I should share with you."

"What does that mean?"

They came to the landing, and he turned left. The walls returned to the same beautiful paneling. The floors were still wood but with a carpet runner in a burgundy and gold pattern. The first several doors they passed were closed. He led her into a room.

She stood in front of him. "Tell me what you're thinking," she demanded.

His square jaw clenched. Finally, he said, "I've found the best way to move someone's focus is to give them something else to worry about. Something larger."

"You want to intentionally cause problems for Michael

Dinetti. Are you insane?"

"I won't cause any problems. Simply shed light on problems he's created for himself."

"I told you I won't go to the police."

"Who said anything about the police?"

She shifted a step back.

But he moved and blocked her path to the door. "I can get things done quietly. I won't put anyone innocent in danger."

"Including yourself." It came out more as a demand than a question.

He hesitated, meeting her gaze with that empty stare. Except, it wasn't quite empty. There was something there, but she couldn't quite decipher it.

"Promise me," she demanded.

"On one condition."

She waited.

"You make the same promise," he said.

"This is my problem to deal with."

"No. This is a problem forced on you. You didn't cause it."

"I caused it by participating in gambling and cheating."

"I won't disagree that cheating is wrong, and you shouldn't have done that."

She was a little surprised—and somehow relieved—that he agreed on that.

Then he added, "But your father selling you and Dinetti believing he owns you are their wrongs. Not yours."

She'd never separated it all in her head like that. It helped. She could recognize her own failings, which she felt a deep need to do—or else she could never improve and be the person she wanted to be—but that didn't make her responsible for *everything*.

Her voice was muted. "Thank you."

He hesitated. "Will you stay?"

She nodded.

He motioned toward the room. "Sheets are fresh, as are the towels. Though I'm sure most things won't be to your liking, you can use anything in the bathroom that you find useful."

She glanced around the room, the attached bathroom, and the attached dressing room—an actual old-fashioned dressing room.

Then she turned back to him. "This is your room."

"Use anything you want." He shifted, about to turn and leave.

"I'm not taking your personal bedroom."

"You'll have to. There are no other beds in the house."

"I can sleep somewhere else. I'm not picky."

"I'm sure you're not. But I'm not about to sleep in a bed and let my guest suffer."

She wanted to argue more. But then something told her she had much larger battles to fight with him. She sighed but nodded.

He turned for the door.

Before he made it to the hall, she asked, "Why do you ignore me?"

He paused but didn't turn.

She was half-surprised he hadn't simply kept walking as if she hadn't said anything.

"Why?" she pushed.

He remained turned away. "I have reasons for everything I do." He walked out of the room.

CHAPTER 8

Cali washed up the best she could. The bathroom was a good size. It had probably originally been a bedroom or perhaps another dressing room. Whoever had done the update had tried to match the style of the rest of the house—cabinets and counters similar to the kitchen and a classic subway tile in the shower.

Then she sat down on the edge of the bed and thought.

No matter how she turned things around in her head, she couldn't find a better way of handling things. If she ran away, she truly believed he'd still go after Michael. If she stayed, she could help and hopefully keep Asher out of danger.

It felt different to think of him as Asher, not Mr. Cross. But not odd or wrong, just different.

She stood and looked out one of the windows into the dark forest behind the house. Directly behind the house was a steep incline. If anyone wanted to get to this room, they'd have to go through the house, which would mean they'd have to get by Asher. Was that part of the reason he'd given her this room?

***

Asher headed to the library and brought up the cameras on his computer screen. He checked all of them—the ones at the house as well as the ones hidden in the trees farther out. Everything looked quiet.

Then he took out his phone. He'd seen Cali had turned off her phone on the drive here, which had been smart. Who knew how much Dinetti had on her? But Asher knew his phone was secure.

He tapped on a contact in his phone saved as "information."

After two rings, the line picked up. "Didn't think I'd hear from you again any time soon."

"Neither did I."

"What can I do for you?"

"I need everything you can find on Michael Dinetti."

"The mob boss from Chicago? What—"

"Can you get it for me?"

There was a pause. "I'm on it. Give me until morning."

"I want everything. Dig until he bleeds. I'll pay whatever you need."

"Understood."

Asher ended the call.

***

Cali bolted upright.

She'd fallen asleep at some point, lying on top of the covers. Something had woken her. A sound. Footsteps rushing up the stairs.

She jumped from the bed and grabbed her gun out of her purse, but before she could get to the door, it swung open.

Even in the darkness, she recognized Asher's form.

"What's going on?" she asked.

He closed and locked the door. "Sensors around the house went off. Cameras show multiple men approaching the house."

It had to be Michael.

"How—"

"I have only one theory." Then he added, "But no time for that."

"Can we run?"

The sound of glass shattering somewhere downstairs answered her question.

She wanted to say she was sorry, but that seemed irrelevant at this point. But she wasn't about to cower behind him while he put himself in harm's way. She stood next to him, his right side. He didn't immediately try to push her behind him, which she was sure he'd do. She looked up at him. Then he looked down at her. He turned his head more than was necessary. More than was necessary…unless he didn't see well out of his right eye. That made sense—the scarring came right up to his eye, so it stood to reason his vision had been damaged along with his skin.

"They're not taking you," he growled. It sounded more like a warning than an assurance. Then she realized he was warning her not to give herself up to help him.

"I'm a fighter," she answered.

He nodded once, curtly, barely a movement, and turned back to the door.

She didn't add that she would fight to protect him just as much, if not more, than he'd do for her.

"Do you have any weapons?" she asked.

"Not upstairs. There's a gun safe in the billiard room."

She wished he'd gone there instead of coming straight up to her. She racked her 9mm and checked that the safety was off.

A floorboard creaked somewhere.

"Do you know how to handle that?" he asked.

"I've taken several classes, and I go to the range all the time."

"Good. Shoot anything that comes at you."

Footsteps in the upstairs hall.

"Where's Willow?"

"She's in a cabinet in the library. She's smart enough to keep hidden until I come get her."

She nodded, and they both faced the door.

The sound of a door slamming against a wall—they were checking the other rooms.

"Fire as soon as the door opens," he said.

She held her gun up and supported her right hand with her left, steady, sights fixed on the door. He glanced at her and then back to the door, apparently approving of her technique.

Heavy booted footsteps approached the door.

She was thankful her hand didn't shake. While she'd failed at completely extinguishing her fear, she'd succeeded in being able to control it when needed. *Focus on the immediate situation. Nothing else.*

The doorknob turned. The door remained closed. The door was solid wood, but the lock wasn't anything special. It probably wouldn't take long for them to break it down.

"I know you're in there, you pretty little thing," a man's voice called. She recognized the voice. Carl. One of Michael's top men. "Come out, come out, wherever you are!"

Asher lowered his chin and strengthened his stance.

Cali kept her sights locked on the door.

Carl pounded on the door, sounded like a booted foot.

Then again.

Asher remained completely still.

Focus, Cali.

Carl slammed the door again, and this time, it flung open and hit the wall with a thud.

Cali fired, but Carl had been ready and moved out of the way just in time. But then he cursed, and she realized she must have winged him.

She called, "Circumstances are different than they were last time. You should've taken more time to understand the situation. You always were hotheaded."

She almost felt his annoyance radiating off him.

Asher moved slowly toward the door. She wanted to demand he stay put but worried if they started arguing they would both be distracted. His footsteps were impressively silent.

He stopped just beside the door and turned his left ear toward the hall. Perhaps his hearing in his right ear had also been damaged.

Faster than a snake striking, he reached around the doorframe and dragged Carl into the room by the front of his jacket. With his other hand, he punched Carl so hard in the face she was afraid his neck would break from the force.

Then Asher threw Carl into the hallway. Carl hit the opposite wall like a pile of dirty laundry and slid to the floor. Blood covered his inanimate face.

She stared at Asher. She'd seen plenty of violence in her life but had never seen anything like that before.

"Carl?" someone called from down the hall.

Asher called out, more of a roar, "Come and take her!"

She heard Michael's men talking to each other. "I thought he was half blind and deaf."

"I may be half blind," Asher called. "But I assure you that has never stopped me from making a man bleed."

A pause.

She hoped they decided to cut their losses and leave. But she knew as well as they did what they'd face if they went back to Michael empty-handed.

Footsteps proceeded slowly closer.

Asher shifted back, next to her. "Shoot as soon as you see them. You know to aim center mass?"

She nodded. She knew she had the right to defend herself, but she didn't actually want to kill anyone. Shooting Carl made it feel all the more real. *Focus, Cali.* She aimed her gun at the door.

Asher was watching her.

He pushed her gun down toward the floor and moved toward the door.

"Asher," she whispered.

He ignored her.

Just as a man appeared in the doorway, Asher tackled him into the hall.

She hurried closer, gun still pointed toward the floor, carefully not aimed at Asher. But if she could use the gun to defend him, she would not hesitate.

The man he'd tackled was young, someone she'd never met before. He was just as big as Asher and a good fighter. He was on the ground, pinned by Asher straddling him, but he managed to land a strong shot across Asher's jaw. The shot turned Asher's head to the left, which meant Asher had to depend on his right eye to see him—his damaged eye. The man immediately shifted to push Asher off, roll him to the left.

Cali rammed her foot between his legs to his groin.

The young man cried out in pain, and Asher resumed punching him in the face.

The other man approached. He was older, probably in his forties. Cali remembered him. Jimmy. He wasn't as high a rank as Carl, but it wasn't for lack of ferocity. What he trailed behind Carl in intelligence, he made up for in brutality and a complete lack of conscience.

Jimmy reared back a foot, obviously aiming at Asher's head. She could see he was wearing steel toe boots.

She couldn't get past Asher and the young man splayed out in the middle of the hall, struggling with each other. There was no other choice.

Over Asher's head, she aimed and fired.

While she'd taken plenty of courses on proper use of a gun in self-defense and knew you should always aim at center mass, that aiming for limbs was generally stupid because the chance of missing was so high, she took the chance and aimed at his base leg. Since that leg wasn't moving and she was so close, she figured her chance of hitting it was at least a little higher. It would at least, hopefully, pause his attack on Asher.

She was lucky. The bullet hit the center of his knee.

He went down.

He grabbed either side of his knee and yelled out in pain.

Asher punched the young man one more time across the jaw, and this time, he went still, finally knocked out.

Jimmy reached for his ankle holster—another reason she knew she should aim for center mass, not a limb. If she'd have shot him in the chest, he wouldn't be reaching for an ankle holster. She would've been surprised he didn't have his weapon drawn to begin with if she hadn't known him. Known how he liked to attack with his bare hands, watch his victim struggle face-to-face, listen to their pleas, savor their pain.

Now that the young man was still, she could move closer, next to Asher. She aimed at Jimmy, this time at his chest.

Asher pushed her gun hand away and launched himself at Jimmy.

Due to his preference for hand-to-hand, Jimmy was excellent at it. And he'd obviously figured out that it was Asher's right side that was not as strong. He punched that side of Asher's face, turning his good eye and ear away. And then he punched again.

For a split second, she worried Jimmy would knock Asher out. And then he'd surely shoot him. While Jimmy liked to watch a man die slowly and painfully, he was smart enough to know when it was best to do it expediently.

But then Asher grabbed Jimmy by the throat and slammed him against the floor. The thud reverberated through the house. And then he slammed him again.

Jimmy's head bounced off the wood floor. The sound made Cali's stomach turn.

Asher slammed him again and again. There was blood on the floor under Jimmy's head.

But when Asher lifted Jimmy again and Jimmy was limp in his hands, Asher stopped slamming him and set him down, almost gently.

Asher stood and grabbed Cali's hand. He led her down the hall and down the back steps.

At the bottom of the steps, they paused. They had no idea how many men Michael had sent. Asher turned his left ear and listened.

"How many do you think he would've sent?" he whispered to Cali.

"If it were just me and not a public place where there might be other circumstances to control, probably just two."

"With me added to the mix?"

"They seemed to think they had more of an advantage than they actually did with you. He might've thought three was enough, but I wouldn't be surprised if he sent one or two more, probably outside."

"Contingency. Control the location."

She nodded.

"With all that noise we just made," he said, "they'll probably breach about now."

She nodded.

"Hand me your gun," he said.

She hesitated for only half a second and handed it to him.

"Stay close," he said. "Watch my six. If you see something, call out and then duck."

So he could shoot. She nodded.

He moved quickly and silently through the kitchen, and she followed, just as quietly as him. Silence was one of the first self-defense skills she'd learned.

They made it to the library. She closed the double doors behind them, but there was no lock. The left door faintly creaked, not enough to be heard from any distance.

"In here." He pulled at the edge of one of the shelves, and the entire shelf swung open. There was a small dark room. She could just see Willow standing in the corner, looking ready to pounce. Cali walked inside, but instead of following her in, Asher closed the hidden door. She pushed, but he was apparently holding it closed. She couldn't make any noise and risk calling attention to this room, to Asher. She pushed as hard as she could, but he was far too strong.

A creak. The left library door.

She stopped pushing and looked around for other options.

There was a slight amount of light on the floor, a narrow line. She got down on her knees. Instead of shelves, the lower portion of this wall had cabinet doors, which opened directly into this space. She crawled forward and peeked through the slim gap in the doors.

Two men entered the room.

CHAPTER 9

Asher shot one of the men and then dove to the side to avoid the second man's bullet.

The man moved slowly forward. Cali guessed Asher had dived behind the wingback chairs and table to that side of the room.

Just as the man approached the cabinet doors, she burst forth, tackled his legs, and took him to the ground. She was much smaller than the man, so instead of trying to wrestle him, she kneed him in the groin and got back to her feet. She kicked his groin.

He pulled his knees together and rolled to his side, probably trying to get up.

She slammed the ball of her foot into his stomach. And then again. And again.

And then Asher was there. He grabbed the man's jacket in both fists and lifted him up off the ground, as if the grown man weighed nothing more than a child.

"You tell Michael Dinetti," Asher growled, "she is not his property. Leave her alone, or he and I will have a major problem."

The man blinked.

Asher shook him. "Do you understand me?"

"I'll tell him. I'll tell him."

Asher threw him across the room. Literally across the large room. He slammed into the wall next to the doors. The other man he'd shot was lying by him, writhing in pain.

"Go!" Asher roared.

Both men crawled for the door, pushing each other out of the way. The second man got to his feet and ran, and the man who'd been shot stumbled but managed to follow. He'd been shot in the upper chest/shoulder area, and while he looked to be losing a lot of blood, he stood and moved reasonably quickly. Surely due to being properly motivated.

Then the sounds of running from upstairs.

Asher went over to his computer and pulled up multiple cameras on his three large screens. The three men from upstairs ran out the kitchen side door, and the other two men sprinted out the front door. The man who'd been shot barely made it to the big black SUV before its tires spewed gravel and took off up the drive.

Asher stood. "I need to secure the house."

She noticed… "You're bleeding." The side of his mouth, his left ear, and a cut near his right eye. Where Jimmy had landed some shots.

"I'm fine," Asher growled and kept moving.

She couldn't stop him—she was fully realizing how hard it was to stop Asher Cross—so she stayed with him to help.

The front door locks—two deadbolts—seemed to be functioning. She guessed they'd picked them, which was a skill several of Michael's men had, including Carl.

They went to the kitchen door. As she followed Asher, she noticed he'd tucked her 9mm in his waistband. The kitchen door had apparently been kicked in. The doorframe was broken. Asher grabbed a large, worn, solid-wood sideboard from the other side of the room and shoved it against the door. She helped, though he obviously didn't need it. Based on the weight, she guessed the sideboard was packed full with cooking bowls and pans, probably more mostly-worthless items left behind by the former owner's family.

"Now, let me help with your injuries," she said.

He was already walking away.

"Asher."

He kept walking.

"I understand you're angry," she said. "But you should let me help anyway."

He turned to face her, anger in his eyes. Though his brows were also slightly pulled together. He paused. "I'm not angry with you."

Instead of asking questions or arguing, she focused on making sure he was all right. "Sit down so I can clean you up."

"I'm fine."

"You know better than to let injuries get infected." Surely, he'd been well trained in the SEALs to make sure his injuries were tended so they didn't get worse and weaken him.

He pulled out a kitchen chair and sat. His movement was stiff—probably a broken rib.

While she found a dishrag and soap, he made a call. "I want five guards sent." … "I understand the others will have to work double-shifts."

Surely, he was talking about the security guards at his main office building downtown.

He gave the address and explained how to get to his house. "I want them here within the hour," he said. "No excuses." He ended the call and set his phone on the table.

She came over with a large bowl of hot, soapy water and a clean dishrag.

He stared straight ahead. She felt like she was approaching a rabid wolf, but she would not be dissuaded from making sure he was all right.

She gently dabbed at his right ear to clean off the

blood. Thankfully, it'd stopped bleeding.

"Can you hear out of this ear?" she asked.

"No."

She rinsed the cloth and started on the cut near his eye, even more gently.

"I can clean it myself," he said and pulled his head away.

She pushed his shoulder and ordered. "Stay put."

He looked up at her. "It's all right if it bothers you."

"Your scars? That doesn't bother me at all." She added, "I just want to make sure I don't hurt you worse."

He hesitated, meeting her gaze. Then he turned his head and resumed staring straight ahead, across the kitchen.

Willow came hesitantly down the hall. In the doorway, she looked at Asher, trotted over to him, and jumped on his lap. She stayed on her feet and watched the doorway, obviously nervous, but she leaned into Asher. He held her against him with a strong hand.

"Poor thing," Cali said.

"She's tough. She'll be fine."

Cali still felt guilty.

She rinsed the cloth and dabbed at the corner of his mouth. It was bleeding, though slowly. "This is the worst place."

"You've been cut there?"

She rinsed out the cloth.

"Your turn to ignore me?" he asked.

She continued to rinse out the cloth. "Michael punched me for mouthing off last time he caught me."

The muscles in his jaw worked.

"Now for the ribs," she said.

He stood, holding Willow, and headed for the hallway.

She grabbed his hand. "Nope. No ignoring me this time. I can see you have broken ribs."

"They're probably just bruised. Nothing you can do anyway."

"We can ice them."

"It's fine." He shifted to keep walking.

She gripped his hand harder. "Please."

He paused, facing away from her.

She pulled at his hand, and he followed her to the refrigerator.

"Ice in the bottom drawer." He grabbed a large Ziploc bag from a cabinet.

She filled it with ice and took a hand towel out of the same drawer where she'd found the dishcloth. Then she looked at him, assessing.

He held his hand out for the bag of ice.

"You don't have a couch anywhere, do you?"

"No."

"Upstairs it is, then." She motioned for him to go up the back stairs, and she walked up behind him.

At his bedroom door, he held his hand out again for the ice.

"Yeah, I'm going to trust you to ice your ribs," she scoffed.

"I have been injured before," he said. "This isn't new to me."

"I know, but you should relax properly. I just… I need to help in some way."

He paused but then went into the room.

"Lie back," she said.

He set Willow down next to him and did as Cali ordered.

She carefully untucked his white dress shirt from his black slacks and unbuttoned the shirt. He turned his head toward the window. Cali saw the bruising starting already—she guessed at least two ribs were badly bruised. She gently rested the ice on his skin. And tried not to notice his well-formed abs.

Willow finally relaxed and cuddled up against his side. He rested a hand on her and gently rubbed her fur with his thumb.

Cali sat on the edge of the bed, careful not to shift him too much.

Quiet.

The silence was, shockingly, not awkward. Or at least it didn't seem awkward for her. She'd gotten much better at interpersonal relations over time with a lot of concerted effort, but she'd been terrible at it as a child. She still sometimes didn't trust that she read situations completely correctly.

He continued to look out the window to the now-dark forest.

"It's pretty," she said.

He turned his head to look at her. Then he turned back to the window. "Yes."

There was a beep. He slid his phone from his pocket.

"Security is here?" she asked.

"Yes. Setting up surrounding the house."

"I don't think Michael will try again right away."

"I agree."

"He thought he could overpower the two of us. And definitely hugely underestimated you."

No response.

Quiet.

Finally, she said, "I'm sorry."

He continued looking out the window. "We've already discussed you have nothing to apologize for. Your father's and Dinetti's actions are not your fault."

"I meant... I wasn't properly prepared to use my gun. I've taken so many courses, and I go to the range all the time."

He looked at her, and his voice was surprisingly soft. "You should never apologize for not wanting to take another person's life."

She nodded.

"Do you understand me, Cali? Don't ever lose that."

She met his gaze. Her heart beat faster.

"I'm here," he continued. "You don't have to hurt

anyone."

"I should be able to take care of myself."

"You do take care of yourself. And you helped me. Most people would've cowered in the corner, but you helped make sure I didn't get blindsided. You figured out my limitations and helped compensate."

He sighed and rested his head back, now focused on the ceiling.

"What's wrong?" she asked.

Silence. She figured he was back to ignoring her. Every time he started to open up, he inevitably shut back down. He'd saved her life twice today, so she was determined to give him space. At least for now.

She asked him one more question. "Why did you shoot that man in the shoulder, rather than center mass?"

No response.

"You were a SEAL. I know you can shoot very well."

"Yes," he said.

She opened her mouth, about to ask why, but then she closed it. She'd always been too curious. She had to remind herself to step back sometimes. People were not like ciphers. She couldn't push them until they cracked. Or rather, she *shouldn't*.

They were quiet.

She made sure to hold the ice steady.

Willow purred, tucked into his other side.

"I think that's enough." He took her hand and lifted the ice off his ribs and sat up.

"I know you have secrets."

He paused and looked at her.

"I'm guessing they're really big secrets," she said.

He watched her.

"I dig into secrets," she said. "It's my thing. It's always been my thing—figuring things out. Everything I've studied—math, languages, geography, history—it's all geared toward deciphering secrets."

He made no response, only watched her.

"But I'm not going to treat you like a code to be broken. Not anymore. I was warranted in pushing you before—rude sometimes, but warranted."

"And now?"

"You've earned respect," she said. "And trust."

He raised one brow, the only indication of emotion on his face.

"Not blind trust, granted, but a healthy amount."

A pause.

"The real question is," she said, "why are you trusting me? You don't know me, and the only things you know about the situation are what I've told you."

CHAPTER 10

Asher slid Willow out of the way and stood, opposite side of the bed from Cali. Cali watched him, waiting for an answer. Why did he trust her? She wasn't getting an answer to that question. Out of everything he kept to himself, that was the least likely ever to be pulled out of him.

"You should get some sleep." He walked out of the room.

Willow trotted after him a few seconds later.

He went outside and spoke to the security detail, made sure they had clear directions. On the front drive, he turned back toward the house and noticed Cali standing at an upstairs window, watching him.

He ignored her and went inside and to the library.

He knew he could not tell her the things she wanted to know, the questions that were incessantly buzzing in that mind of hers. He just hoped his lack of openness with her didn't drive her away from his protection. If anything happened to her, if Dinetti hurt her, his avoidance of killing anyone for her sake would stop abruptly.

***

The rest of the night passed slowly. Cali tried to sleep but wasn't very successful. Before the sun peeked through the trees outside, she turned on the shower. He'd said she could use whatever he had, so she used the soap and shampoo he had sitting on the shower ledge. The bar soap was a little on the masculine side, but the scent seemed to wear off shortly after she dried. The shampoo didn't have much scent at all.

He didn't have a brush, of course, but he did have a comb. She did the best she could combing out her long, wavy hair. By the time she put back on the same clothes, her hair was mostly dry. She didn't put it up like she usually did. It was easier to work with when it was completely dry.

She went downstairs and found Asher in the library, already awake. Or perhaps he hadn't slept. There were no blankets or pillows on the wingback chairs or on the floor.

He didn't look up from his computer when she walked in.

"Do you mind if I make breakfast?" she asked.

He still didn't look over. "Help yourself."

She walked back down the hall toward the kitchen. In the refrigerator, she found some eggs and butter. And in a cabinet, she found some bread. The only meat she found was frozen ground turkey and chicken tenderloins, not exactly breakfast food. *Eggs and toast it is.*

It took a few minutes to cook some over-easy eggs and buttered toast. She left it on the counter and went back to the library. He was still at his computer.

"It's ready."

He looked over, and she swore he hesitated half a second before answering, "What's ready?"

"Breakfast."

"I didn't intend for you to cook for me."

"I know. But I did, and if you don't eat it, I'll have my feelings hurt."

"I think the real consequences would be the wrath of

Callista Lebeau."

She grinned. "Probably." She turned and headed back down the hall. Sometimes she saw that glimpse of humor and fun in him, and she worried why it came out so rarely.

She heard his quiet footsteps follow.

"Sit." She pointed to the table tucked in the bay window and then grabbed the two plates she'd put together.

He actually listened and sat at the table, the same chair he'd sat in last night when he'd let her tend his injuries. She set a plate in front of him, as well as a fork and paper towel.

Then she took a seat, one chair between them at the round table. The sun filtered into the room through the trees outside and then the large bay windows. The forest looked ethereal with mist lurking along the ground and up into the trees. Many of the leaves had turned colors—reds, oranges, yellows—and the sunlight hit certain leaves and made the color glow.

She took a bite of toast and then a sip of water—she hadn't found anything else in the refrigerator to drink. "How're you feeling this morning? Looks like all the bleeding stopped."

He nodded and took a bite of egg.

"How about your ribs?"

"Fine."

"We should ice them again."

No response. She'd figured that was the reaction she'd get.

Her appetite ran out sooner than usual, and she set her fork down. She put to words everything she'd been going over and over in her head last night. "I think I should leave."

He finally looked at her.

"You should go to the doctor."

"What does one have to do with the other?"

"You've been a good man and protected me. You've

done a lot more for me than you should. It's time for me to do something for you."

"Leaving is not doing something for me."

"I can take care of myself. I've been doing it for a long time. I'll be fine." She took a breath. "But I won't be fine if you get hurt again."

He leaned back in his chair and crossed his arms over his broad chest.

"You can give me that dead stare all you want. I'm not scared of you."

He smirked. "That I know."

"You find that amusing?"

"Little bit."

"You expected the little blonde to be terrified like in some fairytale?"

"If you think about it, it's pretty rare to see a terrified heroine in a fairytale."

She paused to consider. "You're right. Not always the brightest, but usually reasonably brave."

"I would argue kind and perhaps overly trusting, usually stemming from that kindness, but not dumb."

"Maybe." Then she straightened her back. "But we're not talking about a fairytale. I don't need a prince to save me."

"Good thing I'm no prince."

"A prince hiding behind the façade of a beast."

He gave no response, but she thought she saw something in his eyes. Before she could figure it out, he looked away, out the window.

She stood and took both their plates to the kitchen and then washed them in the sink.

He walked over and stood a few feet away from her.

"You can't leave," he said.

"Who says?"

"You *shouldn't* leave."

She picked up a towel off the counter and dried the plates.

"What I said yesterday still stands," he said. "I'll go after Dinetti myself. If you stay, you can guide my actions, make chance of success much higher."

She'd thought about that and had determined he would likely not actually follow through. Why would he? Or maybe he'd try to hire a private detective to look into things, but that wouldn't do any good—no private detective who had half a brain would get involved in investigating Michael Dinetti. And then Asher would lose drive or get busy with the thousand other things he had going on, and he'd let it go.

Asher moved closer, took the plate out her hand, and set it on the counter with a clink. With both hands on her upper arms, he turned her to face him. His grip was gentle enough that she could easily pull away, but she didn't.

His voice was more of a rumble from deep in his chest. "I will not stop, Cali. Do you understand me? *Nothing* will stop me."

She stared up at him.

"You have two options," he said. "You leave or you help me."

"Why?"

A long pause. They held eye contact.

Finally, he said, "You don't need to know why. Just that I will not stop."

"I need to understand." He wasn't making any logical sense, and she didn't do well with illogical.

He let go of her and backed up a step. He shifted his gaze to the window. "You promised you wouldn't treat me like another of your ciphers. Can you do that?"

She heard a sound from outside. Before she could register what it was, he picked her up and moved her away from the window.

CHAPTER 11

Asher turned to look out the window, shielding Cali. The guards outside yelled, "What're you doing here? This is private property." And then, "Exit the vehicle. Now!"

"Who is it?" She shifted to look around Asher's shoulder. She recognized the car—she'd driven that car. "Tell them not to hurt him."

"That's the same car you drove here before," Asher said.

"Yes, I borrowed it from a friend. Please tell them not to hurt him." She started for the hall toward the front door.

He was faster and walked outside just ahead of her. "Lower your weapons." Three of his guards had surrounded the car, aiming semiautomatic handguns at it. They didn't hold themselves like merely guards, more like police or military.

All three men did as he ordered, but they kept both hands on their weapons, ready, and they kept position around the car.

Asher walked up to the driver's door and opened it. "Out."

Floyd glanced at the guards as he stood from the car.

Asher grabbed Floyd's jacket in both fists and lifted him up to Asher's eye level. Floyd wasn't exactly short, but being so thin and compared to how tall and thick Asher was, Floyd looked like a rat in the mouth of a lion.

"No," Cali said. "Put him down."

Asher continued to glare at Floyd. "Who did you give my address to?"

Floyd hesitated, and then he flickered his gaze over to Cali.

"I asked him to get it for me," Cali said. "I'm sorry."

Asher looked over at her, and his tone wasn't as harsh. "Your knowing where I live doesn't concern me. Never has." He turned back to Floyd. "But someone gave my address to someone else, someone who should not have it."

"He wouldn't." Cali tugged on Asher's forearm, trying to get him to lower Floyd.

"Who did you give it to?" Asher yelled.

"Just Cali." Floyd's eyes were wider than usual, but Cali was impressed his voice didn't shake.

"Someone gave my address out. You're the only one who knows it."

Floyd glanced at the guards around them.

"They didn't know until last night when I called them in. After someone attacked my home."

Floyd turned to Cali. "Were you here? Are you okay?"

"I'm fine." She tugged harder on Asher's arm. "But *someone* has bruised ribs he's going to aggravate."

Asher set Floyd down on the ground but didn't let go of his jacket.

Floyd continued to address Cali. "Who attacked?"

Cali opened her mouth, but Asher spoke first. "You don't need to know that."

"Was it Dinetti?" Floyd asked Cali.

"How do you know about Michael Dinetti?" She'd never told the Gray Hats—not for lack of trust so much as an attempt to protect them.

"Are you positive it was Dinetti?" Floyd asked.

"Okay, timeout," Cali said. "Both of you are not telling me something, and I have a feeling it's several somethings."

There was a pause.

And then Asher let go of Floyd with a shove. Floyd bumped into his car but then straightened. He closed his car door and then slid closer to Cali, away from Asher, who had not moved, had not given Floyd any more room.

One of the guards murmured to Asher, "Mr. Cross, would you like us to resume our posts?"

"No. Stay here," he answered.

Why in the world was Asher being so touchy about Floyd? He was one of the least physically threatening men she'd ever met—cross between a poet, comedian, and tech geek.

"First," Cali said to Floyd, "tell me how you know who Michael Dinetti is." She did *not* want Floyd or the others getting involved in this.

Floyd hesitated. Then he glanced back at Asher.

"He won't hurt you," Cali assured. At least she was pretty sure he wouldn't.

When Floyd didn't answer, she pushed, "Tell me."

"You know how we won't ever tell anyone what information we looked up for you?"

"Who asked you to research Michael Dinetti? You need to steer clear of him."

"Trust me, we're steering clear."

She softened her voice. "Will you please tell me who asked you to research him?"

Floyd looked at her with that puppy dog look he got sometimes.

Asher stepped forward. "For goodness' sake, you're going to make the poor man melt right here in my driveway. Go easy on him."

"What?" She was going easy on Floyd. "You're the one flinging him around."

"He researched Dinetti at my request," Asher said.

"How in the world do you know Floyd?"

Asher turned to Floyd. "What did you find?"

"It's in the car." He opened his car door and grabbed a thumb drive out of the console. He handed it to Asher. "I promise I did not give your address to anyone but Cali."

Asher continued to sound extremely direct. "What about your friends?"

"No way. We're not stupid."

"That's the illusion I've been operating under," Asher said. "But *some*one gave Dinetti my address."

"If Dinetti is coming after you, why is Cali here? She needs to be out of harm's way."

Asher growled, "That's why she's here."

"Dinetti is after me." Then Cali added, "But I don't want you guys involved in this. Make sure no one follows your online trail, and don't talk about this to anyone. I'd rather you not even think about it." Then she turned to Asher, "How do you know Floyd? That night you appeared out of nowhere, were you going to see him? Is that why you were in their neighborhood?"

"Cross has never been to our place," Floyd said. "What's going on? Why is Dinetti after you? What happened?"

"It's a long story you don't need to know. I'm keeping you out of this."

"The heck you are. We've got your back. You know that."

"Yeah. And I've got your back too. You are staying *out*."

"Cali—"

"No."

"You realize I don't require your permission."

She softened her voice. "I'm asking as your friend."

He got that puppy dog look again. And then he blinked. "My Lovely Lady Lavender, you are a truly good soul. We do not abandon good souls."

She crossed her arms. Then she turned her sights on Asher. "How do you know Floyd?"

"Uh-uh," Floyd said. "I need to know why a mobster like Dinetti is after someone like you."

Before she could shut him down, Asher answered, "He's under the misguided belief that he owns her talents as well as her physically."

Floyd scowled. She'd never seen his expression turn so dark. Then he called Michael several bad names that she didn't particularly disagree with. "Why would he possibly think that? And how does he know what you can do anyway? You don't exactly advertise the level of your skill."

"This is exactly why she doesn't advertise it," Asher said.

Floyd lifted his chin in understanding. "You've been running from him for a while." Then he asked, "How did Cross get involved?"

"Michael caught up to me on the sidewalk not far from work. Asher was driving by and, I guess, noticed something was wrong." Then she turned to Asher. "Why were you driving by? That was the opposite direction of your house."

Asher addressed Floyd and held up the thumb drive. "Did you find anything useful?"

"Maybe. Kind of depends, I guess. We'll keep looking for more."

"No, you will not," Cali said.

Floyd raised a brow. "Why is it he gets to help but I don't?"

"Don't be too offended," Asher said. "She's tried to push my help away just as hard." Then he added, "Who could've possibly figured out where I live?"

"I don't know, man. It's not exactly easy to figure out. It took all three of us sorting through all your corporations and then all the holdings of those corporations. And then we looked up each address on Google Earth to come up with the most likely options."

"This house does not appear on Google Earth, and how would that tell you anything?"

"Well, the fact that it's *not* on Google Earth kind of gave it away. You're not the kind of guy to live in a pretty little neighborhood with lots of people. And…we might have hacked traffic cameras and followed your car."

"How hard is that to do?"

"If you're asking if that could be how Dinetti found her, I seriously don't think so. I've dug enough into him to see he's not a tech guy, nor are any of his people."

"I could've told you that," Cali said. "He doesn't like anything recorded, especially electronically. He keeps track of things in ledgers using code." Then she added, "And that's why you should back off—you won't find anything anyway."

Floyd grinned. "Everyone is online whether they want to be or not. You just have to know where to look."

She sighed. Then she turned to Asher. "How do you know Floyd?"

"I told you I have connections."

"The Gray Hats aren't your normal connection. It's not like they advertise who they are. They're careful to keep a low profile, and no one can do that better than they can."

He met her gaze with zero emotion in his eyes.

As she looked at him, she furrowed her brow. "You're trying not to lie to me."

He gave no response.

"That's it, isn't it? Why you just don't answer—you don't want to lie."

Floyd spoke up—trying to redirect the conversation? "Why would you need to lie if you can just scare the tar out of people instead?"

She continued to focus on Asher. "The problem with that is I'm not scared of you."

Asher's voice was quiet. "I know."

She touched his arm with her fingertips. "How do you

know Floyd?"

He paused. "A couple of years ago, I needed information on someone. I knew someone with very high skill had completed a bug bounty assignment for the company. I made inquiries."

"We found those inquiries," Floyd said, "looked into him to make sure we didn't find anything concerning, and then we reached out to him."

"That wasn't so hard." Though she pretended to be appeased, she knew there was something more. But other things were more important right now. She turned to Floyd, "Why're you here? You never drop off thumb drives—you always do everything online."

"I've been looking for you. When you didn't answer your phone, and I didn't find you at home last night, I decided to try here. I was hoping you were here harassing Cross again."

"Why were you looking for me?"

"I really hate to add anything more to your plate. But we've found murmurs online about a cryptologist. Most of the messages are in code, but it's that same terrorist group we've been tracking."

"The one I've been deciphering."

"Yeah. We keep seeing stuff about a cryptologist. At least, we're pretty sure that's what they're talking about."

"And you think they might mean me."

"Yeah."

"Do you have the coded messages?"

He took some folded papers out of his pocket and handed them to her. "We've seen enough to be worried. And…we've figured out…they appear to have some kind of connection to the NSA."

Asher said, "You think a terrorist group that's infiltrated the NSA is after Cali."

"Yeah. We do."

CHAPTER 12

Cali turned and walked into the house. She heard Asher and Floyd following, but she ignored them.

"Where're you going?" Asher asked.

"Do you have an idea?" Floyd asked.

She went upstairs to Asher's room and grabbed her purse. When she turned, she noticed Floyd glancing around with raised brows. He probably thought she'd stayed in this room *with* Asher. She didn't care enough to set him straight.

She slipped by Floyd, but Asher obviously understood what she was doing and stood in the way. "I'll take you away, but you're not leaving without me."

"I have no idea what I'm even up against. There is no way I'm letting anyone else get in the middle."

"I'm already in the middle," Floyd said. "We gave you those messages to decode."

"And I'm planting myself in the middle." Asher stared down at her. "All the same arguments I presented earlier still apply. Perhaps more so now."

"Use that beautiful brain of yours," Floyd said. "You can't do all of this alone."

She spun around and yelled, "You don't get it, do

you?!"

Floyd stared at her with wide eyes. She'd never lost her temper with him. Usually, working with the Gray Hats was a haven from reality. A place she could feel useful.

Asher's voice was quiet. "I get it."

She felt her posture deflate.

"I get it," Asher repeated. "Ever since you were a child, your primary goal in life, in all of your interactions, has been to not make things worse for others. And you feel like you're failing monumentally."

She stood there, gaze on the floor, while she tried to think around reality.

Asher moved in front of her and gently held her shoulders. "Trust me," he murmured, "you make things better for others." Then his voice returned to normal. "All the same arguments I presented earlier still apply. You really have only one option."

She dug through her brain to find options. A way to keep these good men out of her mess. Anything.

Asher's rough but gentle hand lifted her chin. His voice barely made a sound. "You have only one option."

She felt all the determination slip out of her expression as she looked up at him.

"I'll pack some things," he said. "And we'll leave in five minutes."

"What about the Gray Hats? They're my friends…"

"I'll take care of them. I'll either move them someplace safe or leave a security detail with them."

"No way, man," Floyd said. "We have a lot of work in our setup, and we work alone."

She knew it would be hard for them to move. She wasn't sure if it was really to do with their technical setup or with Mt Dew's crippling anxiety. He hadn't left the apartment in years, though he did his best to try to hide that fact, and both Floyd and Bl@ze would protect and support him no matter what. And they would never let outsiders into their apartment. What they did was too sensitive.

She met Asher's gaze, asking for his help for her friends.

Turned away from Floyd, he mouthed, "I'll take care of them."

Barely a movement, she nodded.

"Give me five minutes." Asher let go of her shoulders and walked into his closet. He grabbed a duffle off a shelf and started filling it.

Then he headed downstairs to the library. She and Floyd followed. Asher moved books out of the way and revealed a safe tucked into one of the shelves. He opened it and took out stacks of cash.

"Take a few books if you'd like," Asher said as he zipped the duffle.

Instead of getting books, she got his laptop ready to go. There was a backpack leaned against his desk, the same backpack she'd seen him bring to the office. She put the computer and anything else she thought might be handy in the bag.

"We should grab some food as well." Asher went to the kitchen and dumped a few food items into a trash bag. Then he grabbed the two gallon jugs of water he had in the refrigerator and set it all on the counter.

"What about Willow?" she asked.

"Who's Willow?" Floyd asked.

Asher looked over at Willow sitting on a kitchen chair and paused.

Floyd followed Asher's gaze. Then he said to Cali, "I didn't know you had a cat."

"I don't."

Floyd looked at Asher. "I never imagined *The Beast* having a sweet little furry friend."

"Don't call him The Beast," Cali said.

Floyd held his hands up. "No offense, I promise."

Cali hedged, "Would you take her while we're gone?" She glanced at Asher to see if he had any major problems with the idea.

"Um…" Floyd said. "I guess that would be okay. Bl@ze keeps talking about getting a dog. A cat will have to do, at least temporarily."

Asher gave no indication how he felt, but he did hand Floyd a bag of Willow's food. Cali had a feeling Asher was more attached to Willow than he would admit.

Floyd walked over, let Willow smell his hand, and then picked her up. She had that annoyed look on her face and didn't relax in his hands, but she didn't struggle. She watched Asher as he moved closer. He petted her head and murmured, "Be good."

Then he grabbed everything off the counter and headed for the door. Cali tried to help, but he ignored her attempts.

Outside, he opened the garage door and then put everything in the back of a black Ford Bronco. Then he motioned for one of his security staff to come over.

"You are to organize a contingent. Follow Floyd back to his apartment. He and his two friends are never to be unprotected."

"Yes, sir."

"But they cannot realize you're there. And you will not look into what they do. They will maintain complete privacy."

The man paused. "It's not going to be easy."

"I realize that."

"They all live together? Do they often split up?"

Cali spoke up. "Floyd is the only one with a car. He does most of the chores like buying food and other supplies. The one who always looks annoyed never leaves the apartment. Literally never."

"And the third?"

"He's the most level-headed of the three, and also probably the smartest. He doesn't talk much about his life offline. He may simply not have much of one."

"Any names other than Floyd?" the man asked.

Cali shook her head. "I only know their handles, and I swore I'd never share that." She was shocked Floyd had used Bl@ze's name in front of Asher. That told her something about what the Gray Hats thought about Asher.

Or maybe they knew each other better than she'd realized?

"Do you have it?" Asher asked his man.

The man lifted his unshaven chin. "Yes, sir." He walked away and spoke quietly to one of the other men.

"Are you ready?" Asher asked Cali.

She huffed out a breath. "I guess I have to be." She waved toward Floyd, who had just put Willow in the front seat of his car.

"Keep us in the loop," he called.

She nodded. Then she got in the passenger seat of Asher's Bronco while he took the driver's seat. He started the engine.

"How good is your security?" she asked.

"All ex-SEALs, Rangers, and Green Beret."

She nodded.

He backed out of the garage, but instead of starting up the long drive, he drove around the back of the garage. There was a trail she hadn't noticed before. If the word *trail* could really be used. It didn't have major trees in the way, but it was covered over in foliage, even a few saplings. The truck bumped over tree roots and rocks.

"The car won't be damaged?"

"It's made to handle the terrain." He made a hard turn to avoid a huge oak tree.

She remained quiet and let him focus.

All she could think was *I have to be crazy*. Here she was driving through the forest alone with a man she barely knew. Pulling this man deeper into her mess of a life. She looked out the window and let her thoughts travel up to God. He would tell her if she were making a horrible mistake, right?

***

Asher glanced over at Cali, at her long, loosely curly hair. This morning was the first time he'd ever seen her hair down. Then he refocused on the trail in front of the truck.

He was thankful she had decided to be quiet for a while. His thoughts were too tumultuous. He wasn't entirely sure he was doing the right thing. If it was wise.

But he'd seen no other options.

And he had a responsibility to make sure she was safe. The terrorist group probably would not be targeting her if not for him.

***

After a few miles, Cali finally asked, "Where are we going?"

Asher paused long enough she figured he was going to ignore her. She wasn't going to have patience for that any longer. She opened her mouth.

Then he answered, "It's possible Dinetti found the house by having people stationed around town. I know his Mercedes didn't follow me, but perhaps he had enough people stationed that he found me anyway. We have to assume the house is being watched."

She nodded, "So, we're leaving in an unexpected route."

"Yes."

"But where are we going?"

He paused again. She wasn't sure if he was avoiding talking to her or just very focused on the rough terrain. They bumped along for a few seconds until they came to a shallow creek. Once on the other side, he finally answered, "I own property across the country."

"I thought it was centered in this region."

"Most of it is, but I have more."

"Where?"

"Anywhere I find historical properties."

"Have you taken classes on giving vague answers?"

He gave an annoyed sigh. "The ownership of my historical properties is purposefully more difficult to track."

"Why?" Perhaps he was used to people getting tired of pulling information out of him, but she didn't tire so easily.

"I don't want the historical significance to be overshadowed."

"By your fame, and by people's hatred of you."

He glanced over at her.

"Yes, I know people hate you. I'm not a gossiper, but I'm a listener."

He hesitated, gaze again locked on the now-nonexistent path in front of them. "Do you?"

"Hate you? Definitely not—people have to give me a direct reason to hate them. I'm not scared of you either, but I used to feel cautious."

He didn't respond, but she could feel the question burning through his skull.

"I don't feel that same caution anymore," she said.

"A different kind of caution."

"I feel some degree of caution around everyone."

"I understand that."

"But if I didn't feel some amount of trust, I wouldn't be in this car."

"I think you're in this car to protect me more than to protect yourself."

She didn't deny it but wondered if he was annoyed to have someone, a woman especially, protecting him. Warrior types like him sometimes had a hard time with that idea—not in a sexist way necessarily. More like they felt they had to be the protector, and if they weren't, they believed they were failing those around them.

Quiet.

"We're going to a property in Black Mountain," he

said.

"That's near Asheville, right?"

He nodded.

"Well, then," she said. "That was an awful lot of work to get that little bit of information out of you." She didn't expect him to respond and looked out the side window.

But then he said, "I'm used to being in control of every conversation I'm in."

She thought about that. "Because you have to be."

He glanced at her.

"You don't talk to anyone outside work, so it seems anyway. And at work, you have to be in control—you have a lot of people depending on you for their livelihood." She paused as she looked at him. "You take that very seriously."

He nodded once.

"I don't want you to feel that kind of pressure with me," she said. "I was your employee, but you're not responsible for me. You can walk away at any time. I mean that."

He gave zero response.

She turned her head to look back out the side window, at the brightly colored leaves brushing against the glass.

Several minutes later, the truck paused, and she looked out the windshield. They were at a road, looked like a tiny country road made of pitted asphalt.

"About two hours to Black Mountain?" she asked.

"Maybe more. I plan to take an indirect route." He turned onto the road.

They drove for a while. He offered for her to turn on music if she wanted. She didn't feel like music. Her mind was way too active to be able to absorb music properly. It would just annoy her.

When she started getting a headache, she opened the glovebox and took out the vehicle owner's manual.

"Something wrong?" he asked.

"Just occupying myself." She flipped to the beginning

of the manual.

He looked over at her. "By reading the truck's owner's manual?"

"I know it's weird." She didn't offer further explanation. No one understood why she liked to read what she did, and she'd learned a long time ago not to try to explain herself—just accept no one else got it.

He glanced at her occasionally but didn't ask her why she was reading it. She appreciated that. She let her mind focus on the technical aspects of the vehicle. She liked older cars better because they were more mechanical, less computer-driven. She understood mechanical components better than computers. It was easier to visualize.

They drove in silence for a long time. She finished reading the manual and put it back in the glove box.

"Any interesting features I should know about?" He didn't sound like he was merely making conversation, and definitely not making light of her quirky behavior, more like he honestly wanted to know.

"Most of the cool stuff are the off-road abilities, but you obviously have a good handle on that."

More quiet.

"You gave the information to Ms. Banks, didn't you?" he asked.

She looked over at him. "Huh?"

"About Bob Walsh."

She hesitated. "I left breadcrumbs. She's smart. She may have found it all anyway."

The corner of his mouth twitched into a slight smirk.

"Why'd you bring me in on that?"

"You're intelligent."

"I was a bookkeeper. You didn't know me from Adam."

"I know who all of my employees are. And I understand their capabilities."

She raised her eyebrow. "Every single employee? How about the secretary for Elaine Jones?"

"Jody Harris. She has a bachelor's degree but hasn't been able to make it out of the secretary role. She thinks it's due to people not understanding her talent."

Now Cali raised both her brows. "But that's not it."

"She tends to find the problems but not the solutions. Finding problems is important, but it's a worthless ability if you can't or won't find solutions."

"How do you know all that?"

"I read performance reviews. And I pay attention."

She assessed for a moment, and she came back to, "Because people rely on you, and you don't want to let them down."

He didn't respond.

"So, what do you know about me?" she asked.

He looked over at her, met her eyes, and then turned back to the road. "Your résumé did not include your full educational background."

"You don't have to have a fancy formal education to be intelligent. You're a prime example. No college degree and yet one of the most powerful men in the country."

"I agree a formal education is not required to be intelligent."

"How do you know that about me?"

"Are you admitting you omitted information off your résumé?"

She sighed. "Fine. Yes, I didn't include my entire educational background."

"In order to maintain a low profile and stay hidden from Dinetti."

"Yes." Then she added, "How did you know that about me?"

"I suspected, and you just confirmed." He kept his gaze on the road.

She wasn't buying it. There was something more. But she wanted to try not to treat him like a code to be broken. Or at least save her really aggressive questions for when it truly mattered.

But she did want to talk to him, try to be friendly. She hadn't had the opportunity to be truly friendly in a long time. "Will you tell me about Rose?"

His jaw tightened all the way up to his temple, and the air inside of the truck seemed to drop thirty degrees. He barely slit his mouth open. "No."

CHAPTER 13

Cali allowed Asher's silence. She hadn't thought Rose would be a difficult subject. She'd thought the opposite— maybe that it would put him at ease and be one thing he'd be comfortable sharing.

But then, she shouldn't assume family was a safe subject. It certainly wasn't for her. It was hard to admit what her father had done. Humiliating. Weren't fathers supposed to protect daughters at all costs? What did it mean that her father was not only not willing to protect her but willing to sell her for his own gain? She tried to convince herself that it was his addiction that had made him do it. But sacrificing his daughter hadn't been his only option, yet that was the one he'd chosen. And addiction or not, he was responsible for his actions.

And her mother. That subject might be even worse.

Asher turned the truck off a country road onto a gravel drive. The gravel looked white and new, unlike his home in Charlotte. Huge trees, thick with red-and-gold-tinged leaves that hadn't yet started falling, lined the drive and obscured the view. After a couple of minutes, the trees opened to a vast green field, in the middle of which sat an old plantation house, fresh white paint gleaming in the sun.

A two-story portico centered on the flat façade framed the front door. The house was lovely and large, surely once owned by a wealthy family, but there was a humility to it that she liked—no grand double doors, no fancy iron railing, not even decorative shutters.

The drive made a circle in front of the house, but instead of stopping at the front door, Asher took a smaller drive around the back and parked by a simple porch that spanned the back side of the house. There was no garage, but she saw many outer buildings in the distance, also white like the main house.

Asher turned off the engine and got out of the car. He hadn't uttered a single word since she'd mentioned Rose.

She got out as well and helped grab some items out of the back of the vehicle. Then she followed him up the steps.

He opened a lockbox hanging off the door handle, took out a key, and opened the door into a farmhouse-style kitchen with white antique cabinets and butcher-block counters.

He set his bags on the table in the middle of the room and then took her items out of her hands.

"Are you hungry?" he asked.

"No."

"There are several rooms upstairs. Take your pick."

Is that a dismissal?

Then he added, "There are shelves in the front room but not an extensive selection of books."

"Is this your vacation home?"

"No." Then he kept talking, as if trying to force himself to be polite. "I just finished restoring it. I plan to monetize it as a vacation rental. Or perhaps make it a bed and breakfast if I can find the right couple to manage it."

She looked around at the smooth plaster walls and the dinged but freshly painted cabinets. "You have a thing for history."

He turned and opened a cabinet and looked at each

shelf of dishes, perhaps checking that it'd been stocked per his directions. Then he moved on to the next cabinet.

She meandered over to the doorway, which led to a central hall, which led to the front door and main stairs. The old wood floors creaked under her shoes. When she found the bookshelves, she paused to read the titles. She pulled a book off the shelf—Black Mountain history and lore—and browsed it.

"You are permitted to sit."

She looked up to see Asher standing next to her. She realized she'd been standing there reading for a while.

"I brought in the computer," he said. "I thought you might like to go through the thumb drive Floyd dropped off."

She snapped the book closed and put it back on the shelf.

He led her over to a small desk at the side of the room and turned on his laptop. He set the thumb drive next to it and turned to leave.

"You're not curious?" she asked.

He kept walking. "You'll understand it better than I will."

She sat and looked through everything on the thumb drive. Most of it was nothing of great consequence, things she already knew or suspected. And nothing that would do any real harm to Michael in court. He was too careful.

There was one email, though, that was interesting.

She picked up the laptop and walked back through the house. She had no idea where Asher was—until she heard a loud noise. She followed the sound and found him outside. He raised an axe and slammed it down to split a log. Perhaps there was no central heating in this very old house, or maybe he just enjoyed a crackling fireplace.

The difference hit her—the Mr. Cross who wore a suit, ran board meetings, and felt a million miles away, and then the Asher whose arms and chest strained the fabric of his t-shirt as he chopped wood to make a fire to keep them warm tonight.

He stopped and looked over at her. "Find something interesting?"

She brought the computer over to him. He set the axe down and leaned closer to look at the screen. "Deposit confirmation?"

"Huge deposit from very early this morning."

"Someone like Dinetti probably has money flowing all over, correct?"

"Yes." She knew a fair amount about Michael's business and financial practices. "But not usually such a large amount at once. He's usually more careful than that."

"Who did it come from?"

She shook her head. "Don't know. I can only find the institution. But I don't think they're adept at moving money, at least not sums this large. They didn't even use an offshore account. Unless... I was assuming the money was ill begotten."

"From someone just as shady as Michael, someone who would have used an offshore account."

"Yes. But they would manage funds more adeptly."

"What legitimate person would give Dinetti almost two million dollars?"

"I suppose it could be someone he's extorting from, but he usually forces them to follow his transfer directions." She paused. "I have a theory, but I'm not sure it fits."

He opened his mouth but paused at a sound coming from the house. From this distance, it was muted, but it sounded like someone knocking on the front door.

They headed in the back door and through the house.

Before opening the door, he murmured, "Will you stay to the side?"

She moved to the sitting room doorway, where she could see Asher, but the door would block anyone's view of her. She didn't want anyone seeing her with Asher, linking them together any further.

Asher opened the door. "How may I help you, officer?"

Officer?

"Hello, Mr. Cross. Mighty nice what you've done with the old broken-down plantation."

How does the officer know Asher owns it?

"We've had plenty of discussions in town about who was investing in this place. We were a mite surprised to find that Asher Cross owns a little piece of our Black Mountain paradise."

Cali couldn't tell if the officer liked having Asher as part of the community or if it set him on edge. Maybe a little bit of both.

"It's a lovely community," Asher said. "Is there something I can help you with?"

"We received an anonymous tip, you see, and well, I need to search these premises."

"What kind of anonymous tip?" Asher didn't feign surprise, just continued talking in his usual direct manner.

"Fugitive from justice holed up on this property. A Miss Callista Lebeau."

"Fugitive? What is she accused of doing?"

"Attempted murder. If you'll just let me and my deputy inside to look around, we can clear this up right quick."

She couldn't decide if the officer was a little simple or really slick. She was leaning toward the latter—he used his southern drawl to lull unsuspecting city folk into thinking he was just a country bumpkin. But Asher wasn't so easily lulled.

"May I see the warrant?"

The slight rustle of paper.

Asher paused long enough that she was certain the warrant appeared to be legitimate, and he was trying to think of a way around it.

She walked over to the door. "I'm Callista Lebeau."

Asher rested his hand on her waist, as if ready to snatch her away. His touch sent a sensation through her that she couldn't quite process. Maybe due to the current circumstances, maybe because she'd never felt anything like that before.

She looked up at Asher. "We know what's probably happening. Will you please call my friends?" He would understand whom she meant.

His jaw tightened, but he nodded.

"Miss Lebeau, you're under arrest for the attempted murder of Jonathan Sikes."

She had no idea who in the world Jonathan Sikes was—it was not someone she knew from Michael's circle. She let the officer handcuff her and then lead her to a police cruiser parked in the circular drive in front of the house. She sat in the back seat and looked at Asher standing on the front porch.

He was staring down the cruiser as if he could make it burst into flames.

She forced a small smile and nodded at him.

He nodded once curtly in return.

Somehow, she felt that they understood each other exactly.

***

It took all of Asher's self-control to stand there.

Asher watched the cruiser take Cali, and he dialed Floyd's number.

Floyd answered before the second ring. "Cali okay?"

"How would someone fake an arrest warrant?"

Floyd took the phone away from his mouth and said, presumably to the other hackers, "Cali. Arrest warrant." Then he said to Asher, "Did you get her away?"

"She surrendered herself when the officers came to the door. Said they got a tip a fugitive was there."

"So, they found your safehouse."

He'd been to this house only a couple of times. He'd never even stopped in town. Only one contractor knew he owned the place, a contractor he trusted.

Asher's hand shook with rage.

He heard voices in the background, and then Floyd said, "Who's Jonathan Sikes?"

"No idea."

Floyd said to his friends, "Find out everything about Jonathan Sikes."

"I'm calling a lawyer," Asher said. "Tell me when you have something."

"We're on it. We're getting her out."

Not if I get her out first.

Asher headed back through the house to his truck. He dialed another number and slammed on the gas. He gave directions to his attorney as he drove and demanded he stop everything and focus just on getting Cali out.

A little while later, he pulled into the driveway of a small house in a cute little neighborhood. The front door was open.

Asher ran into the house. "Jim!" he called.

A groan came from the next room.

Asher turned the corner to find his contractor lying on the kitchen floor bleeding. He'd been brutally beaten. He slit open his swollen eyes. "Mr. Cross. I…"

Asher dropped to his knees next to Jim. The bleeding seemed to have stopped, thankfully. He dialed 911 and directed them to send an ambulance.

"Mr. Cross," Jim said. "You gotta git outta here. They were looking for you."

"Who was it?"

He started to shake his head but then groaned. "Didn't catch any names. Gangster types." His expression strained with stress. "I tried not to say anythin'. But then I thought the house was just standing vacant, so…"

Jim hadn't thought Asher was even in town. He had no reason to.

Jim continued, stress now shaking his voice, "Then they said somethin' about finding a girl."

It all clicked together in Asher's head. He texted Floyd, "Jonathan Sikes linked to the terrorist group." Dinetti didn't have the right connections to pull off a fake arrest warrant. Dinetti had tracked down Asher's location—his skills at tracking people down was better than he'd given him credit for, probably from all those years of tracking Cali—with the assumption Cali would be with him, and then he'd sold that to the terrorist group. That explained that large deposit. She'd proven too difficult, not worth the effort of trying to control and use her. Dinetti had recouped his losses, so Cali was likely free of him, but now an even more powerful force had her.

Some protector I'm turning out to be. Fury roared through him.

"Mr. Cross," Jim said. "I don't know what's goin' on, but you gotta git outta here. Go help that girl they're after, whoever she is."

"I need to make sure you're—"

"You called an ambulance. I'll be all right. Had worse when I was ridin' bulls. Go."

Asher hesitated.

"Please," Jim said.

Asher looked him square in the eye. "You call me if you need anything." Then he added, "It's not your fault, you understand? This is my fault."

"Please help that girl they're lookin' for."

"I promise you I will make sure she's safe."

Jim nodded, one small movement. "Go."

Asher left. He could hear the ambulance siren about a block over. He'd left only for Cali's sake. If he got too mixed up with Jim, with what'd happened, it might hinder his ability to help Cali.

Help Cali…

What he wanted to do was storm the station and carry her out, like he'd done back in the SEALs, all those off-the-books assignments.

He stopped back at the house, loaded everything they'd

brought back into his truck in less than two minutes, and then headed for the police station. He was getting her out one way or another.

CHAPTER 14

It took a little while for the officers to process her. They weren't friendly by any means, but they treated her with basic respect. She wouldn't expect anything better. As far as they knew, she'd tried to kill a man.

Finally, she was taken to a phone.

She remembered the number. Asher had told her it in the car just in case. She hadn't thought she'd need it. But she did remember it. Numbers tended to stick in her head, whether she wanted them to or not.

She dialed.

He answered before the first ring ended. "Hello."

"It's me."

"Are you all right?"

"Yes. The officers have been professional."

"I wasn't sure if you'd call me or your friend." Meaning Floyd or one of the other Gray Hats.

"I called to ask you to—"

"No."

"You—"

"We've had this discussion before. It's a waste of time to have it again and come to the same conclusion."

She sighed.

"I'm still able to annoy you. You must be holding up quite well."

She suppressed a laugh. Since when was Asher Cross funny? But then…she didn't really know him that well. No one did. Maybe Willow heard all the jokes.

"I've called my attorney," he continued. "Your friends are also looking into the circumstances. We'll get this cleared up. I'm waiting right here for you."

She wanted to ask if they'd found anything about Jonathan Sikes yet, but she couldn't discuss freely here.

"I'll get you more information as I'm able," he said.

"Thank you."

He added very quietly, "If there is an issue in there, someone trying to hurt you, make a commotion."

She wasn't sure what he meant.

They ended the call with his assurance his attorney and her friends were doing everything possible to clear this up.

One of the officers led her back to a cell. On the way, past an area filled with multiple desks, she overheard two officers talking. "…standing right there in the lobby."

"Didn't he play in the NFL?"

"Yep."

"And he's just standing out there? Is he waiting to talk to someone?"

"I think he was harboring that murderer we just brought in."

They were faced away from her and obviously didn't notice her being led through by another officer.

"I think we're gonna have to tell him this ain't a campground."

The officer led her through a metal door and then into a cinderblock hallway. He indicated a cell, she entered, and he closed the door with a clang.

She sat down on the hard cot. Why was Asher just standing out there? It wasn't as if he could do anything here, other than potentially annoy the police.

But somehow…she felt better knowing he was here.

She didn't need anyone to take care of her. Never had. She was the one who got things done, fixed problems, and generally figured things out. But now, she didn't have much choice but to rely on others. It felt alien, and she didn't particularly like it.

But she appreciated that he wanted to help. That someone was putting her at the top of the priority list. She'd never had that.

She stared across the cell at the gray cinderblock wall.

Or…was he simply feeling guilty? The only way anyone could have found her was through some connection to him.

She slouched back against the cold wall.

Then she shook her head and focused. Jonathan Sikes…she definitely did not know the name. And given her current circumstances, she had a theory about that large deposit into Michael Dinetti's account.

She took a breath, closed her eyes, and let her mind zoom through all logical theories.

Two things she'd learned long ago: getting upset didn't help anything, and if she didn't get herself out of trouble, no one else would.

***

After speaking to his attorney again on the phone, Asher went back inside the police station. The desk sergeant looked up. Asher continued to ignore him. Asher knew he was starting to annoy him, but he was not leaving this station without Cali.

The day passed.

He spoke to his attorney again. All the attorney could find was that the warrant appeared to be legitimate, though she wasn't able to get much more information than that.

He also spoke to Floyd. "Looks like it's legit," Floyd said. "A judge signed off. We checked on him, real deep dive. He's clean."

Asher closed his eyes and clenched his jaw. He'd assumed the warrant had been the work of hackers, that the Gray Hats might be able to just make it disappear.

"Do you think the charges could be valid?" Floyd asked. He quickly followed with, "I trust Cali's a good person. I'm not saying she's necessarily in the wrong."

"But perhaps justified."

"Yeah."

Could that be why she was so bent on keeping Asher out of this? The charges were legitimate?

Floyd added, "There's a lot we don't know about her past."

"She said she doesn't know the name."

"Jonathan Sikes could be anyone. If Dinetti sent some hired goon after her, she might not know the name. If she defended herself and ran, she might not have even realized how bad she hurt him."

Asher knew she had trained in self-defense and carried a weapon. But he'd seen in her eyes she hadn't wanted to use that weapon on the men who'd attacked his house. Was that because she didn't have a killer instinct or because she'd almost killed once and couldn't live with it again?

Finally, Asher answered, "It doesn't matter one way or the other."

Floyd paused. "All right." Then he asked about what Asher's attorney had found, and they ended the call.

The night passed slowly.

There was no actual waiting area, no chairs, so he sat on the floor with his back leaned against the wall and his arms rested on his knees.

He fought memories. It was always harder when he was stressed or angry. And he wasn't as good as he used to be at staying awake. He hadn't slept at all the night before, so he only made it to about four a.m. before he started to doze.

Dreams invaded, like they usually did. He never dreamt

about the incident that'd given him his scars and gotten him discharged. He always dreamed about those he'd failed to save. Their terrified eyes. Their screams. Their blood.

He woke with a start.

The desk sergeant was staring at him.

He wasn't sure if he'd done or said anything in his sleep. At least, he was still seated on the same spot on the floor. Rose had told him that he sometimes yelled and thrashed in his sleep. Her presence had helped calm the dreams, but he didn't have her anymore. Her memory only added to the nightmares.

He stood and went outside to try to calm down.

Flashes of the dreams stuck with him. They were different. The same terrors of his past but a different person.

He pulled shaking hands through his hair.

An officer passed him on the walkway and watched him carefully, as if concerned he was mentally unstable. Sometimes he felt like he was.

After a few minutes, he grabbed a protein bar out of the back of his truck and then went back inside.

In the desk area behind the glass, three officers were talking in a huddle. With the bulletproof glass in the way, their voices were muffled, but the tone was definitely agitated.

"Where could it have gone?" one of them asked.

Another glanced over at Asher and indicated to the others that they should move this conversation elsewhere. They exited the desk area through a side door.

***

The good thing about having been arrested in a small town was that the police building was also small. Cali sat perfectly still and listened. Thankfully, the few people in the other cells were apparently still asleep and being silent.

123

She could just catch some of the conversation a few officers were having in the next room.

"I don't see that we have any other choice."

"...should call the D.A."

"Already did. He..."

"I know it was there."

A couple of sentences too muffled to hear.

"...no other choice."

CHAPTER 15

About a minute later, an officer came into the holding cell area and unlocked Cali's door. "You're out, Lebeau."

Cali stood and followed the officer. Questions threatened to overwhelm her, but it was usually best not to question something like this too much. Just accept the good fortune and get out of there.

At the end of the hall, another officer stood in the way of the heavy door leading to the public reception area. *Too good to be true* rang through her head. As she approached, she noticed his name tag said Chief of Police.

"Ms. Lebeau," he addressed her with a professionally detached tone. "There appears to be some kind of error, and the warrant for your arrest has disappeared from the system."

She controlled her thousands of questions and just nodded.

"I've never seen anything of the sort happen before," he continued. "Please know this: if something nefarious has happened, we will get to the bottom of it."

She nodded. "Yes, sir."

"But if it was a clerical error being corrected and the warrant was never valid to begin with, please accept my apologies."

"None needed, sir. Your officers have been nothing but professional."

He nodded and stepped out of the way. The officer escorting her opened the door and let her walk out.

Asher was standing there with his arms crossed.

"They said I can leave," she said.

He moved quickly to the door leading outside and held it for her. They both went across the parking lot, got in his truck, and were down the road in less than a minute.

He jumped on I40 and headed west. Rain started falling and made the view out the windows fuzzy.

"What did you do?" she finally asked.

"I didn't do anything. My attorney and Floyd both said the warrant appeared to be legitimate."

She looked over at him. "Legitimate? Floyd said that?"

He nodded, focused on the road.

A long pause.

"Do you remember the name Jonathan Sikes?" he asked.

She realized why he was asking that again. Trying to determine if she'd done what she was accused of. She blinked hard to banish the prickly sensation she felt on the backs of her eyes, and she turned to look out the side window at the fuzzy rain.

Several minutes passed. She calculated what to do next—most likely wait until they stopped next and find a way to ditch him, which shouldn't be that hard if he thought she was a murderer. The thought made her posture sag for some reason. Probably because he was the first person whom she thought actually might care about her, not as a useful tool, but as a person.

Suck it up, buttercup, she told herself. *You don't need anyone.*

But as the years had passed, she'd realized that wasn't really true.

Nevertheless, it was reality.

He spoke again, but quieter, "Whatever you tell me, I'll

believe you."

She looked over at him. He continued to focus out the windshield.

She hesitated. "I've never killed anyone. I've never even come close to killing anyone. I've trained to defend myself physically, but I prefer to stay one step ahead and avoid violence if at all possible."

He nodded once, a simple but decisive gesture.

And that was it. He said nothing more, didn't even look over at her.

He continued driving.

They were quiet for a long time.

She truly did not understand Asher Cross. He was not the type to believe anyone so simply, let alone some random bookkeeper who used to work for him. In business, he was shrewd and calculating and aggressive—not blindly trusting. She was missing something, and she had no idea what it was.

Sometime later, Asher finally asked, "What did they tell you? When they said you could go?"

"I didn't ask questions, but they said the warrant was just gone. I overheard that they asked the D.A., and there weren't any other options but to release me."

He took his phone out of his jeans pocket and handed it to her. "You should ask Floyd to look into it. Email, phone, and text are all secure on that phone." He added, "They'll want to know you're all right anyway."

She opted for email and typed a short message.

"I'm not reading any of your emails," she said. "But it looks like you have a bunch from people at work."

"My assistant will text me about anything truly urgent."

She handed his phone back to him. "You own the company. Isn't everything urgent?"

"My department heads are very capable."

"Since when do you not run that company with an iron fist? I don't mean that in a bad way. I mean you're involved with everything important."

"Since I have something more important to do." He continued to keep his focus on the road.

"Where are we going?" she asked. "Or are you just driving to get away from Black Mountain?"

"The warrant came from Louisiana. I think we should have a discussion with that judge."

"Is that a good idea?"

"Floyd said the judge seems to be upstanding. I'd like to know why he signed a warrant to arrest an innocent woman."

They were quiet again. This drive was going to be much longer. She'd already read the car's manual, so she just watched the scenery flash by.

He opened something on his phone and handed it to her. "The manual for my other car."

She hesitated but then took the phone.

After a few hours, they stopped for gas and grabbed a snack at the convenience store. Then they drove hours more.

She offered to drive a few times, but he answered simply, "I'm fine," and continued driving in silence. She didn't let herself fall asleep in an attempt to keep him company, but the couple of times she tried to start a conversation, he gave nothing more than one-word answers.

In total, the drive was over ten hours. Other than stopping for gas and food, he drove straight through, like a machine.

There was an almost-tangible distance between them, as there pretty much always had been. It started with him completely ignoring her, and now he continued it by refusing even to glance in her direction. But there had been moments when the distance had receded. She wondered why. But mostly, she wondered why he was so bent on helping her if he didn't even want to interact with her.

Dusk was falling when he turned off into a manicured

gravel drive. It was winding and trees blocked sightlines. He pulled to a stop in what appeared to be a parking lot. She saw a path through trees just ahead.

Asher turned off the ignition and got out of the car. Cali followed.

As they walked through the trees, they came into a courtyard. It was dominated by a huge fountain in the center, with water shooting fifteen feet up into the air. Around that was a pathway of what looked a lot like soapstone. And around the outer edge of the path sat beds of architectural landscaping, perfectly shaped hedges and trees.

To the right sat a house. A two-level porch appeared to wrap all the way around the house. Up the back steps, they paused at the door while Asher opened a lockbox and took out the key. They entered into a grand hall. When she glanced at the kitchen to the left and then noticed double doors at the other end of the hall, she realized this was the back door. Quite an entrance for the back of the house. The hall came to an octagonal vestibule in the center of the house, and the stairs were off that.

Asher started up the stairs, so she followed. Old but polished wood floors creaked under their feet. She tried not to be distracted by the intricate molding, amazing artwork on the walls, and lavish antique furnishings.

He led her to a huge bedroom, probably almost a quarter the size of the whole floor. A four-poster canopy bed dominated the room.

"I'll bring in the food we brought with us and put it in the kitchen. Feel free to wander, eat, or rest." He walked back out of the room.

She allowed herself a few minutes to look around. A bathroom and dressing room were attached to the main room.

While she'd barely slept in the jail cell last night, she wasn't ready for sleep. She headed back downstairs.

The food had already been deposited in the kitchen.

She put the jugs of water in the refrigerator. The kitchen had been restored accurately for an early 1800s house—the hearth and worktable took up most of the space. Modern appliances were set to the side and didn't really fit in.

She looked around the house, expecting to find Asher somewhere, but he was nowhere to be seen.

Eventually, she went back upstairs.

Back in the room he'd given her, there were a few clothes laid out on the bed. She'd been wearing the same clothes for three days. She was desperate to change, even if it was into one of Asher's shirts. A scribbled note lay next to the clothes.

There is a laundry room in the outbuilding.

She closed the door and changed into the t-shirt Asher had left. He'd also left a pair of jeans, but they were ridiculous. He had insanely long legs. She had long legs for her height, but the pants were a foot too long. So, she stuck with just the t-shirt, which fit like a short dress. She grabbed all her clothes, all the way down to her socks, and headed outside. They'd come from the path on the left of the courtyard, so she headed toward the one to the right. The path was well lit with small, decorative pole lights, unlike the courtyard. She found the outbuilding just outside the tree line that surrounded the courtyard. It included the laundry room, as well as a huge commercial kitchen. She guessed he rented this house for events like weddings, so the caterer would need a proper kitchen, more than the mid-1800s kitchen in the main house. She put her clothes in the wash and meandered outside in the courtyard.

***

Asher stood at the railing of the second floor of the wrap-around porch. Cali had found the laundry, and now she was walking around the courtyard. Light slowly burned out of the sky, replaced by darkness and the glow of the moon. The courtyard had lighting, but it was low, designed for romantic pictures of newly married couples.

With her slender legs and feet bare, fair skin catching the low light, she walked around and admired the splashing fountain and the manicured garden.

He'd chosen this house partially due to its location close to New Orleans and partially because he thought the setting might help put her at ease after all she'd been dealing with the last couple of days. Including dealing with him. She'd been trying to talk to him, but he'd continued to ignore her as much as he could, no matter how hard it was. He owed her that much.

He forced himself to turn and go back into the house.

***

She had no idea where Asher disappeared to. After finishing washing her clothes and then finding something to eat, she walked through the house again, this time the second floor as well, but she didn't see him. She even checked to make sure his truck was still here.

Finally, she lay down in the huge bed, still wearing his t-shirt.

She was exhausted, but her mind refused to calm down. There were too many questions. Her mind could not let go of trying to figure everything out. She closed her eyes and tried to force herself to sleep. If she didn't rest, she wouldn't be useful in deciphering the mysteries currently swirling around her.

It was useless. She stared at the dark ceiling and listed out all the facts she knew, all the questions she still had, and possible plans of attack.

Yelling.

She bolted upright and sprang from bed. Quiet.

Then she heard it again and looked up at the ceiling. It

was coming from upstairs, the third floor.

She had no idea where Asher was. Could that possibly be him yelling? No. She couldn't hear words, but the voice sounded too unsettled to be the brick wall that was Asher.

At the door, she glanced up and down the hall, and then she headed for the stairs and climbed up to the third floor. She'd figured it was just attic space, storage, but it was finished with hallways and rooms, though much simpler than the rest of the house—hallway narrower, rooms smaller, and plain white walls. The old servants' quarters?

She followed the yelling to a room at the opposite corner of the house from her room. The door was closed.

"Rose!" he roared. She could barely tell that it was Asher's voice. She'd heard him angry, but she'd never heard fear laced through the anger like that.

She paused. He was obviously having a nightmare. Would he want her to ignore him? Probably.

He yelled again. Anger still pulsed through his voice, but it didn't block the sound of pain. Deep soul-wrenching pain.

She cracked the door and peered inside.

He was lying in a small bed in the corner of the room. No blankets or even a pillow. He was bare-chested but wore his jeans. The bruising at his ribs from when Michael's men had attacked the house was much worse—it had to hurt.

He grunted, and his whole body tensed, as if he were withstanding a beating. A memory?

Then he twisted, face turned away, and his voice came out in a strained whisper. "Ca…" She couldn't understand what he said, but she'd never heard so much pain in a person's voice.

She moved closer, not sure how to approach him. If he lashed out in his sleep from being startled and hit her on accident, she knew he'd feel terrible.

"Asher," she said in a calm voice. "Asher, wake up."

Nothing.

She moved even closer and knelt on the floor. His hand shifted, and she took the opportunity and gently held his hand.

He squeezed her hand back, but his eyes were still closed.

She rested her other hand on top of his. "Asher, wake up." She stroked her hand up his forearm. "Asher, please. Everything is okay."

His eyes flew open, and he stared at her. His breathing was heavy. He looked at her as if he wasn't sure what he was seeing.

"It's okay," she said. "You were just dreaming."

He took a deep breath and closed his eyes. "Dreaming."

She rubbed her thumb over the back of his hand.

He pulled his hand away and stood, faced away from her toward the window.

She allowed a minute or so to pass.

He didn't move.

She asked, "Are you all right?"

"Get out of here."

She stood but hesitated.

"I said get out of here," he growled.

She still hesitated.

He turned and glared. "Go!"

She backed up and slipped out the door. As she turned to head back down the hall, she caught a glimpse of him dropping his head into his hands.

CHAPTER 16

Cali was furious. She wanted to slam doors, but she'd learned to have iron-fisted self-control over her actions.

Her emotions, though, those were sometimes a different story. Most of the time, she was fine. Slights at work, rude people at the grocery store, that stuff slid off her back. She truly didn't care.

But sometimes, rage slipped into the cracks of her heart and infected her.

In her room, she dropped to her knees and bowed her head. *Please.* She reached out to God, but she didn't calm like she usually did.

She opened her eyes and stared at the beautiful antique rug under her knees. Deep breaths. She continued to reach out to God.

And then she realized… Anger wasn't the problem. It was hurt. She felt like pain was searing her in half.

She clasped her hands and squeezed her eyes shut. *Please, God.* She needed her focus. She couldn't get mired in emotion. Her freedom depended on it. Asher's safety depended on it.

She stayed there on the floor for a long time. Hours.

When the sun started to rise and streamed in from

between the heavy drapes, she was lying on the floor, curled up. She wasn't sure if she'd slept or gotten lost in prayer. Perhaps somewhere in between.

She sat there and stared at how the sunlight brightened the reds and golds of the rug.

Then she got up and went through the motions of showering and dressing. The room was stocked with mini soaps and towels, like a hotel.

She decided she would find Asher's computer and do some research. She needed to free him, and in order to do that, she needed to understand what was going on a lot better. He'd shown very clearly that, while he did not want her company, he would not leave her until she was safe.

In the kitchen, she found the bag with his computer. She pulled up a stool, found a notebook, and started working.

A little while later, Asher walked by the kitchen and out the back door. He didn't speak to her, didn't even pause. She stood and followed as far as the porch. He walked across the courtyard toward his truck, didn't look back. She wondered if perhaps he was leaving her. For good.

He didn't have any bags with him, but perhaps he was so angry he was simply leaving everything and driving straight back home. This was his property after all, so it wasn't as if he couldn't get everything back, and she doubted anything here was of any deep importance to him, nothing a billionaire like him couldn't replace with the snap of his fingers.

Her posture slouched. She rejected the urge to call after him and ask where he was going. If he was leaving, that was for the best.

She went back to the kitchen and continued her research. If he had left, she needed to get her plan together, needed to gather all the information she could before she no longer had the use of a computer.

After some digging, she found a man named Jonathan Sikes who might just be the man she was looking for. It would have been easy for the Gray Hats to overlook him.

She heard footsteps on the porch stairs and looked up.

Asher walked inside. He set a cell phone on the table next to her, turned and walked back out to the hallway. But then he paused.

Without turning to look at her, he said, "It was inexcusable of me to raise my voice at you. I'm sorry."

She opened her mouth to reply, but he walked away before she could say anything.

She looked after him for a few seconds.

Then she picked up the cell phone. It looked brand new, the latest model. He'd gotten a secure phone for her? Why?

She pondered whether to go find him and talk to him. But in the end, she decided to leave him alone. He'd been very clear he had no interest in talking with her.

After reading Jonathan Sikes' extremely interesting Facebook posts, which appeared to have stopped abruptly, she started planning how to meet him.

Footsteps.

She looked up to see Asher in the doorway. "I'm going out for a while. I programmed my number in your phone in case you need anything."

So, he wasn't planning on ditching her. She felt...oddly relieved. Since when did she not prefer to be alone?

He didn't wait for a response and walked out the door.

It was only a few minutes later that she met a cab in the parking lot.

***

Asher parked in a garage next to a government building and sat for a few minutes. He felt stressed and agitated, and he needed to get that under control, at least properly hidden. He was used to being alone much of the time, except for Willow. He didn't like to admit to himself how much he missed that cat—she made him feel a little less alone but never asked him about his nightmares or about Rose. He never had to explain himself. Or apologize.

That was what was causing his agitation—how he'd treated Cali. It had been the only thing he could think to do to get her to go away. To protect her.

He needed to focus on the task at hand, the bigger picture, what was most important. His pain was irrelevant.

He got out of the truck and headed into the building. After going through security, he headed upstairs to where the judges' chambers were. He'd done his research and had a plan on how to approach this. To the clerk, he gave his name and told him he was interested in discussing a property the judge had for sale, a multimillion-dollar property that was getting pretty much no interest from buyers.

The clerk, an awkward young man, stared a bit intensely at Asher, and his eyes widened at his name. Asher was concerned about being seen—the people after Cali knew she was with him. And he'd had no alternative but to leave her alone at the house. He didn't have reliable contacts in this area of the country. He could get someone here, but it would take several hours. And Cali probably wouldn't like it—she'd feel she was being babysat. The last thing he wanted to do was anger her even more than he already had.

Asher said to the clerk, "I don't care if you gossip about my being here, but I ask that you please wait until after I've gone. I won't take much of the judge's time, and then I'll leave."

The clerk lowered his brows. "I would never talk about the judge's interactions."

"But you'll mention to close friends that you saw me, even if you don't give details of the circumstances. You can tell your friends I fulfill the name The Beast perfectly. I don't care. Just wait until I've gone."

The clerk nodded and then went into the judge's chambers.

A couple of minutes later, the clerk allowed Asher into the chambers and went back to his desk. The judge looked like the standard upstanding older man—gray hair, rimless glasses, clean shave, classic blue suit. He stood and greeted Asher with a solid handshake. And his gaze did not linger on Asher's scars, like the clerk's had, no matter how much he'd tried to hide it. Asher didn't care if people looked at his physical scars, as long as they didn't ask questions, but he found over the years that whether a person stared or not gave Asher an indication of how best to deal with them.

"I'm certainly surprised to hear Asher Cross is interested in my little property," the judge said. "I thought you dealt in commercial properties." He motioned for Asher to take a seat and resumed his own chair.

"I do. For the most part. But I'm looking for a vacation spot in the area." Although the property the judge was selling was too flashy for Asher's taste—resort-style pool, multiple guest suites, pool house, etc.

"Ah, well, it's a great vacation place. Plenty of room for guests and parties." Then he moved on quickly, surely thinking either Asher had no friends for parties or assuming Asher's parties were not the sort the judge wanted to discuss. People tended to think Asher was some combination of brute and womanizer. "Have you looked at the listing pictures?"

"I'm guessing you bought the place when your kids were younger, and now that they're in college, you don't need all that space." And he surely needed the money to pay for two Ivy League college educations.

"Yes, exactly." The judge smiled. "What kinds of questions do you have about the place?"

Asher paused. "The question I'd really like an answer to is why did you sign an arrest warrant for Callista Lebeau?"

Anger clouded the judges' eyes, and he started to stand.

"I know you're a good man," Asher said. "Your record

shows you have a level head and a good grasp of the law. You don't insert your own agenda. You're a good judge."

The judge sat back down but said, "You need to leave now, Mr. Cross."

"Are you being blackmailed? If you are, I may be able to help."

The judge appraised him intensely. Asher met his gaze openly.

After a good full minute, the judge said, "Are you representing Miss Lebeau?"

"Yes. My personal attorney is handling any of her legal needs."

"What is your relationship with Miss Lebeau?"

"She was an employee until just recently."

The judge lifted his gray brows. "And you do this kind of thing for all your employees?"

"No," Asher admitted.

"Why this one?"

"She has more need." He couldn't tell him the whole truth, but he added, "She is truly a good person. And no, other than helping her with this, I have no personal relationship with her."

The judge leaned back in his chair, and the leather shifted against his back. "I heard the warrant disappeared from the system."

"Do you know why?"

"Technical glitch, I'm told. When I reached out to the D.A.'s office, they informed me a key bit of evidence disappeared from their system as well."

"So they can't request a new warrant."

"Correct."

"Can you tell me what that evidence was? I know she did not commit this crime, so knowing what that evidence was could be helpful in figuring out what's going on."

"I can't discuss specifics like that with a private citizen such as yourself." Then he added, "It was just enough to justify a warrant."

"But not yet enough to convict."

The judge sat forward in his chair. "I didn't say any of this."

"Understood."

"Whatever is going on, perhaps someone with your connections and resources can dig up the truth. I don't take kindly to outside forces tampering with the justice system—whoever is doing it needs stopped."

"That's the plan." Asher stood. "Have a nice day, Judge Anderson."

The judge nodded, and Asher walked out of his office and back to his truck.

Before heading to the house, Asher made a quick stop at a store, and a short while later, he parked at his property. He brought the bags in, expecting to find Cali in the kitchen on his computer still, or perhaps with a notebook in front of her filled with notes and theories. But she wasn't there. He went up to her room. He looked in the open door to find it empty. He set the bags on her still-made bed and continued through the rest of the house and then the outbuilding.

She wasn't on the property.

Nothing in the house was disturbed, so he felt confident no one had found this place and grabbed her. She would never go quietly—she would leave a trail of destruction.

Which meant she'd left on her own.

On his way back through the courtyard, he sat on one of the low walls. Had she left for good?

CHAPTER 17

Cali paid the cab driver—thankfully, she had enough cash—and walked up to the "behavioral health center," which was a pretty way of saying mental hospital/rehab center. It was a sprawling beige brick building, probably built in the 60s or 70s, that looked like it had been a church in another life. She found the main entrance and walked up to the reception desk. Now to do something she hated—lie.

She smiled at the nurse. "Hi. I'm here to see my cousin."

"Name?"

"Chester McDonald." She'd gotten the name from the Gray Hats.

The nurse typed something on her computer, presumably checking that Chester was allowed visitors. She looked back up at Cali. "I.D. please."

Cali huffed out a breath. "That's a problem. I was mugged yesterday. They took my wallet, everything. I can't even drive because I don't have my license—I had to take a cab to get here."

"I'm sorry, miss. I can't let you see a patient if you don't have I.D."

"Oh, dear." Cali wrung her hands. "I promised Chester I'd visit. I was supposed to come yesterday, but I had to make the police report, and I was so distraught. And I'm worried he'll feel abandoned, and his recovery will be set back. His mom and brother had already turned their backs on him. I just... I can't be responsible for another setback for him."

The nurse stood. "Let me go talk to his doctor." She walked away.

A couple of minutes later, an older woman in a lab coat came out. She introduced herself, asked Cali's name—Cali gave a fake name—and asked when she'd last seen her cousin. Cali had the impression she was evaluating her.

"Not since before he was admitted, so a little over a week ago," Cali answered. The Gray Hats had told her when he'd been admitted. "I promised him I'd come on my first day off. That was yesterday."

"But your purse and I.D. were stolen. I'm sorry to hear that." The doctor paused, surely still assessing Cali, determining if it was in Chester's best interest to let her see him. "Would you allow us to search your bag?"

Cali smiled. "To make sure no illicit substances are brought in. Sure. I support anything that can be done to help him get well." The Gray Hats had let her know Chester was in for alcohol addiction. She'd left her wallet in a drawer at Asher's house in anticipation of a request like this. All she had in her small bag was some cash, a little notebook, and a hairbrush.

The nurse handed Cali's bag back after looking quickly through it.

The doctor said, "I'll take you back to see Chester." She stepped out from behind the reception desk and led Cali down a hall. The walls were ugly cinderblock but painted a sunny yellow.

The doctor led her through an open door into a small but tidy room. A young man looked up from his seat on the narrow bed. "Hey, doc." He was too thin and had heavy bags under his eyes, but his smile was kind, though a little sad, like a beaten dog.

Cali spoke up, "Hey, cuz. Sorry I didn't come yesterday like I promised."

Chester looked at her and hesitated.

Cali added, "Please don't be mad."

Chester smiled. "'Course I'm not mad. I'm happy to see a friendly face."

The doctor said to Chester, "Group session is in an hour."

"I'll be there."

The doctor walked back down the hall.

Cali sat in the chair in the corner.

"I must have been really, really drunk when we met. I'd think I'd remember meeting someone who looks like you." Then he added, "Or something interesting is going on."

"I have it on good authority that you're a nice person, so I'm going to be pretty honest. I told the doctor I'm your cousin in order to gain access. I actually need to see someone in the psych ward."

"Who's this 'good authority'? And why didn't you tell the doc you're the cousin of the person you really need to see? Why are you sneaking into a psych hospital? People usually sneak *out* of these places, not in."

"It's someone who's being watched, and I worry any record of a visitation, even one under a false name, will be flagged and scrutinized by the wrong people. People I think have tried to hurt this person. No one can know I was here."

"And who's the 'good authority'?"

"My hacker friends. Good hackers, I promise. They said you've been struggling with alcohol addiction for a long time, but you have no arrest record, and all your employer reviews speak of your work ethic and teamwork."

"They found my old employer reviews? Who are these guys? What're you involved in?"

"I can't tell you everything, for your own safety. But I'll tell you I'm not trying to hurt anyone, just getting to the bottom of who is chasing me."

Chester raised his brows. "Old jealous boyfriend?"

"Much, much bigger than that. Please don't tell anyone about what I've said. I don't want you getting in the middle of anything." Cali stood. "I need to go. If the doctor asks, will you tell her I went to the restroom?"

"I don't like lying to the doc. She's the only one who thinks I'm worth any effort." He paused. "But if you stop in the ladies' room, it won't actually be a lie."

"Deal."

"It's down the hall on the left." Then he added, "Psych ward is in the back section. Take the last right turn at the end of the hall."

"Thank you, Chester." She paused at the door and looked back. "You are worth the effort. God is with you. He's sitting right there with you holding your hand."

Chester opened his mouth but said nothing. Then she noticed he squeezed his right hand tight, as if holding onto God.

"You can do it." Cali left the room.

She did stop at the restroom just so Chester wouldn't have to lie. Then she moved quickly down the hall. She worried the entrance to the psychiatric ward might be locked, but it wasn't. Now to find Jonathan Sikes. She had found his picture on his social media page, so at least she could search for him based on sight and didn't have to ask names. She glanced in a few patient rooms and then a common room. Thankfully, the orderly in there had his back turned. Finally, she found a man, probably early sixties, sitting alone in a room looking out a window to the courtyard.

"Hello, Professor Sikes."

His head snapped up. He had graying hair, a bit unkempt, though it was well trimmed. He was slouched, but his eyes were alert when he looked at her. "No one's called me that in years. Who're you?"

She took the chair next to him. "I'd like to hear about The Lost Library." Based on his social media, that appeared to be the object of his obsession, but Cali had no idea if it was connected to anything. If nothing else, it might serve as a way to get him to open up.

He glanced at the doorway and whispered, "I'm not supposed to talk about that."

She tilted her head. "Who says?"

"If he hears me talking about the library, it'll be bad."

"Bad how?"

"I'll have to go to the hospital again."

"What happened the last time?"

"He made me drink something, something worse than usual." He put his hands on the arms of his chair, about to get up.

Cali put her hand on his. "They framed me for trying to kill you. Please help me."

He stared at her for a moment and then settled back into his chair. He glanced again at the doorway.

"Do you have any idea what's going on?" she asked.

He shook his head.

"I'll try to help. What's his name? When's the first time you saw him?"

He hesitated and then went on in a rush. "Marcus. He's an orderly. He came to my house. Made me drink something. I felt so strange, and I did weird things, things I'd never do. He said I can't tell anyone, or he'll hurt them. Please be careful. Please."

"And then you got sent here."

He nodded.

Obviously, this Marcus was drugging him, but thankfully, he seemed lucid right now, just scared. "Does Marcus tell you not to talk about anything other than The Lost Library?"

He shook his head. "That and the drinks."

So, that had to be why he was being targeted and

possibly related to why *she* was being targeted. "What is The Lost Library?" She'd seen lots of his social media posts about it, but she hadn't researched it in depth yet.

"Ancient texts from the Libraries of Constantinople and Alexandria."

"The Library at Alexandria? Are you serious?"

He nodded. "Greek, Latin, and even Chinese works were in the original library. It's grown since then."

"Where is it?"

He raised a brow.

"It's called The Lost Library for a reason," she surmised.

He nodded. "It's also called the Golden Library. It was originally assembled by Grand Duke Ivan III."

"Ivan the Great of Russia."

"And Ivan IV made it lost."

"Ivan the Terrible."

He nodded.

"Other than the obvious historical significance, why would someone want The Lost Library? Why would someone be going to such lengths?"

Footsteps in the hall.

"Hide," he whispered.

Cali slid quickly under the bed.

A female voice came from the doorway. "Dinner time."

Jonathan said, "I'm coming. Thanks."

The footsteps moved away.

Jonathan whispered, "You need to go."

Cali slid out from under the bed. "I need whatever information you can give me. Have you published papers on this that I can look up?"

He shook his head. "That'll give you the basics but not the real truth."

Cali wasn't entirely sure the guy wasn't actually nuts, but her gut said to follow this lead. "Can you tell me?"

He glanced at the doorway and fidgeted with his hands.

"You need to go." Then he added, "Check out *Atlas of Fictional Places* at the Louisiana State Library. It's all there. Trust me. Now, go."

He was growing more agitated, so Cali slipped out of the room and back down the hall. She smiled at Chester on the way by and headed back out past the reception desk, where she thanked the nurse.

She didn't want to hang out at the behavioral center any more than necessary, just in case Jonathan Sikes was being watched, so she walked down the street to a gas station, where she talked the clerk into calling a cab for her. It was twilight by the time she got back to Asher's house. She paid the cab driver and headed through the courtyard.

Asher stood from his seat on the low wall surrounding the fountain. "Are you okay?"

She stopped and tried to read his expression, but it was too shadowed. "Yes."

He turned and walked around the fountain toward the back door of the house. Had he been waiting for her? If yes, why did he walk away without a conversation? She followed him into the house.

THE LOST LIBRARY

CHAPTER 18

Cali walked through the house down the central hall. Asher was nowhere in sight. She paused at the stairs—he'd most likely retreat as far from her as possible, right? That was usually his MO. But she followed her gut and checked the rest of the downstairs first. She found him at the front of the house in a room the original owners surely had called the parlor. Though it had tall windows looking out to the front veranda, it was too dark outside to allow in much light. And the little that did struggle into the room was sucked up by the dark green walls, dark wood mantle, and brown leather wingback chairs.

Asher stood in the corner by the window, hands half-covering his face and fingers pulled through his hair. She could see his shoulders and biceps were strained.

She made her voice quiet but kept her concern out of her tone. "Are you okay?"

He dropped his hands, and she barely caught a glimpse of his expression before he wiped it clean—worry, maybe even fear.

He tried to walk past her out of the room, but she stood in his way.

He kept his gaze above her head, on the wall behind

her. "Move please."

"What's wrong?"

"I'm tired. Now, if you'll let me by."

"If you're so tired, why'd you come here instead of going straight up to bed?"

His jaw flexed.

"Because you didn't think I'd look for you here. You were trying to avoid me," she surmised. "Why?"

No answer.

"Are you mad at me?" she asked.

He finally looked down at her. "No."

She tried to remind herself of her promise not to treat him like a mystery to be torn apart and solved. He'd done so much for her, more than anyone in her life.

She met his gaze and admitted, "I don't understand you, and that's really hard for me."

His tone was quiet, almost gentle. "I know."

Silence.

He didn't look away, and neither did she. There was something in the air between them. She could almost grasp it.

A sound in the distance, a dog barking somewhere, broke the silence. Asher stepped back.

"May I ask where you went?" he said. "Did you learn anything?"

For some reason, she had an urge to stay in this room, close to him. "I found Jonathan Sikes. He's in a mental hospital." She waited for him to ask a bunch of questions—had she been careful? Did she really think it was a good idea to get close to the man she was accused of trying to murder? Had anyone seen her?

But he said, "Did you learn anything useful?"

"Maybe. I have a bunch more research to do. He's obsessed with something called The Lost Library or the Golden Library. And an orderly might be drugging him. But I don't know if any of it is the ravings of an insane man or something else altogether."

"What's The Lost Library?"

She gave him the basics Jonathan Sikes had told her. Then she said, "Can I ask where you went? Did you learn anything?"

He explained that he'd gone to meet the judge and what he'd told him. "It sounds like you're safe from being arrested again," he said. "At least for this particular charge."

"But someone might try to make up something else. What's interesting is that there appears to be more than one force lurking in the background."

"Whoever framed you and whoever made the warrant and evidence disappear."

"I don't see how it could be the same people doing both. It wouldn't make sense."

"Unless something really complicated is going on." Then he said, "I'm sure your fingers are itching to start researching." He shifted to walk around her out of the room.

She stood in his path. "Will you tell me what was wrong? Did I upset you?"

He stopped.

Then he rested a hand on her upper arm. The sensation jolted through her, silenced all her thoughts.

He barely murmured, "Please."

With slight pressure from his hand, she stepped out of his way. He escaped out of the room and disappeared down the hall.

She took a step to follow but then stopped.

Instead of following him, she made herself go to the kitchen. His computer was still sitting there, the phone he'd given her next to it. Maybe the fact that she hadn't told him where she was going and that she'd left the phone made him think she'd run away from him. Maybe he'd thought his yelling at her had made her want to leave. Yes, she'd been hurt, but she also knew he was a good person who'd had a bad moment. Maybe he'd been upset because he felt bad for yelling at her.

She stood to go tell him she was fine. He'd apologized, and she felt he'd meant it.

Then her phone rang. Floyd's number. She'd called him from the phone earlier when she'd asked for information on a different patient so she could use that to get into the behavioral center.

"Hey," she answered. "It went fine. I got in. No issues."

"Good. We were starting to worry."

She explained what she'd learned.

"The Lost Library you said?"

"Yeah," she said. "Or the Golden Library."

She heard Bl@ze in the background. "We're on it."

"Thank you," she said.

"I bet all that lying was really hard for you," Floyd said. "I'm sorry for that."

Misplaced puzzle pieces vibrated in her brain, begging to be put into place. She'd been doing her best to let certain things lie, not treat the people around her like enigmas to be solved.

She'd given the Gray Hats a lot of leeway, but maybe that'd been a mistake.

"How did you know lying is hard for me?" She failed at making her tone sound light.

Floyd paused.

"Don't try to think up a lie," she warned. "I haven't shared that part of me with you. There's no way you'd know. Unless you'd dug into my background."

Floyd continued to be quiet. The typing in the background stopped as well.

"I expected that you'd have done a basic search," she said. "Make sure I don't have a criminal record before you trusted me with helping you decipher. But this is more than that. It would've had to have been extremely invasive to dig up such a personal tidbit."

"Cali…"

"This is how you found me, isn't it? You didn't happen to run into me at the library and strike up a random conversation. You knew who I was. You knew my skillset, and you created an 'incidental' meeting."

"You're invaluable. You've done so much to help—"

"Floyd," she demanded.

"You know how we operate. Hacker-client privilege."

"Someone hired you." She looked up at the ceiling, as if she could make her vision laser through the floors of the house. "Asher. He hired you, not just to research Dinetti, but to research me, before you and I met in the library. That's how he knew my educational background. That's how he knows more than he should." She'd been hoping he was just extremely observant.

She could almost feel Floyd sweating through the phone. He was usually very calm and collected. Was he more scared of Asher or her? Asher was powerful, but she knew a lot of their secrets.

"I'm hanging up now," Cali said.

"What're you going to do?"

"You know me so well—you should already know." She ended the call.

She dropped the phone on the counter with a clatter and walked calmly up the stairs. At the third floor, she headed down the hall to the room Asher was using. *Why is he using this tiny room all the way up here?*

The door was closed, of course.

She knocked. "I'm coming in." She gave it a few seconds in case he wasn't decent and then opened the door.

The room was dark but for the moonlight streaming in. Asher was sitting on the bed, facing the window, away from her. He didn't turn or even acknowledge her.

"Did you have the Gray Hats do a background check on me?"

A couple of seconds of quiet. "Yes." He still didn't turn or move at all.

"An extremely invasive background check."

"Yes."

She waited for more reaction, explanation, something.

He continued to sit there unmoving, gaze focused out the window.

She moved around the bed so she could see the side of his face, and she realized his gaze wasn't focused out the window, but on the plain white wall.

"Asher."

"I've told you what you wanted to know."

"I want to know why."

Quiet.

She moved closer, standing at the end of the bed.

His gaze shifted in her direction, but didn't make it to her.

She took a slow breath and reminded herself of all he'd done for her, more than he should've ever done. Her tone was calm. "Please tell me why. Do you do background checks on all your employees?" *Please say yes.*

"No."

"Why me?"

He took a breath that made his back expand and fill out his shirt even more. "I saw differences in some of the reports, especially the account notes. Astute observations. Too astute. You were the only variable that had changed."

"You did a background check because I was too good at my job?"

"Things have happened," he said. "In the past. I've learned the necessity of being overly cautious of those around me."

She could understand a sense of caution given his position. "Why not a standard background check from a standard company? Why the Gray Hats? Why so invasive?"

Quiet.

Finally, he looked over at her. "There are things I can't tell you."

She had no idea what that meant. Maybe… "About your service? Your scars?" She had no idea how that would have anything to do with this conversation, but she'd always assumed the story behind his injuries was traumatic.

"My scars bother everyone else a lot more than they bother me."

"Why—"

"I never read it," he said. "I picked it up from Floyd. I had it for a few days. Put the thumb drive in my computer a couple of times. But I never opened any of the files. Eventually, I put the thumb drive in my fireplace."

"Why didn't you read the files?"

"I couldn't bring myself to…" He turned back to the wall. "I couldn't invade your life like that."

"But you've paid attention."

"Yes." He paused. "I realized you were special. I've pieced together enough to realize you are far more educated than your résumé indicated, whether that was formal education or experience. And you also go to great lengths to hide it. I had several theories as to why."

"Were you close? Your theories?"

"Yes."

"Why didn't you fire me?"

He looked over at her with his brows lowered.

"I've brought trouble right to your doorstep. It could affect your whole company."

His jaw clenched, tightening muscles from neck to temple, and he turned back toward the wall.

"Are you angry?" she asked.

"Yes."

"Why?"

He paused. "I'm *The Beast*. I suppose you would think I'd do something like that."

"I just meant you need to protect your company and employees."

"I think I've proven I mean to protect you as much as

anyone else."

Her voice lowered to a murmur. "You're right. You have."

Several seconds of quiet.

Finally, she shifted back a step.

"If you feel the need to leave me," he said, "will you accept my help from a distance?"

CHAPTER 19

"I—" A realization hit Cali. She hadn't seen it coming, and it plowed into her like a semi. "I'm not leaving."

Asher turned his head a few inches in her direction but didn't look at her. Another pause. "We were both out in public today. We should leave first thing in the morning."

"I'll be ready." She turned, walked out of the room, and closed the door.

She headed down to her room and walked in to see several shopping bags on the bed, as well as a new suitcase. In the bags, she found clothes and toiletries. The clothes were the right sizes and the kinds of things she would've picked for herself—simple and modest but pretty in an understated way.

She closed the door and sat down on the bed.

There was too much in her mind to sort. Too many things she didn't fully understand and had no idea how to feel about. She felt a migraine coming on.

But one thing kept coming back to the surface. No matter how much she tried to push it away.

She was developing feelings for Asher.

Feelings she shouldn't be having. Feelings she'd never had before, had never been free enough to develop before, and was ill-equipped to deal with.

She forced herself to stand and keep moving. She removed the tags off the clothes, folded them, and packed them in the suitcase. Then she got a shower. She couldn't fathom sleep, so she found a notebook and started plotting out their next steps.

*

Asher stayed seated on the bed. He wouldn't be sleeping tonight—he couldn't risk waking Cali with his nightmares again. Especially since his nightmares had begun to morph, as if his mind was reaching out to the one thing that might be able to help him deal with his demons. But that wasn't an option.

No sleep meant he had to withstand his thoughts. Not much easier.

His phone rang. Floyd. He didn't answer.

A while later, it rang again. His assistant this time. He answered. She apologized for calling late and said there were a few emails that needed his attention.

Relieved to have a distraction, he went downstairs to the kitchen, logged into his computer, and buried himself in work.

Floyd called a few more times. Finally, Asher texted him, "She hasn't left. At least not yet. We'll see how it goes from here."

***

Cali woke early, before sunrise. She was thankful to put on fresh clothes—jeans and a fitted knit top. Then she took her new suitcase downstairs, still before the sun had risen. She planned to prepare some kind of simple breakfast for Asher, even if it was just toast.

Asher was already in the kitchen. He shut his laptop. "Ready?"

"How early did you get up?"

He took her suitcase from her and headed for the door.

Did he not sleep? Perhaps he hadn't wanted to risk it, risk having more nightmares after what'd happened the night before.

She followed him out to the car. He'd already loaded his bag and the food they'd brought inside, so they got in the car and started down the road.

"Head to the Louisiana State Library?" he asked.

She nodded. "Jonathan Sikes may be nothing but a delusional man, but we should check it out anyway."

He entered the directions into his phone. It took a little more than an hour to get from New Orleans to Baton Rouge, and then they grabbed something to eat. By the time they arrived, the library had just opened. Thankfully, it was pretty much deserted other than the old lady behind the front desk. Based on the thickness of her glasses and how she held the paper she was reading close to her face, she probably couldn't see her and Asher very well as they walked by. It wouldn't be helpful if someone recognized Asher and posted on social media about it.

"He said *Atlas of Fictional Places*, correct?" Asher asked.

She nodded and glanced around at the signs. A few minutes later, she found the book on a shelf in the back of the reference section. It was hard back with cloth covering and no dust jacket. It was an old book but obviously hadn't been checked out very often—the pages were yellowed but were otherwise in excellent condition. She sat down right where she was and set the thick book in her lap. She looked through the publishing information and the forward before looking up at Asher.

He was standing over her, watching.

"We can go find a table to sit at," she said.

"This is your natural habitat. Sit wherever you want. I'm fine."

"My natural habitat?"

"Do you deny it?"

"No." As she turned back to the book, she thought she spied the corner of his mouth tweak into a slight smile.

He walked away but not far. She heard him make a phone call but didn't pay attention to who he was talking to.

She started with going through the table of contents and the rest of the book's front matter. Then she started looking through each section. The book basically theorized the most likely locations of various fictional places based on writings, legend, and hard facts and realities. It included a lot of maps, of course, but also plenty of written background and reasoning.

There was an entire section just for Atlantis, a section for mythology, one for American legends... When she got to the section on fairy tales, she stopped. There was mention of Russia where there shouldn't be, at least to the best of her knowledge.

She looked more closely through the section.

The binding had been changed, a page added. Some of the text had been modified. It almost all focused on one particular story. The more she looked, the more she realized she needed to study this more in depth. And she could not leave it here for someone else to find. She hadn't ruled out Jonathan Sikes being legitimately off his rocker, but she also didn't want to risk the wrong person finding something potentially valuable.

She stood and took the book with her. She found Asher in a small open area. He was just sliding his phone back into his pocket.

"Work?" she asked.

"I got him moved to a more secure facility."

Jonathan Sikes. "Thank you. He may truly belong in an institution, but—"

"We shouldn't take a chance."

"How about the Gray Hats? Your security is watching over them?" She was still angry, but she certainly didn't want them hurt.

He nodded. "They haven't seemed to catch on yet."

She worried it was only a matter of time.

He nodded toward the book in her hands. "Find anything interesting?"

"Interesting, yes. Whether or not it's the ravings of a madman, who knows." Then she added more quietly, just in case anyone lurked in the rows of shelves around them, "We shouldn't leave it here."

He held his hand out, and she handed him the book. He had a jacket on today, a black wool jacket in a style that was somewhere between professional and casual. He tucked the book in his jacket, under his arm. Thankfully, the book wasn't as huge as a lot of atlases, though it was definitely too thick for her to be able to hide it against her small frame.

He led her back toward the main entrance. On the way out, he dropped a hundred-dollar bill in the donation box.

In the car, he handed her back the book.

"Thank you for paying for it," she said.

"It would've killed you to steal from a library." He started the engine and pulled out of the lot.

He was right, but she had no idea how he understood these things about her.

A few minutes later, he merged onto the freeway.

"Where to?" she asked.

"I have two other currently vacant properties—a 1920s restored Hollywood mansion and a Victorian in a small town in Ohio. Do you have a preference?"

She wasn't an L.A. kind of girl, and definitely not an L.A. mansion kind of girl. "Ohio it is."

The map program on his phone told him to make a turn, and she realized he'd already set the directions. "How'd you know I'd pick Ohio?"

"I can't imagine you in a Hollywood mansion."

That was funny. People tended to take one look at her and assume she had aspirations to be in movies or the cover of magazines. How did Asher know her so well if he hadn't read the background check? How close attention had he been paying to her?

After stopping at a gas station, they got on the freeway. She offered to drive, a little worried about him not sleeping, but he declined. And he seemed fine, perfectly alert.

Still, she tried to think of something to talk about. But he never seemed to like to talk, especially not with her.

Finally, she decided to take a risk. "Can I ask about how you were hurt?"

He paused. "You mean my scars."

"You said they bother everyone else more than you. But you don't have to talk about it if you don't want to."

He paused again. So long she figured that was all she was going to get. She looked out the side window.

"Child suicide bomber. In Syria."

She looked over at him. "The child died?"

"No. His injuries weren't severe."

Asher's injuries were all on his right side—hand arm, side of his face, neck, and his eye. And he was right-handed. "You took the bomb off the boy. I'm guessing there was a kill switch. When you took if off the boy, the bomb exploded. You'd thrown it, but it went off too close to you."

His gaze flicked to her and then back to the road. She could see she'd gotten it right.

"Your injuries were why you were discharged from the Navy SEALs?"

"Yes." He looked in the rearview mirror for a second longer than he usually did.

She sat straighter and glanced in the side mirror. "Which car?"

He didn't answer.

"Something has you on alert. Which car is it?"

"Blue Ford Taurus. Two cars back."

"Reckless driving or following us?"

"It's been with us since we got on the freeway. Always two cars back."

"Should we exit off?" She'd studied a lot of different

kinds of defense, but this was not one of them. While she could drive pretty much anything with wheels, she'd never owned a car. These kinds of tactics had never seemed pertinent enough to spend time learning.

"Help me keep an eye for a little while longer. But don't turn around to look. Mirror only."

She nodded. Then she asked, "Reporters follow you all the time, right?"

"Frequently."

"And you manage to lose them?"

"They haven't figured out the location of my house." Then he added, "But you did."

"The Gray Hats did." She kept her gaze locked on the side mirror. The Taurus stayed in its position two cars back, no swerving, not following too close.

"You're not the first one to ask them to find that information."

She'd known they sometimes took private investigation work. "But they report the request to you instead."

He looked in the mirror again. "I pay better."

She still wasn't sure what to think about them, how to feel. It wasn't as if she hadn't known that some of what they did fell in the gray area. They were "Gray Hats," not "white hats," for a reason.

"You've never had real friends."

She looked over at Asher.

"You've never let yourself have real friends," he clarified. "They were the first ones to come close. That's what's bothering you." He glanced in the rearview mirror.

She turned her head to look out the side mirror. He was right. She wasn't always good at deciphering her own emotions, but he'd nailed it.

"Would you be mad at them if it was someone other than you?"

She sat back against the seat and thought about that, while keeping an eye on the side mirror. That way of thinking about it helped her analyze more effectively—take herself and her emotions out of the equation.

Asher glanced in his side mirror.

"Still there?" she asked.

"One car back now. The car directly behind us exited." A few seconds passed. He kept his gaze on the road. "Why do you seem to be less angry at me than the Gray Hats?"

She looked out the side window.

He didn't push.

She noticed the Taurus dropped back a bit, until another car moved in front, and then it picked up speed to match again.

She noticed a sign on the side of the road. "I have an idea."

He tilted his head to show he was listening.

"Pull off at the rest stop."

A few seconds later, he flipped on his blinker and took the exit. They both glanced in the mirrors—the Taurus exited as well.

"Park down at the end," Cali said.

Asher did as she asked and put the truck in park. "What's your idea?"

Cali explained.

She got out of the car and left Asher there while she walked up the sidewalk toward the building. She purposefully did not look around, pretending to be oblivious, but still using her ears and peripheral vision.

She paused at the vending machine area, which was really just a freestanding wall facing the bathroom entrances. The wall was lined with machines selling everything from snack cakes and chips to Pepsi and Mountain Dew.

Footsteps stopped a few feet back and to the side. One set of footsteps. Male based on the weight and stride, but not a huge man.

After a few seconds, she let out a huff, as if nothing in the machines appealed to her, and she started down another sidewalk, the one that led past the machines and restrooms across an expanse of grass and trees to picnic tables, currently unoccupied due to the nippy temperatures.

She moved slowly, close to the wall of vending machines.

The footsteps quietly followed. He was pretty good at being quiet, but not good enough.

She passed the wall and didn't let herself look anywhere but straight ahead.

At the sound of shuffling feet, she turned.

Asher, who was behind the wall, secluded in shrubbery, had grabbed the man by the neck and was pressing him against the block wall.

The man struggled. Asher took a gun from the back of his waistband and held it to the man's forehead. The man stopped struggling.

Asher's voice was calm but deadly. "Why are you following her?"

CHAPTER 20

"I'm a reporter. Gossip columnist. I was following you."

"Then why did you walk after her instead of approaching me while I was still in my truck?" Asher asked.

Part of the plan had been for Asher to stay in the truck for a few minutes, separate from her, so they could determine who the target was.

The man opened his mouth but said nothing.

Asher growled, "Answer me."

The man tried to turn his head to look at Cali.

Asher pressed the barrel of the gun harder against his forehead. "You and I are having a conversation. You don't get to look at her."

The man's Adam's apple bobbed. Cali scanned him for anything of interest. He definitely wasn't one of Michael's men. He didn't have that hardness in his eyes, the brutality lingering just below the surface. Either this man did not have brutality in him, or he was a lot better at hiding it. Or maybe his ugliness was different from what she was used to.

She lifted his suede jacket to check for weapons.

Nothing in his pockets or tucked in his waistband.

"We're too civilized for guns and knives," the man said, though he still couldn't turn his head to look at her.

"Seems to me that guns and knives in the hands of good people are what keep evil people in check," she said.

"And which is your friend here?"

"I suggest you not push his limits and find out," she said. "Now answer his question. Why were you following me?"

He pressed his lips together.

"I really don't think you want to push my friend's limits."

"Need a man to do the heavy lifting?"

"Don't try to make me angry and say more than I intend to. That doesn't work on me," she said. "Why are you following me?"

No answer.

Asher continued to hold him there. She appreciated that he didn't try to take the lead. He was used to being in charge, so she understood it might feel unnatural for him to step back.

She tried something else. Sometimes, the best way to get information was to give information and watch the reaction closely. "We know about The Lost Library."

His eyes widened slightly, and a muscle in his temple twitched.

"Also known as the Golden Library."

His fingers twitched against his pant leg.

"Looks like I'm on the right track," she said.

His jaw tightened.

"You don't really think it exists, do you? After all the searching that's been done?"

His breathing increased. His reactions up to now seemed more like nerves, but now, it looked more like anger. Good—she could work with that. "The real question is why do you think I have anything to do with anything? I'm nothing but a simple bookkeeper."

"A bookkeeper who hangs out with Asher Cross. What's the deal with that? Sleeping with him in order to get protection?"

Asher growled and shifted even closer. "Insult her again," he challenged.

"Sleeping with you is an insult?"

Asher glared. She was almost surprised the man's flesh didn't melt off his face.

"Why are you following me?" she asked again calmly.

He didn't answer, too busy staring at Asher.

Asher growled, "Answer her."

"We…we…"

"Spit it out."

"I was just told she's important and not to lose her."

Cali believed him. "How about The Lost Library?"

He pressed his lips together.

"So, you know about it, but there is someone you're more scared of than Asher. Interesting. Asher's pretty scary. This other person must be terrifying." She amended, "Or group." Then she added, "I've deciphered enough to know there are quite a few people involved, and they're located all over the world. They appear to communicate exclusively in coded messages on forums and such. That tells me there probably isn't a lot of trust, and there is probably a select group, perhaps a single person, who controls all information. There are no cell phone numbers or addresses for this select special group or person."

She watched him closely. There was frustration, fear, and anger in his expression. She was on the mark.

She looked at Asher. "I don't think he knows anything else." She guessed he was a lackey who had been given just enough information to make him feel important but not enough to be a liability, which meant he wasn't that useful to them.

"We can't let him follow us," he said.

"I know. Any ideas?"

Asher tilted his head as he glared at the man. The man

visibly shook. Asher twisted the barrel of the gun.

Asher said to Cali, "Can you slash his tires without anyone noticing?"

She took a few steps to the side until she could see the man's car. Then she stepped back over to Asher. "Yes."

"There's a knife in my back pocket."

She looked at his backside and hesitated. Then she slipped her hand in his pocket carefully, trying not to touch him any more than necessary. She tucked the knife in her pocket and walked quickly away, toward the man's car. He'd parked across the drive lane, along the tree line, backed into the parking space.

She casually approached the car and pretended to check the state of the front passenger tire and then moved to the back. She pressed the button for the automatic knife, held it inverted, and slammed it into the tire. She had to wiggle the knife to get it to dislodge. Air leaked out of the tire with a whizzing sound. She walked around the back of the car and slashed that one as well.

Then she hit the button to pull the blade back into the knife handle, slipped it into her pocket, and walked back over to where Asher was still holding the man. "Done."

"Go get in the truck. I'll make sure our friend knows the consequences of yelling for help or trying to follow us again in the future."

"What're you going to do?"

He turned his head toward her and squinted his right eye, the best wink he could probably do with that eye. At that angle, the man couldn't see the wink.

"Okay," she said, with feigned caution, and walked away quickly.

He followed behind her about a minute later, got in the truck, started it, and pulled out of the parking space and back onto the freeway.

"What'd you do to him?" she asked.

"Nothing he won't survive."

She didn't question further. Maybe because she didn't

want to know.

Asher drove for hours.

Cali tried to think of things to talk to him about, something safe. When she asked questions, he gave one-word answers. She commented about the landscape or other things she saw out the window a few times. He always looked over at whatever she was talking about, as if interested, but then never commented back.

About five hours into the trip, she said, "You should let me drive for a while."

"I'm fine."

He *looked* fine, but she worried. "You didn't sleep last night, did you?"

No response.

She touched her fingertips to his forearm. "Please."

His gaze flickered to her hand, but he didn't say anything.

But then he pulled off at the next exit, stopped on the shoulder, and opened his car door. She walked around the front of the car, and he walked around the back.

When she got in the driver's seat, she couldn't reach the pedals and had to take a minute to adjust the seat. Then she put the truck in drive and got back on the freeway.

Asher looked out the side window and continued not talking.

About an hour later, she glanced over at him and realized he'd fallen asleep. His head was leaned on the headrest but still turned toward the window so she couldn't see his face. When she had to make a turn, she did it slowly to try not to wake him. She had a feeling he was the type to wake at the slightest sound or movement. He obviously didn't let himself sleep much, and she wanted him to sleep as much as possible.

A little while later, he jerked up.

She didn't let herself look at him, allowing him to recover from whatever he'd been dreaming with as much privacy as she could give him. But she could see peripherally as he looked over at her. For several seconds. Long enough that she started to worry.

Then he rubbed his hands over his face and through his hair.

He remained silent but didn't fall asleep again.

CHAPTER 21

About an hour later, Asher said, "We're getting close. Let me drive."

"We're going to a small town, right? People who might scrutinize every passing car. You should slouch down in your seat. Some people might be up this early to get to work. We don't need anyone recognizing you."

"I'll explain how to get to the garage for the house."

They entered the small town, drove past a Dairy Queen, over railroad tracks, past a very small main street, and up a steep hill lined by old wood-sided houses with front porches. The directions stopped at a beautiful Victorian house that was probably once considered a mansion, with a third story turret on the right side.

"Turn left at the next street," Asher said. "Then another left at the next stop sign."

When she turned the second corner, he pointed. "There."

Apparently, the property for the house spanned the length of the entire block. She pulled into a dirt drive secluded by tall pine trees. Asher got out and opened one of the garage doors, more like a carriage house than a garage. She pulled in, and he closed the door and then found the light switch. They unloaded only their clothing and a couple of food items.

There was a door at the side of the garage that opened to a gravel path that led up to the back of the house.

Inside, Asher showed her to a bedroom upstairs, the biggest one by her estimation, and then he disappeared somewhere. She slipped her shoes off and lay down.

When she woke up, light was shining through the tall narrow window. After a quick shower, she went downstairs and found a surface to work on. There was a desk in the front room. She sat down and started poring through *Atlas of Fictional Places*, the book they'd taken from the library.

"You should eat."

She blinked and looked up to see Asher standing in the doorway. The angle of the light hitting him from the window told her she'd been sitting there several hours. "I'm okay."

"You should eat." He walked over and set a plate on the desk. Then he turned and walked back out.

On the plate were a couple of grain and fruit bars. She picked one up and resumed her analysis.

At some point, he set a glass of water next to her as well.

"What've you figured out?" Asher was back.

She rubbed the bridge of her nose and turned to look at him.

"Whoever did it made the changes to the book expertly."

"You don't think Sikes made the changes?"

"I haven't ruled that out." She stifled a yawn. "He may have just discovered it."

"Wouldn't he have taken the book then?"

"He might've thought leaving it in the library was the safest thing to do. Or maybe he found it someplace else and got it added to the library to hide it."

He nodded.

"Some names in here match the deciphering I've done for the Gray Hats." She turned back to her notes. "The publisher's name was changed to Golden Palace Publishing. I looked up that name—it's not a publishing house."

He moved closer and looked over her shoulder. "Could it simply be defunct? It's an old book. How could someone change the type in a book?"

"I couldn't find it even when looking for old defunct publishing houses. I'm guessing there is some kind of chemical treatment to remove the original print and not damage the paper."

"You saw that name in the things you deciphered for the Gray Hats?"

"Golden Palace. I know it's not that uncommon a name for certain types of businesses, but the context wasn't anything like that. Plus there's this." She flipped pages. "This says the most likely location of the tale of *Beauty and the Beast* is Saint-Émilion in Bordeaux, which is in southwest France. But my independent research puts its most likely location in one of the quaint old villages in the northeast, maybe Ribeauvillé or Riquewihr." She looked up at him. "You're probably thinking it's fiction, so it could be set anywhere. But the rest of the book aligns perfectly with other research."

"You researched all the other entries in the book to see how accurate they are?"

She nodded. "Thank you for the phone, by the way, it's been really helpful with this." She turned back to the book. "That got me looking more closely at the *Beauty and the Beast* entry, and I found this." She pressed down on one of the pages close to the spine.

Asher leaned closer, and she could smell his soap. "An added page?"

"Yes. I had to abuse the book a bit, but you can just see where it was glued in. I'm guessing it was artificially aged to match the rest of the book."

"What's on that page?"

She flipped it back to show him the front side of the page, a map of Saint-Émilion. Then she flipped back to the other side, which was all text. "This is about how The Beast was originally from Russia, how he is said to have made his fortune, and why he built his castle. Then how he moved all his prized possessions away from Saint-Émilion to protect them. None of that is in the original tale."

"That's where The Lost Library was, at least for a time. Some castle or estate in Saint-Émilion."

"Exactly what I think."

"Does it say to where he moved?"

"It doesn't say *he* moved, just that he moved his most prized possessions. Though, based on how it's worded, the average reader would assume he and Beauty moved, along with all his riches, to start a new life together." She touched her fingertip to a line on the page. "'To start anew, to be safe.' But it doesn't say explicitly *where*."

"Not explicitly…"

She grinned and then touched her fingertip to another line on the page. "'He searched for just the right Chateaux in a new land, bilt for grandeur fitting his treasures.' Bilt spelled BILT."

"Bilt?"

"What's the one piece of real estate in your home state of North Carolina that you would—presumably—love to own but most likely never will?" While his company made money mostly in the commercial sphere, he obviously had a love of grand old homes.

He raised his brows. "Biltmore?" Then he added, "But what about the other Vanderbilt homes? There are several all over the country. BILT could be referencing anything related to the Vanderbilts."

She touched her fingertip to a line on the page. "'Someplace temperate like his beloved Bordeaux.' The other Vanderbilt houses are mostly in the northeast—New York, Rhode Island. Not exactly known for being temperate. There are a few in Florida, but again, not temperate like Bordeaux. Biltmore is the only one that fits."

"So, you think The Lost Library is in Biltmore?"

"I think it was there at one point. I can't say for sure now. Being that it's such a major tourist attraction—the largest house in America—and there are curators paid to know everything about the estate, I find it a little far-fetched that it could still be there."

"Even so, the people looking for it would love to have that information. Might give us something to bargain with."

She assumed he meant bargain her safety for this information, but she wasn't sure she was willing to do that. If The Lost Library was real, it needed to be protected.

Asher set his computer, which she hadn't noticed he was holding, on the desk. "Floyd sent Sikes' research. You should also have them check into Biltmore to see if they find anything interesting."

She pulled the computer closer, and Asher walked out of the room.

Time passed as she reviewed. It was all papers that had been published in legitimate academic journals, so nothing that even hinted at conspiracy or terrorist groups tracking it. But they gave her a solid understanding of the history, what was proven truth and what was considered legend.

A light clicked on, and Cali realized it was getting dark. And then Asher set a bowl of oatmeal next to her.

"Thank you."

"Please eat."

She reached for the spoon. If she didn't make herself stop right now, she'd forget the oatmeal was even there. She took a bite and then rubbed her eyes with her other hand.

"Anything interesting?"

"I think I have a solid grasp on the accepted history of The Lost Library. Like Jonathan Sikes had told me, it was started by Ivan the Great and made lost by Ivan the Terrible."

"By lost they mean hidden?"

"Yes. I'm assuming it had grown to be so valuable that he didn't let anyone see it. It's said to have been hidden underneath the Kremlin in Moscow."

"Then how did it end up in France? If we take that inserted page in the book to be true."

"Well, when Napoleon took Moscow in 1812, it's said he looked for the library but didn't find it. But he wouldn't have advertised that he found it if it's as valuable as legend says."

"So, maybe Napoleon took it to France."

"That's my best guess. Again, assuming we take *The Atlas of Fictional Places* seriously."

"Whoever altered *The Atlas* spent a lot of effort on it. It's not likely someone would do that much work for a hoax and then just leave it there buried in a random library."

"I agree—it seems it was put there in order to hide and protect that information. Whoever put it there believed it was accurate and extremely important. Whether or not they were a conspiracy nut, we have no way of knowing."

"Agreed." She took another bite of oatmeal. "Have you eaten?"

"I will after I make sure you eat."

She rolled her eyes. "There are several accounts of people throughout history claiming to have seen the library. Or finding a catalog of books that belonged to the Russian Czars."

"Books from the Library at Alexandria and Constantinople, right?"

She nodded. "Some unheard-of authors but also Plato, Virgil, Livy's entire 142-volume history of Rome, ancient Chinese texts."

He shook his head. "Priceless. If it does exist, I would hate to see someone get their hands on it and sell it off piece by piece on the black market. All that history lost."

"But… I don't think that's what the terrorists the Gray Hats are following want to do. I think they want to keep it for themselves. I think they believe it holds some kind of power."

"I have a feeling you don't mean the power of knowledge."

She shook her head. "They seem cult-like."

"What do you mean 'cult-like'?"

"There are mentions of 'power of the ages.' I got the impression they think whoever possesses the library will rule the world. They think they uniquely have the ability and right to rule over the 'simple masses.'"

"If the library does exist and if they were to get it, I wonder what they would do in order to obtain the power they seem to think they deserve."

"Cults aren't known for letting things go." She turned back to the computer. "I'm going to ask the Gray Hats to send me any further communications or information they've found. We need to have a better understanding of their capabilities." She still wasn't happy with the Gray Hats, but they were the best resource they had. She brought up an email and started typing.

Asher walked out of the room.

She sighed. She wanted to talk to him more. Talking was helping her work things out in her head. That was unusual—she usually worked better in silence and alone.

She continued typing the email, vaguely aware of hearing Asher's phone ring in another room. She clicked the send button and rubbed her eyes again.

At the sound of a crash, she bolted up out of her chair.

CHAPTER 22

Cali ran out of the room toward the sound of the crash, the same direction the sound of Asher's phone had come from.

In the kitchen, she had to walk around a large pile of shattered pottery. Had he thrown it at the wall?

"Asher?"

He was faced away from her, his phone on the floor next to him.

"Asher, what's wrong?" She approached him tentatively, not out of fear of him but out of concern he might not want her around while he was obviously upset.

Nothing.

She paused to allow him time to calm down.

She wanted to rest a hand on his back, but she didn't. He often didn't seem to like her being around, but she couldn't get herself to leave him alone. And she didn't know if it was something personal or if it was related to The Lost Library—did they need to get out of here?

His shoulders rippled as he pulled both hands through his hair.

"Asher?"

His voice was tight. "Please go away."

She took a step back and started to turn.

But then she barely heard him whisper under his breath. "Please forgive me." She didn't think he was talking to her. Maybe to God?

She hesitated. "He always forgives."

He lowered his head even more, and she could barely hear him. "Not me. Not what I've done."

"You do so much good," she said. "I've never met anyone who does as much good as you."

He turned and looked at her. No, glared. "Jonathan Sikes is dead."

"What happened?"

"I had him moved to a different facility."

"I know. He wasn't safe with that orderly there. It was the right thing."

"He's dead. Do you think it was the right thing now? I pulled strings, used my influence, and now the man is dead. His family will never see him again. He had a daughter and a granddaughter—did you know that? Now, they'll never see him again."

She hadn't known he had a family. She should have checked, should have made sure they were safe. What had she learned about not involving others? About protecting innocents? Nothing, apparently. Tears pricked the backs of her eyes.

"Now, you know why they call me The Beast." He moved to walk past her out the door.

She grabbed his arm.

He stopped but didn't look at her.

"You're not a beast," she said.

"It's a well-earned moniker, I assure you."

"It's not."

He turned his head and glared. "How can you not see it? You with your brilliant mind, and you can't see the obvious."

"You're right—sometimes I miss things that are obvious to everyone else. But this is not one of them. I've studied you. You don't let people really understand you, but I've seen how you put everyone ahead of yourself." She paused. "I have no doubt you would die to protect a stranger. Your scars are proof."

He gave no response, but his glare slowly fell away into lack of expression. She almost wanted his glare back. In a way, it hurt less than that empty expression, the wall he kept up between them, that kept her away. Always away.

A tear escaped her lash line. She took a breath to control herself.

He moved his hand to rest it on her cheek, and he used his thumb to gently wipe the tear away. "I'm sorry I failed. Again." He took his hand away and moved to leave.

"What do you mean 'again'?" She still had a hold of his arm and didn't let go.

"I'm surprised you don't already know. I assume you researched me."

"Only the things that aren't personal."

"Of course. You're too good a person. You should've ripped through my past. Maybe then you'd know better than to be near me."

Though he wasn't actually telling her much, he was talking more than he'd ever done. Maybe he needed to talk. Maybe that would help him heal. "Tell me."

Silence while they held eye contact.

"Your opinion means too much to me," he said.

"My opinion doesn't mean anything. But I'm here to listen."

"Your opinion is everything."

They held eye contact. There was something between them. She didn't understand it. She felt something was there, something massive. But she had such difficulty with emotions, especially big, complex emotions.

She whispered, "Tell me."

"Rose."

"Your sister."

"She's dead because of me."

"What happened?"

He looked away.

"Please." Then she added, "I won't give you empty platitudes. If something was your fault, I won't try telling you it wasn't."

He turned back to her.

"I've seen enough to know you're a man of substance. You don't want empty words or fake sympathy. You would rather have honesty. Even if it hurts."

"There's too much fake in my life as it is."

"I think talking to someone might help. Rose is obviously a very difficult memory, and I doubt you've talked to anyone about it." She added tentatively, "I'm guessing she's part of what causes your nightmares."

He hesitated. "Yes."

"Maybe if you get it out, your nightmares will calm. Even just a little."

He took a slow breath and turned his head toward the window over the sink.

"She was your baby sister, right?"

A long pause.

He turned to face her. "You have the right to know who I am, but I can't risk scaring you away when you're in so much danger. They killed Sikes." His voice quieted. "I can't let them kill you."

"None of this is your responsibility. Not Sikes and certainly not me. You put too much on yourself."

He started to shake his head. She lay a hand on his cheek, and he stopped. She swore she could feel electricity zipping through her hand, and then it traveled up her arm, down her legs, and then settled in her gut.

They moved closer. Very close. She wasn't sure if it was him or her or both. Or something else outside of them pushing them toward each other.

She felt warm, frazzled, content, on the edge of craziness.

Their lips touched.

She closed her eyes.

She felt light-headed. Like she was floating. But also anchored to Asher.

His lips were soft. Warm. The complete opposite of everything she knew about him. There was more to him than even she had yet realized. Secrets. Even lies. But she knew it was all to protect others, not to gain anything for himself.

Their lips moved.

The ball of electricity flipped around in her gut.

She set a hand on his chest and shifted her other hand so that her fingers combed into his hair.

He broke away and stepped quickly back several feet. Through quickened breaths, he said, "I'm sorry."

"Don't." She didn't want him to be sorry. More than any time in her life, she didn't want someone to be sorry for getting close to her.

He moved quickly back to her and held her face gently in both hands. She thought he was going to kiss her again. She'd never wanted anything so much.

He looked her square in the eyes and said, "I'm sorry."

Then he walked away. He was gone before she could even consider what was happening, let alone how to react to it.

Tears came. Her legs gave out, and she sat on the floor.

She looked in the direction he'd walked. He was gone.

Her vision turned blurry.

A sob bubbled out of her chest.

She swallowed hard. She couldn't cry—couldn't let herself cry. She took deep breaths. She didn't sob anymore, but her vision was still blurry. She squeezed her eyes shut and then wiped the tears away.

But she didn't have the strength to get up.

She sat there and stared at the checkerboard floor.

***

Asher walked into the office one room over. He couldn't trust himself to be in the same room with her. But he couldn't get himself to go farther.

He was anchored to her.

He had been for a very long time. No matter how much he fought it.

Her sob.

He couldn't breathe. He'd made her cry. The indestructible, invincible Cali—he'd made her cry. He'd never disputed the moniker *The Beast*, but now he'd fully earned it.

"I'm sorry," he whispered.

He stood there and listened, praying to hear anything other than her tears. He'd rather hear her cursing him or even hear her leaving. There was nothing.

Eventually, he sat down on the floor next to the door with his back against the wall. This was as close to her as he could allow himself to be. He needed to be more careful.

CHAPTER 23

Days passed. Cali continued researching any aspect she could think of. She let herself fall down rabbit holes of reading, sorting through information. Asher didn't come to see her. He didn't bring her food. He didn't ask what she was doing. But she heard the floorboards creak as he walked through the house, and he left food for her on the kitchen counter. She felt like a stray dog that he fed sometimes but was too dirty to keep as a pet. She didn't see him for several days.

Finally, she decided to take a walk. She needed to get out of this stifling house, and perhaps she could come up with a plan of what to do next. Sometimes walking made her brain think better, and maybe she would find a way to leave Asher, find some safe means to leave that would make him confident enough in her safety to drop this and go back to his life.

She threw on her jacket, stepped out onto the front porch, and texted Asher that she was going for a walk. As she stepped down the porch steps onto the front walk, she tucked her phone in her back pocket.

The air was a lot cooler here, but it didn't make her uncomfortable. She'd lived in so many different places she could acclimate to any climate almost immediately.

She heard the front door and looked back.

Asher locked the door and headed down the front walk toward her.

Rather than make him speak to her, she continued down the front walk and left enough room for him to walk next to her. He was obviously worried about her safety. She'd hoped he'd relax since they'd been here several days with no incidents. If they'd been followed or discovered by some other means, something would have happened by now.

They turned right onto the public sidewalk.

She looked at the architecture of the houses, the vibrant leaves on the huge trees, and the occasional passing car.

Finally, she said, "Someone might recognize you."

He shifted the ballcap he was wearing lower on his forehead, and lifted the collar of his jacket up so that it covered his neck and some of his face.

They continued walking.

Asher was silent.

Down a hill, they came to the Main Street of this tiny town. An old three-story brick building on the right held a library, and a one-story brick building on the left held the Post Office. They turned left down Main Street. There were a couple of little stores, but most of the buildings were empty.

She heard voices and looked around. Up ahead, there was a group of people on the corner.

Finally, Asher spoke. "Let's turn around."

Cali had no objection and started to turn.

"Hey!" someone from the group called. "I know you!"

Both Cali and Asher ignored him and headed back the way they'd come.

Quick footsteps from behind them.

Asher spun around and stood between the group and Cali. His voice was calm. "We're just out for a walk."

Cali could just see around Asher that the man who'd yelled was now right in front of Asher, and the rest of the group, probably twenty people, was quickly approaching. They were mostly young, and many wore political slogans on their shirts.

"You're Asher Cross." The young man said it like an accusation.

"We're just out for a walk." Asher's tone was calm, but his stance was straight and solid.

"How can you live with yourself?" the young man asked.

A woman with perfectly curled and bouncy blond hair with a pink streak through it walked up next to the man. "Having that much money is immoral."

"I'm not here to debate fiduciary morality," Asher said. "We're just out for a walk."

"How can you live with yourself?" The young man spit at Asher's feet.

Cali tightened in anger. With his hand at his side, Asher held his palm to her, as if to ask her to stay back.

Instead, she stepped to his side.

He looked at her.

Then he refocused on the crowd that was now surrounding them. "Let my friend go, and you can berate me all you want."

"We can *berate you all we want* right now," the young man said in a mocking tone.

Someone else called, "Another filthy opportunist."

"Living off the backs of workers!" someone else yelled.

"I bet he has platinum utensils and uses a gold toilet!"

Cali wanted to point out Asher's clothes—not designer, not fancy, no watch or jewelry. And even if he did have nice things, that was his business. Just like it wasn't anyone else's business how much the blonde spent on her hairdresser or how much several of the others had spent on their very fancy phones that they were now using to record the scene. But Cali kept her mouth shut and didn't antagonize.

"If you think my employees are unhappy with their benefits packages," Asher said calmly, "I encourage you to reach out to them. They are all employed at-will. Now if you'll excuse us."

No one moved out of the way.

"Why do you feel the need to have that much money? Why aren't you supporting the needy?"

"I support several charities. Reach out to my public relations head, Patricia Simms. She'll provide all the documentation."

"You could feed starving children!"

"That is the primary goal of one of the charities we started many years ago. We feed several thousand underprivileged children every day."

"Tax the rich!" someone yelled from the back, and then everyone started chanting the same thing. "Tax the rich! Tax the rich! Tax the rich!"

Cali rolled her eyes. She'd seen the tax numbers.

A woman with short dark hair rushed forward and screamed incoherently in Cali's face.

Asher shifted, but Cali held him back with a hand on his arm.

The woman ran out of breath, and her scream tapered out.

"Are you done?" Cali asked.

"Tax the rich!" the woman yelled.

The young man in front of Asher demanded of Cali, "Who are you? Some kind of accessory? Like a fancy watch?"

Asher growled, "Don't."

"What do you care?" the man said to Asher. "She's just your toy."

Asher shifted a step forward and seemed to grow even taller. "Don't."

There was fear in the man's eyes. Someone in the back yelled, "What're you gonna do? We're peacefully gathered."

Asher stepped back and addressed the crowd. "If you're peaceful, you won't give us any trouble leaving your little event." He took Cali's hand.

"You're not going anywhere," the young man said, and several other men stepped forward and surrounded Asher.

Asher's voice lowered into deadly. "Back. Off."

"What're you gonna do?" one of the large men asked. "You don't have a lot of choices."

One of the others added, "Let's just see if we can get that taxing done." He looked around Asher to one of the men behind them. "Grab his wallet."

Cali let go of Asher's hand and slid behind him, back-to-back, blocking access to his wallet and phone in his back pockets, as well as the gun tucked in his waistband.

She felt Asher reach for her hand, but in the same moment, one of the men slung her forward onto the ground. She swept the pair of legs closest to her and got up to one knee. She deflected a punch toward her face. Someone behind her grabbed a fistful of her hair and yanked. She felt a patch of hair and possibly scalp come off, and she started to lose her balance. As someone else came at her, she grabbed their hand and used it to pull herself back forward, and then she swept that person to the ground.

She felt hands on both her arms, pulling her back. She had nothing to grab, was off balance, and fell to the ground again. She rolled to try to get up, but there were so many all around—someone else slammed her back down, and before she could get her bearings, there was a boot coming at her head. The last thing she heard was Asher's unintelligible roar.

***

Asher was only vaguely aware of who he was hitting. So many people had squeezed in between him and Cali.

They wouldn't move. He saw her fighting back and thought she might just be able to get away, and then she got thrown down one more time and stopped moving.

"Cali!"

He punched another man who dared get in his way. He stumbled but didn't get out of the way, so Asher grabbed him by the throat and threw him. Another man reached for him from the side, and Asher side-kicked his knee out. He didn't have the capacity to consider the consequences of destroying the man's knee. All he knew was he was in the way of getting to Cali and had to go.

He shoved someone else, and finally, there was Cali.

She was on the ground, face down. A chunk of her hair had been pulled out, and her scalp was bleeding down her cheek. He dropped to his knees and checked her pulse, terrified of what he would feel.

CHAPTER 24

She had a pulse. She was breathing.

"Cali," Asher murmured. "Cali, can you hear me?"

The others, those whom he hadn't knocked out, had stopped attacking him. Perhaps because he'd taken down the largest of the men, and no one else was brave enough to come at him. Someone standing to the side said, "Look what you've done!" She pointed to the men on the ground and called him several expletives.

The men on the ground were only knocked out. He felt confident they'd be fine. And they'd come at him, not the other way around; he'd merely defended himself and Cali.

He looked up at the woman. "She's an innocent."

"No one who associates with the rich is innocent."

He turned back to Cali and gently lifted her into his arms. She was still unconscious, but her breathing remained steady.

What would've happened if she hadn't been able to defend herself as well as she had? He hadn't seen everything, of course, but enough. If there hadn't been so many people, she probably would have handled the attack quite well.

He glanced around at the group still standing, a

warning.

No one moved.

He carried Cali away, careful to make his stride both quick and steady so as not to jostle her. He debated with himself—hospital or no? She had good color and didn't have any major wounds other than where someone had ripped her hair and scalp, and he knew with certainty what she would want. So, he started up the hill back to the house.

But he continued to question if he was doing the right thing. Maybe he could find a private practitioner in town and take her there. He'd get her back to the house, lay her someplace comfortable, and look up local doctors.

He moved as quickly as he could in the hopes of not drawing attention. At the top of the hill, he cut down the side street and took the narrow road that led to the back of the house. He was thankful he'd always continued his rigorous exercise after being discharged—he had no problem carrying her and keeping a quick pace. He hadn't kept up with the training for any noble or even vain reasons. It was simply a way to help him deal with stress and guilt.

Overwhelming, crippling guilt.

He refocused on the task at hand.

Finally, he made it to the back door of the house and somehow managed to unlock it while still holding Cali. Inside, he kicked the door closed with his foot and then headed upstairs. The antique settee in the front room wasn't very big or comfortable. He took her to the room he'd given her to use and gently laid her down. She didn't rouse.

He took his phone out of his pocket and started searching for doctors in town.

She made a sound, a low groan.

He sat down on the edge of the bed. "Cali?"

"Asher," she mumbled.

"I'm here. Are you all right?"

She opened her eyes slowly, as if using all her strength to force them open, and looked right at him. "Are you okay? Your ribs?"

"What hurts? Do you feel dizzy? Headache?"

She glanced over him, surely making sure he was all right.

With his hand on her cheek, he directed her attention back to his eyes. "What hurts?"

She moved her hand slowly. "My hair. Someone pulled out a chunk."

"And pulled off some skin as well. That's the only obvious injury I could see. Anything else?"

"A little groggy. But it's passing quickly." She pushed herself up to a seated position with legs crossed. She gingerly touched the back of her hair, behind her left ear, where her hair had been pulled out.

"I'll get something for that. Does anything else hurt?"

She stretched her back and neck. "No, I'm okay." She looked up at him. "And, no, I'm not going to the doctor."

A part of him wanted to grin at her astuteness. But the gravity of everything came crashing back down. He stood. "I'll be back in a minute."

He headed downstairs. Part of the standard package in his rental houses was a good first-aid kit. It should be in either a downstairs bathroom or the kitchen. He found it quickly and headed back upstairs.

He found her standing at the mirror in the bathroom connected to her room trying to clean the blood off her neck and cheek.

"Come sit down," he said. "I'll take care of that."

She glanced back. He held up the first-aid kit, and she came over and sat on the corner of the bed. "Thank you. I can't see what I'm doing properly."

Seated on the edge of the bed behind her, he took an alcohol wipe and started cleaning the blood off. Then he very carefully cleaned the wound where her hair should be. She winced slightly, but otherwise showed no pain. He applied some antibiotic ointment and then taped some gauze over it, careful to keep the tape on her neck and not in her hair.

He put the tape away and closed the first-aid kit. "I'm sorry."

She twisted in her seat.

Before she could argue, he held a hand up. "I didn't protect you."

"You did. And it's not your job anywa—"

"I'm sorry." He stood and walked out of the room.

"Please don't go."

He didn't pause as he walked down the hall.

***

Cali watched Asher walk away. He'd talked to her, even touched her—she'd hoped he was back to normal, normal for Asher anyway.

She sighed and stared at the rug under her feet.

Why did he feel so responsible for protecting her?

She needed to leave, set him free. Soon.

***

Guilt threatened to destroy him from the inside out.

She'd been hurt. She'd been in danger solely from being in his company—no other reason.

He'd failed her. Just like he'd failed Rose.

He needed to run, massive physical exertion, but he certainly could not leave her. He needed to make plans to get them out of here, but he was having difficulty thinking clearly, too overwhelmed with his raging guilt. And his lack of concentration was making the guilt worse.

On the first floor, he paced in front of the stairs—both standing guard over her and trying to get his mind to calm down. He'd been spotted, and that crowd was made up of the type to post the sighting on social media, including the videos they'd taken. Their location would not remain a secret for long.

He wanted to allow her a little time to rest to be sure she was all right and didn't need a doctor. But he couldn't risk too much time, maybe an hour or so. He wanted to use this time to pack the car, but he also couldn't get himself to leave her alone in the house, even for just a minute at a time.

"Asher?" her voice came from the top of the steps.

He couldn't get himself to stop pacing. He felt on the verge. He probably looked like a crazed madman.

Her soft footsteps descended.

He couldn't get himself to stop pacing.

As he turned to continue the other direction, she was there in his path. She brought him to a halt by gently placing her hands on his upper arms. Her gentleness was what stopped him, the only thing that could stop him. If she'd grabbed him forcefully, he'd have shaken her off.

"I'm all right," she said.

He nodded once stiffly.

She took her hands away. "I'm sorry I didn't defend myself better."

He closed his eyes, jaw tight. "Don't." He opened his eyes and stared down at her, almost a glare. "Don't you dare apologize. You defended yourself well. You are not to blame for anything." He paused. "I am."

"How are you to blame for any of that?"

He turned to walk away, but she grabbed his arm. That blasted gentle touch of hers.

He turned to look at her.

"I haven't amassed wealth for the sake of being powerful," Asher said.

"I know. Because of you, people have jobs and security."

"That's important to me, but that's not why I've worked so hard. It was so that I had resources to protect people."

She hesitated. "Is this about Rose?"

He looked her in the eye. "She died because of me."

***

"I seriously doubt that," Cali said.

His expression hardened. "I killed a terrorist in Afghanistan. His brother crossed the southern border into America illegally solely for the reason of seeking out Rose and killing her. As retribution. For no other reason than her connection to me, because she was important to me."

Cali paused. She would not give him platitudes. That would do nothing but annoy him. "Was he caught?"

"He used the opportunity of being in America to kill more 'infidels.' He drove a vehicle into a crowd of people at a street fair and was killed by an armed bystander. Before he died, he killed seventeen people. Five of them were children. When his family back in Afghanistan learned of what he'd done, they celebrated and handed out candy. He would have never made the effort of coming here if not for avenging his brother."

Cali remembered reading about that attack.

"There are many other people in that family," Asher said, "and many others who are dead because of me, whose families may decide to do the same."

"Especially if you ever get close to anyone again."

He only looked at her. She could feel the sadness radiating off him. The loneliness, the pain. The guilt.

It was amazing he'd lived through all that, on top of the horrors he'd seen in war. But then he really wasn't living, was he? He had no family, no friends. He wouldn't allow it. The only living creature he'd allowed himself to be close to was Willow. And right now, he didn't even have her.

"You have to let me go," she said.

"I'm sorry you don't feel safe with me. I promise my intentions have only ever been to help you. I realized something wasn't right when I saw Dinetti and his men with you on that sidewalk, and I couldn't keep driving and just leave you there."

She opened her mouth to correct him. He was the only person she'd ever felt safe with. Literally the only person.

Before she corrected him, she paused. This was an opportunity to free him. But if she let him think he was the reason she left, he'd have even more guilt to live through. She couldn't add to that. But she still had to find a way to free him. If she was honest with herself, she hadn't put her full effort into it. She'd been selfish.

"I'm sorry I got you into this," she said.

"I chose to get involved. I should have found a different way to help, without making it look like you're close to me."

Making it look like he was close to her. He would never let her be truly close to him. The kiss had been nothing to him. Just a natural reaction of a man who forced himself to live like a monk suddenly in proximity to a willing female. Some tiny part of her, a part she hadn't even let herself acknowledge, had hoped he'd helped her, specifically her, for a reason. But he'd done it for Rose, some misplaced attempt to make up for Rose's death. She swore she could literally feel her heart breaking in half.

"Asher…" She paused, not sure how to go on.

Crash.

The sound of shattering glass came from the kitchen. The back door?

Asher snatched her hand and ran with her toward the front door.

CHAPTER 25

Cali ran with Asher through the front lawn, across the road, to the park. They paused behind a large tree with a trunk so wide they could both fit behind it.

Asher glanced down at their hands and let hers go.

He stood very still and listened, and Cali remained as silent as she could, wishing she'd left him long ago.

Asher squatted and quickly peeked around the tree toward the house. He looked up at her and mouthed, "Two men."

They must have followed them out the front door. She mouthed back, "The same ones from earlier?"

He shook his head. "Older."

Had the group that attacked them earlier posted the scene on social media? She'd noticed some of them shooting video with their phones. She didn't doubt they'd posted the videos immediately, perhaps after some strategic editing to make Asher look bad. And had the terrorist group that was after her already seen the video and tracked them?

"We need to get to the car," he mouthed.

She nodded. Though…other plots were forming in her head.

He glanced around the tree and then back to her. "We're going to run."

She nodded.

He looked around the tree, paused, and then he grabbed her hand and ran. She ran as fast as she could, but she knew she was slowing him down. She jogged all the time, but he was a lot taller and his fitness and training was at an elite level.

They reached a playground and paused behind a large play structure with slides and ladders, and bridges.

"I need to get a better visual of the back of the house," he said.

"But they know we need the car, so I'm sure they'll be waiting." Cali was thankful no children were in the park right now. Perhaps too chilly outside.

Asher looked all around them and pointed. "Between those two houses. Let's go."

They ran between two quaint houses that looked like they came from a 1950s sitcom set.

"If we can get over this fence," he said, "and then across the road, we should be able to see the back of the house from that vacant lot. It has enough trees for cover."

Cali looked up at the six-foot-tall fence.

"I'll lift you up, and then I can scale it myself."

Of course he could. She was again slowing him down. When he offered his interlaced hands, she set her foot into them, and he boosted her up. She was able to clamber over without making a lot of noise. Then he grabbed the top of the fence and hoisted himself up and over.

They ran through a backyard, over another fence, across the tar and gravel road, and into the vacant lot. They squatted behind some brush.

Sure enough, one of the men was walking through the back of the property.

"The other one is probably searching the house," Cali whispered.

Asher nodded. "They might have heard us leave out

MELISSA KOSLIN

the front door but obviously didn't see where we went. This one is watching for us to return to get the car, and the other is probably looking for any indication as to where we might have run to or any other pertinent information."

After a few moments of watching the man walk through the backyard, apparently checking the area to make sure they weren't hiding back there, Asher said, "I'll lead him away, you get the car, and meet me behind the Dairy Queen." He took the key fob from his pocket and handed it to her. "You noticed the Dairy Queen when we drove into town?"

It was a bit of a hike, probably two to three miles, but for him, it wouldn't be anything. She also knew he could easily take out the two men if they didn't get a drop on him with a firearm, probably even still then, but he wasn't going to lead her into a physical confrontation if he could. He would take all the danger on himself.

"Cali," he said. "Are you in agreement?"

Thoughts splintered through her mind—each strategy, its chance for success, possible negative outcomes, her goals as opposed to Asher's goals. It all came down to getting both those men and Asher to do what she wanted. Asher was—by far—the more difficult of the two.

"Okay," she said.

"I'll get him to chase me. He won't fire at me here—too much chance of being seen and caught in this little neighborhood. Once we're out of sight, run to the car and get out of here. Take a different route than the direction I end up going."

Of course—again keeping her out of danger at all costs. She nodded.

He turned and focused on the man in the backyard. When the man walked into the garage, which they'd apparently opened, Asher ran out of the brush and across the road. He slowed as he passed by the garage but then picked up pace again as the man chased after him. They ran through the side yard, and Cali could just see as Asher

205

led him to the left, the opposite direction of Dairy Queen.

Cali ran across the street and into the garage.

She set the fob on the hood of the truck. Out of her pocket, she took the phone Asher had given her, opened the note app, and typed in it. He'd set up the passcode, and she hadn't bothered to change it, so he'd be able to open the phone and read it.

I'm safe, I promise. Please go home and live your life. Thank you for everything. You've done infinitely more than you should have.

She left the phone next to the fob and peeked at the house from around the corner. She saw nothing in any of the windows and ran up to the back door and slipped inside. In the kitchen, she paused to listen.

Footsteps from upstairs, probably from the room she'd been using.

She slipped silently up the stairs, having already noted where all the creaks were so she could avoid them, and stood to the side of the door.

A man with brown hair and streaks of gray and an average build was in the bathroom. She stepped back to remain hidden and listened.

She heard the wheels of the suitcase Asher had given her and then a thump, like something being plopped on the bed. Based on where she'd left the bag, she guessed he'd put the bag on the bed closest to her and was, therefore, probably turned away. She took a quick peek around the corner to confirm, and then she crept up behind him and put him in a submission hold with her arm around his neck, putting pressure on the sides of his neck, not windpipe. The fact that she was shorter actually worked to her advantage on this hold—since she'd gotten him by surprise, he was leaned back against her, off balance, and couldn't out-muscle her, though he tried struggling.

"I'm the one you're looking for," she said.

He paused his struggles.

She kept the pressure on his neck carefully not too tight to knock him out. "I'll surrender. If you call your other man back and leave Asher Cross alone."

His voice came out strained due to the pressure on his neck. "What other man?"

She squeezed tighter, and he made a sound of distress.

"Don't play games," she said. "I know there are two of you. The other man is chasing Cross. Call him back. Once he's here, I'll surrender myself."

"You'll have to…" She eased pressure slightly, and he finished, "…let me go so I can call him."

"Nice try. You can do it just as well from here. Your hands are free."

He grunted an annoyed sigh but then fumbled to get his phone from his pocket. He managed to get it and redialed a recent number.

"Speakerphone," she said.

He pressed the speakerphone button.

"What?" The man who answered sounded winded.

Cali lessened her grip a bit so that the man could talk clearly.

"Come back. I've got the asset."

"What about Cross?"

"He's a hindrance, not the goal. Getting rid of him is a bonus."

"All right. I'm coming back."

"Make it quick. We need to get out of here before he comes back."

"On my way."

The call ended.

The man in her grasp said, "Okay, you can let me go."

"Not until he's here."

They stood there awkwardly for several minutes. It would've been funny under other circumstances.

The sound of a door closing. Sounded like the kitchen door. "Where are you?" a man's voice called.

"Up here," the man she was holding responded.

Cali waited until the man came upstairs and entered the room. At seeing a middle-aged man who looked like he'd traveled aggressively recently and had been running came into the room, she released the other man. He stumbled away.

"Let's get out of here," she said.

"Wait," the man who'd just come in said as he looked at his friend rubbing his neck. "Why are you giving yourself up? Is this some attempt to trick us?"

"I have my reasons. Do you want to risk Cross coming back and having to deal with him? I don't have any tracking devices or anything like that on me. You can search me if you need to."

"Wanted to get rid of The Beast, huh?"

"Something like that."

The first man grabbed her arm above her elbow. "Let's go."

She went with them down the stairs and out the front door. Just across the street, they got in a car in a different house's driveway. The first man got behind the wheel and backed out of the drive.

"Take an alternate route out of town," she said. "Don't pass the Dairy Queen."

The men glanced at each other, and the driver looked at his phone, presumably to find a new route. He made some additional turns, and they left the town without passing Dairy Queen.

***

Asher lost his pursuer, though he wasn't sure how. He took a careful route avoiding any main roads and made it to the Dairy Queen. He went around back, but Cali wasn't there. He'd been confident she'd make it here first. He waited a few minutes but grew more agitated each second.

She should have made it here easily. He trusted that she

was smart enough and quick enough to get the car out of the garage and away from the house before the other man could've gotten out the door and stopped her. He knew her skills quite well, better than he would admit.

Something wasn't right.

He started back toward Walnut Street. He had no idea what could've gone wrong. She wouldn't have purposefully delayed getting to the Dairy Queen. He knew her well enough to know she would never leave him—or anyone— exposed if she could help it. She would do everything she could to keep others out of danger…

He broke into a sprint.

He took the most direct route, no longer caring if someone saw him.

As he approached the back of the house, he slowed to a jog.

The property appeared to be quiet. And his truck was still in the garage. They could be holding her inside the house, waiting to ambush him.

She'd never sit there quietly while they waited. But they could have gagged her…or knocked her out.

He slipped into the garage where he could see the house from the window in the side door.

Then he noticed a key fob and a cell phone sitting on the hood of the truck. The cell phone he'd given Cali. He tried the combination he'd originally set for unlocking the phone, and it worked. The screen had been left on the notes app.

I'm safe, I promise. Please go home and live your life. Thank you for everything. You've done infinitely more than you should have.

He wanted to hurl the phone and curse at her. Instead, he gripped the phone so tightly it might crack.

He wanted to be furious at her, but then he reminded himself she had no idea why he'd involved himself in this. He'd kept it from her to protect her. That'd worked out spectacularly.

She'd said she was safe in the note. For a second, he thought maybe she was. She was astoundingly smart. But as he glanced at the silent house, his hope wilted.

He pocketed the phone and key fob and walked up to the house to confirm his suspicions. He went through every room of the large house, checked every corner. It was empty. Those men wouldn't have left unless they had what they'd come for.

They had Cali.

CHAPTER 26

Asher was barely in control. He'd never felt like this before, and it scared him. But not enough to stop.

He raced out of the small town in the vain hope he might catch up to them, and he called Floyd.

Floyd answered with, "How is Cali?"

"Gone."

"What do you mean 'gone'?"

"As in gone," he growled. "I believe she left with a couple of men who'd tracked us."

"Why would she do that?"

"To get me out of it. She left me a note telling me to go back to my life." Every time he thought about that note, he wanted to rage. How did she expect him just to go back to life and forget about her? She must think he really was a beast. "I need you to find her."

"What do you got for us to go on?"

"She left maybe an hour ago." He provided the address.

"Got a plate or make/model of the car?"

"No."

"A direction of travel?"

"No," he spit out. "I have nothing." He took a breath,

and his tone calmed. "Please, Floyd."

Floyd paused, as if hearing something more in Asher's voice. "We'll do everything we can. We haven't failed you yet."

The call ended. Asher knew he should just pull over and wait for them to get back to him, but he couldn't just stop. So, he drove in circles, not wanting to commit to a direction of travel just for it to end up being the wrong direction.

His hands shook. His mind kept veering off to horrible scenes of Cali being attacked.

Finally, he tried something he hadn't done since Rose died. He prayed.

***

They drove for hours.

Cali watched the scenery flash by in one long blur.

She listened for the men to discuss something, anything of interest, but they said nothing other than where to stop for gas, what food to grab, and how much farther they had to go. One of them received a call that was probably something of interest, but she could hear only his half of the conversation, which didn't give her much of anything. All she deduced was that these men had been the closest to her location when it'd been posted on social media, and they'd been dispatched immediately. They weren't anyone of great importance and probably didn't have a lot of information. She and Asher had already figured that.

She closed her eyes and took a moment to push Asher out of her head. She needed to pretend he didn't exist.

Darkness fell. Based on the amount of time they were spending in the car, she presumed they were not taking her back to where they were from but to someplace altogether different.

Since it seemed pretty clear the men didn't plan to abuse her in any way—they seemed pretty intent on ignoring her most of the time—she allowed herself to get some sleep. Who knew when she'd be safe enough to sleep again.

What felt like several hours later, the gentle slowing of the car woke her. She hadn't slept deeply or peacefully, but it would have to do for now. Out the windows, all she could see were trees. They were exiting off the freeway onto what appeared to be a rural highway.

"How much longer?" She asked it casually, as if they were on a family outing.

The man in the passenger seat didn't turn to look at her, but he did answer, "Less than an hour."

"Thanks." She watched out the windows carefully to be sure she understood where they were as best as possible. They'd made it about halfway across Pennsylvania while she'd been awake. The next route marker she saw was still in the shape of Pennsylvania. After reading a few more signs, she realized they were outside Philadelphia. She'd lived in West Chester for a while, which wasn't far from Philly, so she knew the area pretty well. At this point, she'd lived so many places that she had at least basic knowledge of most of the country.

She wondered if they'd blindfold her, but they kept on driving.

She continued to watch out the windows, carefully noting the main streets and anything that might be helpful. She had a lot of experience with this kind of thing, though Michael Dinetti had quickly learned to blindfold her when transporting her to a new location. Perhaps these two men were inexperienced?

As they drove into a historic area, the man in the passenger seat texted someone. She could just see over the seat that the text read, *2 minutes out*. The name of the recipient was simply WW, and there was no previous conversation that she could see on the screen.

A couple of minutes later, they pulled to a stop in front of a three-story brick colonial. It was old, perhaps even pre-Revolution, and perfectly maintained—fresh paint on the trim and shutters, all brick repointed, spotlessly clean.

An older man in a suit had been waiting on the brick sidewalk and now stepped forward to open her door. "Welcome."

Well, this was certainly different than her experiences being transported by Dinetti. She'd play the game, but she wasn't about to let her guard down. She stood from the car.

The two men who'd driven her stayed in the car, and as soon as the older man closed the door, they drove off.

She followed the older man through the front door encased in fluted molding. The entry was a long hall elegantly attired in molding and hand-painted wallpaper. She didn't know if it was original to the house, but the style certainly harkened back to the early days of America's founding.

The man led her to the left into a sitting room, also adorned in period finishes. He motioned for her to have a seat. He was still and formal but not unkind, definitely a servant, probably held the title "butler." She'd thought butlers were extinct.

"Thank you." She remained standing, and he left the room. She took a good look around.

Another man entered the room, this one with a big smile crinkling his eyes and cheeks. "Miss Lebeau, what an absolute pleasure."

She didn't respond.

He kept smiling as he approached. He wore a tailored blazer and jeans. His charm was palpable—not surprising that he was the one to greet her. "I'm Walter Williams."

The WW the man in the car had texted perhaps?

"Please do sit," he said.

She sat on a settee but stayed on the edge of her seat, ready for anything.

He sat on the other end of the settee. "You must be bursting with questions."

"I'm more interested in your explanation." She'd rather not lead the conversation with questions as much as possible. A person's questions could give quite a bit away. She needed him to give her as much information as possible first.

He sat back and crossed his legs in one elegant yet still masculine movement. "I'm sure a brilliant woman such as yourself has figured out quite a bit."

"Pretend I'm an idiot."

He raised a brow. "Playing inept is often the best way to garner information."

She waited.

He smiled. "I knew I'd like you." He angled toward her and rested his arm on the back of the settee. "First and foremost, you are now completely free of Michael Dinetti. We paid your father's debt and then some."

"Michael isn't that easily stopped. The debt was just an excuse to keep coming after me."

"I agree. But let's just say we handled it."

"Do you really think 'let's just say' is sufficient an explanation for me?"

"Of course not. I forget to whom I speak."

Or he was testing her to see if she was as sharp and unyielding as they suspected. "And I know you paid just shy of two million, not more. What is the 'and then some'?"

"We helped him with a minor matter, or rather a senator friend of ours helped him with a minor matter."

"And in doing so made clear you have influence in very high places and could make his life extremely difficult."

"Two birds, one stone." He continued smiling—it looked so natural and easy on his face. "And now you're here and finally safe."

She raised a questioning brow.

He held his palms out. "I'll explain, I promise. Okay, from the beginning… We paid off your debt because we figured out who you are, that you were decoding our messages—that you're brilliant. It took a lot of work, but we finally found you."

"How?"

"Well, we couldn't identify you—your real name—based on your online activities. You're quite careful and smart online. But Dinetti is not so careful, or rather stopped being careful. He was apparently desperate or angry and blabbed to the right person about who he had a contract out on, and we realized we were looking for the same person. We contacted him and made him that offer he couldn't refuse—large sums of money and senatorial influence are very persuasive."

That was as she'd thought. She waited for him to go on.

"And now you're wondering about Jonathan Sikes. I realize what that all looks like from your point of view."

"My 'point of view' meaning being framed for murder."

"Jonathan is a good man but unwell. He's been gaining attention from the wrong people, and we've been protecting him. That's why he's in that hospital—he's safe there. We have an orderly watching over him. There was some confusion briefly—Dinetti spouting lies that you'd tried to kill Jonathan. It was convincing at first and we did what we could to keep Jonathan safe, but when we realized our mistake, we made the warrant disappear. I apologize for that scare."

Apparently, he didn't know that she knew Jonathan Sikes was dead. She felt sure they were the ones to kill him—who else had the motivation? "How would Dinetti know who Jonathan Sikes is in the first place?"

"That's a question we asked ourselves. At first, we'd assumed he'd learned about Jonathan by watching you, digging into your activities. Obviously, that was incorrect. Honestly, we don't know how Dinetti knew about Jonathan."

Cali showed no reaction to that.

"And now you're wondering about the man who followed you, whom you confronted at the rest stop. We sent out notice to our contacts around the country that we wanted to get to know you better. That particular contact did not handle the interaction well, admittedly, but it did give us a glimpse into the volatility of Asher Cross. That scared us to no end. What if he hurt you?"

She wanted to defend Asher. He would never hurt her. But he was safer if they didn't know anything about him, only the mask he showed to the world—*The Beast*.

"You must be exhausted," Walter said. "Would you allow us to give you a place to rest for a while?"

She'd almost forgotten it was the middle of the night. Though she didn't feel like resting, she decided to play along for a while and nodded.

He stood. "We have a lovely room prepared for you."

She followed him across the hall to the main staircase. He left her in a room overlooking a small but beautiful garden in the back. The old wood floors creaked as she walked over to look out the window.

She continued to note every detail, all while pretending to be at ease.

All while struggling not to worry about Asher.

She'd assured him she was safe and had given him no way to follow her. He'd have to go back home. He'd keep trying for a while, but when he was unsuccessful in finding her, he'd eventually fall back into living his life. If you could call his existence much of a life.

He'd eventually find a way to heal from how Rose had died, right? He was strong, the strongest person she'd ever known. He would be all right.

She knelt on the floor and clasped her hands. "Please, God."

She stayed there for a while trying to lose herself in meditative prayer. Sometimes she would feel a distinct push in a certain direction if she opened herself to God.

But tonight, she was too overwhelmed. She missed

Asher. She worried about if she'd done the right thing, in the right way. She had to protect him. That had become her primary focus.

Because she loved him.

She opened her eyes and sighed. God often helped her see the truth, but it was sometimes a truth she didn't want to admit.

There was no lying to herself anymore. She was in love with him. And it wasn't something she would be able to get over. She was stuck in this precarious position of loving him too much to be with him for the rest of her life.

"Please, God, please help me to be strong enough, smart enough, to protect him." She closed her eyes, bowed her head, and resumed praying.

***

"Give me *some*thing!" Asher roared into the phone.

"Hang on," Floyd said. "Mt Dew says he has something." His voice changed, like he'd taken the phone away from his head. "How do you know that?" Asher couldn't hear the other man's response. "Are you sure?" Floyd said. Then lower, Floyd added, "He'll kill us if we're wrong. This is our only chance to help Cali." This time, Asher could hear the response, "I'm sure. Send him in that direction. He can be there in about five hours. We'll figure out more direction once he gets to Philly."

"Philadelphia." Asher made a turn at too high a speed and barreled toward the freeway. "See what else you can find me. Put anything else you're doing on hold. I'll pay you whatever you need." He hung up and focused on driving. He was on edge. He needed to focus so he didn't wreck.

CHAPTER 27

Morning light had begun to brighten the room when a knock came at the door.

Cali got up and answered the door. Though she was still on guard, she felt confident no one would physically attack her. That obviously wasn't how they wanted to play this.

A young redhead stood in the hallway. Her hair was curly, a bit frizzy, but still pretty in a wild way.

"Did I wake you?" she asked. "I didn't want to, but patience isn't my strong suit. And OMG I am so happy to have another girl around." She glanced down at Cali's clothes. "You're dressed, so I didn't wake you, right? But then, you probably didn't have anything else to change into and so slept in your clothes." She glanced down at her clothes again. "You're smaller than me, but not *that* much. I bet my clothes would work all right. If you want."

Cali resisted the urge to tell the girl to breathe. "I'm Cali. What's your name?"

"Of course you're Cali. Callista Lebeau, actually. That's a super interesting name. I'm not sure which I like better—Callista or Cali. Or maybe something totally different like Ista. Ever considered that?"

"*Ista* is a suffix meaning a strong supporter of someone. I would always feel dependent on others to give my name meaning."

The girl spread her fingers out over her head to indicate mind blown.

"Do I get to know your name?" Cali asked.

"OMG. Of course. I'm Ivy. Well, Ivana really. But Ivy for short. Ivana makes me feel like I'm named after my dad. I mean, I *am*. But it just feels like something you do with your son. Like, hello dad, I'm your *daughter*. I know he loves me, but he secretly wishes he had a son." She said the last part in a stage whisper.

"Sometimes, I think my father felt that way too."

"*Your* dad…" Ivy sucked air through her teeth. "Sorry. I shouldn't say mean things." She pressed her lips together as if that was the only way to get herself to stop talking.

That reaction told Cali that Ivy was included, at least to some extent, in what happened around here. That could be useful.

"Do you think we could get some breakfast?" Cali asked.

"Yes! That's why I came up to get you. Didn't I say that? I'm always getting sidetracked. Follow me." She led her down the hall and then down a back set of stairs.

Cali continued to mentally catalog every detail of the house.

Ivy led her to a dining room, also attired in apparent period décor with an antique table and sideboard and walls covered in a chair rail and light floral wallpaper. Food was set out on the sideboard, and they filled their plates and sat. Ivy motioned for Cali to sit at the head of the table, and she sat at the next chair.

Cali was still deciding if Ivy was very good at playing the game—making it appear that Cali was simply a guest— or if she honestly thought that's all that was going on.

"Do you live in the house?" Cali took a bite of toast.

Ivy sipped her steaming coffee. "A few of us do. It

dates back to the Revolution. Daddy is really into preserving history. He says turning houses like this into museums is a sin. All the traffic destroys the finishes and structure over time. Better for a family, or even a small business, to occupy these important landmarks. We take *such* good care of it. As I'm sure you noticed." She grinned at Cali, possibly having noticed Cali looking around. "Everything that could be preserved has been, and anything that had to be replaced was done with careful attention to proper restoration. We own several other buildings like this. Daddy wants the absolute oldest buildings we can get, but we also have some that are from the Civil War era. They're *so* pretty."

Did Ivy realize what Cali was doing as she looked around, or did she really just think Cali was into history? "I was just staying at an old, restored home before coming here. I don't know what era it was from, but definitely not as old as this place."

"That place was from the 1920s. We don't have anything that new, but I keep telling Daddy it's not just about the age. It's about the value, the craftsmanship. But he's stuck in his ways. I'm sure I'll eventually be able to convince everyone." Ivy grinned and forked a potato.

Everyone... "I'd already determined there was a group involved. Pretty spread out from what I could tell. Do you all have a name?" How would she respond to Cali's directness, and how much would Ivy tell her?

"Libervis. It means something to do with books. As I'm sure you'd guess—and probably already figured. You know lots of languages, right?"

"I'm best with dead languages but can get along well enough in several others." And she understood exactly what Libervis meant. "Are you allowed to talk to me about stuff?"

"Oh yeah! Daddy and the others—they really want to bring you into the fold. You're a kindred spirit. Book lover, history lover, *super* intelligent. We've been *so* worried about you, and we're just relieved you're finally here and safe. I guess I should've led with that, but I know Walter spoke with you last night. But then I know you're cautious, as you should be."

"Okay, let's start with what exactly is Libervis? What do you do?"

Ivy dropped her mouth open and lowered her chin. "You know about the Golden Library, right?"

"I know you're looking for it. Whatever it is."

"You don't know what it is?"

"I've started researching but haven't been able to delve into it as deeply as I'd like. Been kinda busy." Hopefully, she could pull off the lie.

Ivy bumped her head with the heel of her palm. "Of course you have! Okay, get ready for the absolute coolest, craziest story *e-ver*. So, way back when Ivan the Great was ruling Russia, like 1500s, he amassed a huge library filled with Greek, Latin, and Egyptian texts—crazy important works, like scrolls from the Library at Alexandria important. It was hidden under the Kremlin, and he let almost no one see it. Princess Sophia actually made it forbidden for anyone to see the rooms at all. It was more valuable than even the crown jewels. It was handed down to Vasili III and then Ivan IV—AKA Ivan the Terrible."

"Sounds like a cool legend."

"Not legend. It's a real thing." Ivy sat straighter. "Libervis secured and protected the library for hundreds of years."

"How did you get a hold of it if it was hidden and forbidden?"

"We are descended from servants in the Kremlin. Ivan the Terrible—after he tried to have the texts translated to find black magic within them and failed—ordered the library to be burned. But the servants understood the magnitude. They knew what the library was, what it meant. They used hidden tunnels and secreted the library out, one book, one scroll at a time. They miraculously managed not to get caught. When Ivan realized it was gone, he was convinced it was the work of black magic."

"All of Libervis is actual direct descendants of those servants?"

"Only a few direct descendants. My dad is the oldest living direct descendant. The rest are trusted partners brought into the fold to help with our cause. Like you."

"What do these trusted partners do?"

"Anything and everything. Whatever their talents bring to the table."

"Are they all totally trusted?"

"It's like security levels. Everyone agrees with our main objectives, but the depth of knowledge depends on what they need to know to do their part."

"What kind of security level do I get?"

"Pretty high already, actually. You're super valuable."

"Why?"

She raised her brows. "Do you not know how smart you are? You decoded our messages—you probably didn't totally understand them, but you decoded them. We use several levels of code, but cracking just the first level is kind of amazing. I get why you ran. Without getting through all the code levels, you probably thought we were a terror group."

Interesting that Ivy was capable of giving clear direct answers, without rambling, when needed. "Why do you need all those coded messages?"

Ivy took a deep breath. "Okay, time for the really hard part."

"Hard part?"

"The Golden Library—the library of all libraries—was stolen. Several generations ago."

"So, you're hunting it down."

Ivy nodded. "That's why we have people all over the world. That's why we have to communicate in coded messages. That's why we have to be so secretive. We were betrayed by one of our own."

"Why? How? It's a huge library—how does one steal that?"

"We don't know why she did it. My theory is she was freaking nuts. As for how, our best guess is that she did what our ancestors did—secreted it out a little at a time."

"No one noticed it diminishing?"

"It was kept hidden, and only a few people were allowed to actually see it. For security reasons. She waited for the others with access to be away, so she was able to take it out a little at a time over a few weeks. By the time the others came back and checked on the library, it was gone. My great-great-great-grandfather was so upset he died of a heart attack right then and there."

"What happened to the traitor?"

"No idea. She disappeared. There are legends that she died of a curse Ivan the Terrible put on the library. Some say she lived to old age and took the secret of the library's location with her, or that she had a daughter and passed a clue on to her which is passed down over generations. Or that she destroyed it all in a fire." Ivy visibly shuddered.

"I hope not." And that was the truth. Part of Cali really did hope the library was real. *Imagine—scrolls from the Library at Alexandria. Ancient Greek and Latin texts—maybe unknown writings from Socrates, Plato, Homer...* "The thought of all that being destroyed makes me sick."

Ivy smiled and popped another potato into her mouth. "And that's why you're a kindred spirit."

Cali had forgotten there was food in front of her. She continued eating but didn't taste much.

Ivy jabbered on about the homemade marmalade, and Cali glanced out the window. There was a very tall hedge line all around the property, except for the bit directly facing the street, and she could just see the top of a razor wire fence through the hedge. Cali had seen hidden cameras, security guards disguised as maids, and keyed locks on windows. She was a "kindred spirit" locked in a cage.

She wasn't yet sure whether Ivy was a fellow inmate or a guard.

"There you are." Walter walked into the dining room, sat down in the chair on the other side of Cali and set a folded newspaper down on the table. It happened to be folded so that an article about Asher was partially visible. Cali could see a few words—"accusations," "unethical practices." She was sure his laying that newspaper down folded to that part wasn't an accident. They didn't seem to understand what a deep understanding Cali had of Asher's business practices. Yes, he made profits—that's the whole point of business. But along with those profits, the company created employment, with good wages, for thousands of people. His business practices were completely ethical. Cali would not have stayed there if they hadn't been. Yes, he could be intimidating, but that didn't mean he was bad. In his case, it meant he was wounded.

"So, what are we chatting about?" Walter asked.

"The broad strokes of Libervis history," Ivy said. "But then I got going on the marmalade, which led me to whole grain toast vs. white, which led us to baking, which led us to gas vs. electric ranges."

Walter pressed his lips together, suppressing a laugh. "Naturally."

Ivy threw her hands up as if to say *obviously*.

Walter turned to Cali. "Sleep all right?"

Cali nodded.

"More questions for us?"

"Want some coffee?" Ivy asked Walter.

"Sure, thanks," he said and turned back to Cali.

"I'm cataloging questions at the moment," Cali said.

He smiled. "I'm sure you are. I'd expect nothing less." He took a cup of coffee from Ivy with a smile. "Ivan is in town. I thought you might like to meet him."

"Daddy's back?" Ivy asked.

Walter nodded. "He heard about Cali's arrival and took a private plane back. Arrived early this morning. He's resting but will be down in a bit."

"I worry when he pushes himself so hard."

"That's what passionate and dedicated people do. A man like him—if he didn't have something to be passionate about, he'd wither and die. As it stands, I guarantee he'll outlive all of us."

Ivy laughed. "You might be right."

"If you're done with breakfast, I thought Cali might like to browse the archives."

Ivy swung to face Cali. "OMG, you are going to L-O-V-E the archives."

A few minutes later, Ivy led Cali down the basement stairs. At the landing halfway down, they came to a metal door with reinforced hinges. Ivy pressed her thumb to a plate, and the door clicked open.

The basement was one place in this house that had obviously been completely renovated with no concern for historical accuracy. The ceilings were a comfortable height, the floors were concrete, and the walls were block. The ceiling was drywalled over, but Cali would wager there was something more than wood rafters above the drywall, something that would stop someone from simply cutting through the wood floors and subfloors to get into the basement.

To the right were rows of shelves filled with books, and binders, and boxes. To the left looked like a museum— pictures framed on the walls, cases displaying artifacts, and placards giving details on all of it.

Cali guessed why they were willing to show her all of this.

They wanted her to find the library.

***

Asher paced back and forth like a prowling tiger. But he didn't roar. He could hear through the phone how upset Floyd was, and he wouldn't add to that.

"He hasn't stepped foot outside in three years," Floyd said.

"He's a grown man," Asher said. "He'll be all right." Though he had no idea if that was true. He knew the name Mt Dew, but he'd never met him or even spoken to him.

Asher tried not to sound demanding when he asked, "Do you have any idea why he sent me to Philadelphia?" He'd been here a few hours but had no further direction. He'd called Floyd several times with no answer. Floyd's was the only phone number he had, which had never been a problem because Floyd had always answered.

And then Floyd had finally called to admit that Mt Dew had left. He and Bl@ze had gone out looking for him, confident they'd find their socially fearful friend. But they hadn't been able to find him or contact him in any way.

"He wouldn't tell us why he insisted you go to Philly."

"Is it possible he was trying to misdirect me?"

"No." Floyd's voice was almost harsh. "He cares about Cali too. Sometimes a little overprotective, to be honest. He wants to find her and protect her as much as I do, you do."

Asher was sure Floyd truly believed that, and Floyd had proven himself to be exceptionally intelligent.

"Did he take his computer?" Asher asked.

"Yeah. I'd have already hacked in and figured out what's going on."

"What do you know about his past?"

"Not a ton. None of us talk much about that."

Difficult pasts? Perhaps that was part of their bond.

"But he's a fan of the 76ers," Floyd said.

"So, maybe he's from Philadelphia." Sports fans often remained loyal to their hometown team.

"Possibly."

"Any family?"

"He said something about being adopted."

Bl@ze's voice came from the background "No, he mentioned a former adopted family."

Floyd said, "Same difference. But he never talked about them."

"Maybe he meant 'adopted family' as in a group he belonged to, not literal adoptive parents."

Floyd hesitated. "Maybe." Then he added, "I always had the feeling he'd been involved with something big before us. I always figured some secret government job or something."

"Or maybe…" Asher started.

"No," Floyd said emphatically. "He's not a plant for that terror group. He's a good person. I admit I don't know much, but I know that."

Asher heard Bl@ze's agreement in the background.

Quiet for several seconds.

"He's obviously involved in something," Asher said. "Or he wouldn't have abruptly left." Then he added, "Maybe he wasn't a recluse so much as he was hiding."

"Like maybe from that terror group…"

"Not a plant but involved at some point. If he didn't have some kind of background information, how would he even know to send me to Philadelphia? And why would he not tell you why or how he had this information? He chose to reveal it only as a last resort."

Then Bl@ze started talking excitedly. "He said he lived in a Colonial-era house for a while."

The sound of quickly clacking keyboard keys. Floyd said, "Searching for privately-owned, non-museum Colonial houses in Philly."

"Send me the addresses," Asher said. Surely, there were hundreds of such houses in Philadelphia, but he'd knock on every door if he had to.

CHAPTER 28

"Where should we start?" Ivy said, apparently to herself. "I know." She grabbed Cali's hand and led her over to the museum side, to the largest photograph, framed and centered on the wall. "Look at this. A picture of the library before the betrayal. Isn't it magnificent?"

In Cali's imagination, an image of the library had formed, but it looked nothing like the image before her. She'd imagined hand-hewn wooden shelving, with scrolls and books neatly lining them. Simple, honest. But this ornate, gold frame held a photograph of a room with a gilded dome ceiling. The shelving lining the walls had vines climbing all vertical supports with roses sporadically blooming off the vines. Intricate dental molding covered the horizontal shelves. But the books and scrolls were as she'd imagined—varied bindings and sometimes damaged from age but carefully placed on the shelves.

While Cali had observed the picture, Ivy had jabbered on about the details of the photograph. It'd been taken in the late-1800s, the last photograph ever taken of the completely intact Golden Library.

"Why do you say 'completely intact'?" Cali asked.

"Because we cannot trust that the betrayer has

229

maintained it." The voice came from behind Cali, and she spun to see an old man with a cane moving toward them from the stairs. He looked like he had to be in his 90s. His back was hunched, and he shuffled forward leaning on his cane.

Ivy smiled broadly. "Cali, this is my dad, Ivan Volkov, the oldest living descendent of the original saviors of the library. In my opinion, literally the smartest man on the planet."

He smiled, and his papery skin wrinkled. "My daughter may be a bit biased."

She grinned. "Nope." Then she wrapped her arms around him, and they hugged tightly. Before she let go, she said against his cheek, "I'm so glad you're back."

She stepped back, and he laid his hand on her cheek. "I missed you, baby girl."

Cali swallowed a lump in her throat. She'd prayed her whole life for her father to look at her like that.

"Trip successful?" Ivy asked.

"To be seen." He turned to Cali and extended a slightly unsteady hand. "It's lovely to meet you, Miss Lebeau. We are overjoyed to welcome you."

She shook his hand.

"Have you explored the archives?" he asked.

Ivy answered, "We just started. We had a nice breakfast first and got to know each other a bit."

"Some of our history?" he asked.

She nodded.

"Wonderful." He nodded toward the photograph they were just looking at. "Beautiful is it not?"

"Gorgeous."

"My grandfather commissioned those shelves. He designed them himself."

"You still have the shelves, right? And the building where this was taken?"

"Yes, it's one of the estates Libervis owns. But none of us wish to visit it anymore. It tears at our souls not knowing where our precious library is. It's like having a child stolen from your arms. You are not a mother yet, correct, Miss Lebeau?"

"No." And she'd accepted she never would be, no matter how much she wanted it.

"I can tell you there is no greater fear on this earth than a parent whose child has been kidnapped. The library is our child. We will not stop until she is saved. Even if we have to track her down book by book." His expression looked pained.

Ivy tucked her arm in the crook of her father's, the one not holding his cane. "We'll find it, Daddy. We have the best cryptologist in the world." She smiled at Cali. "If she'll agree to help us."

Cali kept quiet about everything she had already discovered. She still felt confident that the library had been at the Biltmore at one time, but she wasn't going to share that. "Show me what you have."

They gave her a thorough tour of the museum section. It was really just a history of Libervis, which was interesting, but didn't help with finding the library.

"May I ask," Cali finally said after looking through pictures of Libervis members at the annual party they held in honor of the saving of the library. It was a lavish black-tie event. "How does Libervis gain funding?"

They were now seated at a small round table in the other area of the basement, near the shelves. Ivan had not been able to stand for an extended period of time.

"We've had benefactors over the years who have donated to the upkeep of the library."

"You shared knowledge of its existence?"

"Only to certain individuals. People we felt were trustworthy and who were kindred. Like yourself. It's very, very rare to allow someone full knowledge, but worth it in certain very special circumstances."

"You realize I've been running from you. Why are you trusting me?"

"Because you are intelligent. We certainly made mistakes" —he looked at Walter— "and we have properly apologized, I trust."

Walter answered, "I explained that mistakes were made, major mistakes."

Ivan turned back to Cali. "And we are deeply sorry for that. It was always with the best intentions, I assure you."

Cali nodded.

"But I think we are on the road to trust," Ivan said. "We are an open book. We are willing to take any risk in order to gain your trust."

"Why?"

"I don't think you truly realize how valuable you are, Miss Lebeau. You solved the final message of Kryptos, correct?"

The sculpture at CIA headquarters in Langley. Cryptologists had been trying to decipher it since 1990. "How could you know that?" She hadn't told anyone.

"You checked a book out of the library about it several years ago. Forgive me, but we have looked into your background extensively. And perhaps even more impressive, you decoded our messages."

"They were quite impressively coded," she admitted. "You must have a master cryptologist working for you."

"Not any longer, sadly. We had someone brilliant, but that was long ago. We still use her cyphers—no one had ever broken them. Until you."

"It was the traitor," Ivy added. "The brilliant cryptologist. The one who stole the library. Such a shame that someone so brilliant could be so awful. But then, I guess a lot of awful people are quite brilliant. Or maybe we know about only the brilliant ones because they accomplished more of their goals." She shrugged.

"Probably," Cali agreed. She almost wondered if Ivan would give some signal to his daughter not to go off on tangents, but he listened to her just as attentively as he had Cali. "So," Cali said. "Am I assuming correctly that you're hoping I'll find the library?"

Ivan pressed his lips together and took a breath. "If I'm being completely honest, yes. That's my hope, anyway. But don't feel pressure. I'm hoping you dig into the archives"—he nodded toward the shelving—"and that brain of yours just can't let go until the puzzle is solved."

"It's as if you know me." Cali grinned.

He raised a brow. "We do. Well, we know your abilities. We're honored to get to know you personally as well."

Ivy chimed in, "And I am sooooo happy to have another girl around. Way too much testosterone in this place. Even the cooking and cleaning staff are guys. Like OMG. Have you ever heard of a male maid? What is that? I swear, I'm going to have you giggling and letting me braid your hair within a week."

Ivan laughed. "What do you say, Walter? Let's leave them to it?"

Walter stood. "I am of absolutely no use braiding hair, I'm ashamed to admit."

"Myself as well." Ivan held up his knobby, wrinkled hands. "Though in my younger years…"

"*That* is a story I need to hear," Walter clapped Ivan on the back, with less force than he would a younger man, surely.

The two men headed up the stairs, Ivan quite slowly as he navigated with his cane.

"Come on," Ivy said. "I'll show you the organization system in the archives. I have a feeling you're absolutely dying to dig in." She led her over to the shelves and started explaining.

Before she knew it, Cali had plopped down on the floor immersed in reading. Ivy left at some point. Cali fleetingly worried about being locked down here alone, but the whole place was a fortress—she was no more a prisoner here as she was in the bedroom she'd been given. And they all seemed bent on bringing her into the fold as a friend, not by force. Though she didn't know what they would do if she stopped accepting their friendliness.

Some small part of her wanted to believe they really did have good intentions. Or maybe she just wanted to think the best of Ivan because he appeared to be a good father.

Ivy came back down the stairs. "Lunch? Oh, you're into the history, I see." She nodded at the book Cali was reading—it was more like an old hand-written journal, one of many, chronicling the known history of the library. "It's a little dry, but interesting to imagine how many times the library was moved. Keeping it safe from war, natural disaster—crazy how close it came to ruin several times. Those old entries, the traitor actually wrote. It's really kind of impressive that they let a woman do something so important, for that time period anyway. Too bad she did everything she could to hurt further upward climbing for women by her actions. But you and I are pushing forward!"

Cali would really rather keep reading, but she decided befriending Ivy was wise. She stood, set the book she was reading on the round table, and followed Ivy back up the stairs.

Cali had expected a simple lunch of sandwiches or maybe soup, but a young man brought out dishes of lobster ravioli. It was divine.

"Can I ask you something?"

Ivy smiled. "That is literally what I'm here for. That and to have someone to talk to. Oh, but don't feel like you have to spend a bunch of time with me. I'm good on my own too. You can lose yourself in the archives all you want. Or ask me questions all day. I'm game for anything."

"Do you mind if I ask a personal question? Just out of curiosity?"

"My dad, right? How is someone in his nineties the father of a twenty-eight-year-old? It's a fair question. He devoted his life to finding the library, but eventually, he realized he needed to have an heir. He didn't want to be responsible for the end of his lineage—he's so proud that his ancestors were brave enough to save the library. So, he finally allowed himself to consider a life outside the quest for the library. He met my mom, who happened to be younger, fell head over heels for her, and married her. It took a couple of years, probably due to my dad's age, but she finally got pregnant with me. My dad always says I'm his miracle." She grinned.

"Can I ask what happened to your mom?"

For the first time, Ivy's expression went from sunshine to cloudy. "She died from cancer when I was eight." She forced a little smile. "I'm just thankful that I remember her."

"I'm glad you have those memories."

"My dad says… This might sound weird, but hear me out. He says he's almost glad in a way that if she had to be taken from us early, that it was the cancer that took her. Just so he knew it was in the family. He's had me screened every year since my mom died."

"You have cancer?"

"When I was sixteen. We caught it really early—because of those screenings. If we hadn't caught it when we did and start aggressive treatment immediately, I had very little chance of making it. I'm in remission now." She leaned her elbows on the table. "Want to know a crazy story? This is what makes me think anything is possible—that we can get the library back."

Cali leaned forward and nodded.

"In the hospital during chemo, I was at the end of my rope. I had tried to make it to the bathroom before getting sick but didn't make it, and then I slipped in my own vomit and hit the floor hard. I remember vividly laying there and wishing it was just over. But then I suddenly got my strength back just long enough to pull myself back to standing and make it to the bathroom to clean up. I swear it felt like someone *helped* me up."

"Like God?"

"I don't believe in God, obviously, never have, but I do believe in angels. I think that's who helped me."

Cali tilted her head. "I don't want to sound cruel, but…where do angels come from if not from God?"

"You believe in God?"

"Yes."

Ivy's face scrunched up. "You? Really?"

"Why not?"

"You're just so smart."

"Smart people can't believe in God?"

"They don't generally. God is like fairy tales." Ivy didn't sound antagonistic at all.

Cali smiled a little. "Actually, I think believing in God is the most rational thing I've ever believed. God is the only thing who lives completely outside space and time. He is the only thing not controlled by the natural world, who is not subject to its laws. How did the universe come to be if not by an outside force? Basic physics tells us something can't come from nothing."

"The Big Bang?"

"So, it's more logical to believe in a random bang that accidentally caused all life in the universe, that accidentally created this perfect balance that is the earth. Did you know that if the Earth's orbit was just a little different, life wouldn't exist? Or if the sun was just a little bigger. Or if trees didn't cover the earth and happen to convert CO_2 to oxygen. There's so much precision in the universe, even within our own bodies—this perfect, delicate balance. I'm too logical *not* to believe in God. I simply don't have the faith required to believe all this was an accident."

Ivy leaned back in her chair. "Wow."

Cali made the same hand motion over her head as Ivy had before, signifying mind blown.

"More like…" Ivy held up both hands and exploded them apart. She sat forward and slapped her palms down on the table. "Okay, just give me a minute to realign my entire way of thinking." She closed her eyes and scrunched her face.

"You should read a few books on it and see what you think. I can make some suggestions."

The young man who'd brought their food out came back in. "Finished? Dessert?"

Ivy opened her eyes and glanced at Cali's empty bowl. "I think we're done." She asked Cali, "Do you want anything else?"

"I'm stuffed."

The man took their bowls and left.

"Can I ask you one more question?" Cali asked.

"I don't know. That last one led to the complete flipping of my entire belief system. I don't know if I'm up for it." Then she grinned. "Shoot."

"What do you do? You don't seem the type to be content with a life of leisure."

"OMG, that would be so boring. Just sit around all day. Ugh. No, I do what I can where I can. Kind of like an apprentice to my dad. I help him with correspondence and plan his travel and stuff like that. All that sounds more like a secretary, but he also consults with me. He says he likes having a younger and fresh perspective. He gets stuck in his ways, understandably, and he thinks it's important not to let that blind him."

"He sounds like a really good dad." It came out more wistful than Cali had intended.

Ivy gave her a kind and understanding smile. "Good dads do exist."

Of course, Ivy knew all about Cali's dad. And surely her mom too.

"Thanks for the amazing lunch." Cali stood. "I guess I'll dive back into the archives."

Ivy let her in the door down to the archives, and Cali lost herself in reading. When Ivy came to offer dinner, Cali tore her eyes from the file she was reading and declined with a smile. As soon as Ivy was gone, she reread the page. *Does this mean what I think it does?*

CHAPTER 29

It was late when Cali headed back upstairs. As she'd figured, Ivy was in the sitting room, which had a view of the stairs.

Ivy looked up from her book reader, as if just happening to notice Cali. "I'm almost surprised you didn't just stay down there all night."

"Tempting. I'll make more progress if I let myself get proper rest." She moved to go upstairs. "Good night."

"Night!"

Although Cali was tired, she didn't let herself lay down but sat on the bed sorting through things.

She'd read a report about Libervis current membership. That hadn't been all that interesting, aside from learning which senator was in their pocket. But she'd also glanced through old reports that were in the same binder. It listed names, security levels, a basic description of what they did for Libervis, and any notes. One in particular had caught her eye.

Matthew Dewer, level 3, hacker

She'd always assumed Mt Dew's handle was due to his obsession with Mountain Dew, the beverage. But if he had been involved with Libervis, wouldn't he have said something once they started tracking them? Maybe he hadn't realized it was them? If he was Matthew Dewer, it was too big a coincidence to ignore.

The notes in his entry stated that he'd gone silent, and he was not included in the next year's member list. Why had he gone silent? Did he truly have crippling social fears and that's why he never left the apartment, or was he hiding from Libervis? If Libervis had doctored the document to hide his involvement from her, they would have removed mention of him entirely.

She couldn't do much about that right now, so she mentally put it to the side.

She'd also found reference to the library having been moved to Bordeaux at one point in the past. She'd gotten excited for a moment—this could be evidence that the clues she'd found in *Atlas of Fictional Places* were accurate, not the ravings of a crazy guy. It was possible the traitor had put those clues together in the book. The book had been quite old, old enough to have been in the possession of the traitor at some point. Cali had figured the pages had been artificially aged so as to match the rest of the book, but perhaps they were almost as old as the book and naturally aged. Had it been sitting in that library all that time until Jonathan Sikes came across it? Perhaps that was even what started his obsession.

Then she reminded herself that even if her theories were true, the library surely wasn't still at the Biltmore. Someone would have found it by now. It was a major tourist attraction, with tourists and curators crawling all over the place on a daily basis. There was no way an entire library could be hidden there.

As she stared at the rug under her feet, she mentally re-reviewed what she'd read.

Wait…

Ivy had said earlier today that the traitor had written the older entries about the movements of the library, including the one about its having been in Bordeaux.

Something about the text in a few places had struck her as familiar but she wasn't sure why exactly. She mentally drilled down into that.

Several minutes later, she looked up and widened her eyes.

That was it.

Her memories of her mom were vague, but there were a few that stuck out. She used to sing a song. Well, it wasn't long enough to be considered a full song, more like a rhyme that she sang.

Beautiful baby Belle
Spoiled of this world
She will quell
In the house built
History doth dwell
As with the yield at Bennett
The righteous will swell
The heir shall learn
The wisdom to rebel

The line "history doth dwell," it was in a few of the entries. It could be a coincidence.

The line "the house built" seemed a little odd. All houses are built; it's a prerequisite of being a house. Otherwise, it's just lumber. Unless…it was supposed to be "bilt," rather than "built." That actually made more sense.

The yield at Bennett… Although most people thought the Civil War ended when Lee surrendered in Virginia, that wasn't actually when the fighting stopped. Confederate generals met at the Bennett farm in North Carolina to agree to a truce. That's when the war was effectively over.

So, it said history—presumably the library—dwelled in the house Bilt, aka a Vanderbilt house, and the reference to the yield at Bennett indicated North Carolina, which narrowed down the Vanderbilt houses to Biltmore.

Was this the clue? The one rumored to have been passed down for generations from the traitor. Was Cali the traitor's heir?

Ivy had said the traitor was a master cryptologist. Perhaps that was where Cali had inherited her skills. It certainly wasn't from her father.

She wished she knew more about her mother. She'd abandoned her when Cali was just four years old. That was what her father had told her, back before he'd been addicted to gambling and had been a decent man. Her mother leaving had been hard on him, and Cali suspected that was part of what had led him to gambling. Her mother hadn't left a note, nothing. She'd just packed her bags and left. Maybe there was more to all of that, some reason she'd left? Perhaps it was just Cali's desperate wish that maybe her mother had actually loved her.

What she needed to do was go through those membership records. She'd gone through several years, but she needed to go back several generations—find the traitor's name and see if she could glean any further information.

She stood from the bed and headed out the door and down the stairs. Perhaps Ivy was still in the sitting room and could let her in the door to the basement.

Halfway down the steps, before the wall ended and railing started and she'd be visible to anyone downstairs, she paused at the sound of voices. It sounded like Ivan and another man whose voice she didn't recognize, likely in the office that was opposite the sitting room at the front of the house.

"Has she agreed to find the library?" the unknown man said.

"We're making headway. My plan to poke her father issues has worked, I believe," Ivan said.

"Trying to become her father figure?"

"Whatever gets her on our side and gets us the library back."

"Whatever gets her to stop getting in the way. I have to say I'm quite impressed. When you pushed to get her released from police custody, I was concerned for your sanity. I started to wonder if you were finally getting too old." He laughed. "It'd taken a lot of doing to get her framed for Sikes."

"She's too valuable to just throw away. We had to try to get her on our side."

A shifting sound, like from someone standing from a leather chair. "Keep us updated on your progress," the unknown man said.

Cali quickly and silently backtracked up the stairs. She certainly wasn't surprised that the pretty mask Ivan and the others wore was covering ugliness, but she needed them to think she was buying it. She needed access to those archives for a few more days.

And then she had to figure out how to escape. She had some ideas, but they were all risky and would require lots of luck. She did not like relying on luck.

She made it back to her room and closed the door. There were cameras all over the house, but the way the upstairs hall camera was positioned in a plant probably would block the view of the stairs. And she wasn't sure if anyone was actively monitoring the cameras. She'd moved at a normal and casual pace, as if just going down the hall to the restroom.

Now she had to sit here the rest of the night. That was going to be tough.

She slipped off her shoes and leaned back against the headboard.

She desperately wanted to talk to Asher. Talking to him helped her sort out everything in her head, and he'd have astute and helpful observations.

Maybe she could talk to him… She closed her eyes and imagined him sitting here next to her. He would never sit so close, but a girl could dream.

She imagined what she would tell him and how he would respond.

He was irritated at the idea Mt Dew may have deceived them. He was quiet while she explained about her mother

243

and the possible clue.

He looked at her more closely. "Something is bothering you."

Though her eyes were still actually closed, she imagined looking down at her hands in her lap. "They used my insecurities against me. My father issues."

"Are you upset?"

She looked up. "Angry."

"Use it. Let it focus your mind, not confuse you."

She nodded.

And finally, she asked the question that made her the most tense, that she'd dreaded asking her whole life. She'd never even asked her father. "Why did my mother leave me?" How could a mother leave her child? What was wrong with Cali?

Asher was quiet while he looked at her with that steady, unnerving gaze of his. "We can't judge her actions before we understand her circumstances and intentions."

She took a slow breath. She rarely needed to be reminded to be logical, but there were a few things that were very difficult for her, namely her parents.

Then her imaginary Asher asked her, "Why did you leave me?"

She sagged against the headboard. She could never say this to Asher in reality. "I love you too much to let you be dragged into this."

"Don't I have the right to choose for myself?"

She opened her eyes and stared out the dark window. "I'm sorry," she whispered. Then she pushed that out of her head. He was surely annoyed that she'd left, but nothing else. Some deep down part of him was probably even a little relieved.

She sat there for a while trying to think but then moved on to prayer.

Someone had left clean clothes on the bed, so well before sunrise, she went to the bathroom down the hall and showered. She was sitting at the dining table when kitchen staff set breakfast out on the sideboard.

"I figured you'd be up way too early," Ivy announced as she walked into the room.

During breakfast, Cali continued to try to get a better read on Ivy.

Then Cali spent the entire day in the archives—thankful for her excellent memory. She wasn't about to write down anything and risk someone stealing her notes or simply reading over her shoulder and realizing she was trying to uncover more than just the location of the library.

She didn't go up for lunch, so Ivy brought her a bottle of water and a sandwich. Cali barely nibbled at the sandwich.

She found the traitor, a widow named Lavinia Florence. She had a daughter named Belle, which fit the song. There wasn't much about her personally, but Cali almost felt like she started to get to know her through her writing—clever word choices and rhythmic tempo—as well as through her cyphers. She was brilliant but understated.

She followed her trail through the archives until it stopped March 11, 1896. Cali had looked up when the Biltmore was built—it had been finished 1895.

And in that last bit of writing, Cali heard something she wagered no one else ever had. It was an unusual bit of opinion at the end of the entry. "We understand the importance and are willing to risk everything."

Libervis had probably read that "we" to mean Libervis, but Cali suspected it meant something else. Lavinia hadn't ever included editorialization—except this one time. But if "we" wasn't Libervis, who else had she been working with?

"Hey, Cali. Can I talk to you?" Ivy had come down. Her tone was more serious than usual.

"Sure."

Ivy plopped down on the floor in front of where Cali sat between rows of shelves. She gripped a tablet in both hands and glanced back over her shoulder.

"Everything okay?" Cali asked

"I've been reading."

Cali grinned and held up the file she was in the middle of.

"I think my reading may actually be more important."

Cali raised a brow, closed the file, and set it in her lap.

Ivy huffed. "I read the book you suggested I start with."

"Already?"

"I'm a fast reader. I… I'm not really sure what to do with it."

"What do you mean?"

"Everything is—suddenly—different. I mean, I grew up so sure all those *Christian* people were idiots believing in a magician in the sky. I never considered anything else. I've missed so much. What else has been right in front of me that I just didn't see? That's kinda scary, you know? Like, how can I trust myself?"

"So, you believe?"

"How can I not? The book laid out each and every argument against God and then demolished it. I know I don't seem like it—way too much of a talker, I know—but I'm a pretty logical person. And now I'm…"

"Scared?"

Ivy's red brows pinched together. "Yeah. Terrified, actually."

Cali reached over and took Ivy's hand. "There's no need to be afraid. Christ died for us. He's already done the heavy lifting."

"But now—all of a sudden—I'm being judged. Well, I've always been judged, just too blind and stupid to see it. Like, how can I possibly make up for all the wrongs I've already done? That time I cheated on a final exam or when I stole an outfit from a store or when I flirted with a guy on a plane who obviously had a girlfriend. I never thought of myself as a bad person, but now, all I can see are all the bad things I've done. And then I'm super scared all that will send me to Hell, and I feel guilty for being more worried about myself than the people I've wronged." Tears glistened in her eyes. "It was so much easier when I thought sin didn't matter, not *really*. I thought when I died I would just stop existing. Maybe that's why I didn't see the truth—it was easier."

Cali took her other hand and squeezed both. "We all sin. It's a fact of humanity. God knows that. That's why he sent his son for us. Christ's sacrifice wiped the slate clean for us—if we accept him, acknowledge our sins, and humbly and honestly ask forgiveness."

A tear rolled down Ivy's cheek. "I don't know how to do that."

Cali smiled a little. "Talk to God. Tell him your fears and insecurities. Ask for guidance. He'll answer. Maybe not in a way you expect or in a way you even understand at first. But you keep talking to him. Be open. Listen. *Let* yourself feel his presence. He's here. He's listening." She squeezed her hands. "He loves you. He loves that you're open-minded enough to listen. He loves that you're trying when this is so hard for you. He even loves that you talk so much."

Through her tears, Ivy laughed. Then she sobered. "Really?"

"Absolutely." Cali held eye contact, willing her to believe, to *hear* God, to *feel* him.

More tears fell. Even though Ivy's face crumpled, Cali could tell they were happy tears. A sob bubbled from Ivy's lips, and Cali pulled her into a hug.

Ivy cried on Cali's shoulder.

Ivy took a breath, and her voice was muffled by Cali's shirt. "Thank you."

Cali heard how deeply that went, could feel how God had changed her, and Cali was honored and humbled that God had seen fit to use her for this. She squeezed her eyes closed. *Thank you.*

Cali whispered in Ivy's ear. "God is here. With us right

now." She paused. "Do you feel him?"

Ivy hesitated so long Cali thought she might not answer. But then her voice wobbled with tears. "Yes."

Cali held her tighter.

***

Cali showered and changed clothes. She'd stayed in the archives late. She was tired, but she probably wouldn't get to sleep tonight. She put on the clothes Ivy had apparently dropped off for her—they'd been sitting on her bed when she'd trudged upstairs. The pants were loose and flowy, and the top was a simple, cotton long-sleeve.

Before walking out of the room, she mentally reviewed the placement of all the cameras she'd spotted in the house. She'd created a mental map of the areas covered by cameras and not. She hadn't seen every area of the house, but she'd gotten a good feel for how the cameras were placed and was confident she could spot them easily. Getting around undetected would be tricky but not impossible.

She slipped out of the room and down the stairs.

There was no one in the office at the front of the house. That struck her as more of a meeting room than a private office. It was a little too perfect. She suspected there was at least one working office somewhere in the house.

Down the main hall, past the dining room, another hall branched off.

Voices. From the other end of the hall.

She headed that direction, careful to look casual just in case she'd missed a camera and someone was watching her.

Thankfully, there was a nook at the end of the hall where a sculpture was displayed. She made a show of examining it, while listening to the voices coming from behind the closed door to her right. She recognized Ivan's voice, as well as Walter. There were two other male voices she didn't recognize—one was very deep and the other a little raspy but not with the waver of age like Ivan's. She'd had a feeling nighttime meetings were common, probably in an attempt to hide them from Cali, with the assumption she'd be asleep this late.

"Isn't it a little cool outside for golf?" Ivan was saying.

Walter scoffed.

The man with the raspy voice said, "It's not snowing yet."

The man with the deeper voice teased, "Finally getting old, Ivan?"

"Didn't you know?" Walter said. "Ivan will live forever."

Walter's tone was lighthearted, teasing, but Ivan's was serious. "That's the plan." Then he added, "What was so important it couldn't wait?"

The man with the deep voice sounded more serious as well. "We received a message through one of our usual forums. Encoded."

"Encoded but not one of our usual contacts?" Ivan asked.

"The message says it's from Matthew Dewer."

Raspy Voice said, "I still say we should have had him killed."

"We can't have too many deaths following us," Walter said.

"You approved the removal of Sikes."

"He had become an immediate threat—talking too much. And that orderly was getting too brazen asking for more money. Sikes' death got him to shut up. Two birds."

"What does Matthew say?" Ivan asked. "And can we be sure it's him?"

"He knew our codes and that we have Callista Lebeau. He wants her released, and he says he'll give himself up in exchange."

Cali was startled when someone laughed. Sounded like

Walter. "He obviously doesn't realize how well we have her in hand."

Deep Voice said, "Ivan has turned our greatest problem into our greatest asset. All by simply stoking her obsessive nature when it comes to riddles."

Walter added, "And by giving her a friend and a father figure. I think those are more persuasive than anything else." He laughed. "Amazing how these tender, fragile people can be controlled so easily."

Raspy Voice said, "Sounds like she'll have the library back in a matter of weeks. What shall we do with her then? Dispose?"

"We'll see how things play out," Ivan said. "She could continue to be useful. Especially with how easy she is to control."

"And what should we do about Matthew?" Deep Voice asked. "Ignore him?"

Walter weighed in. "Hadn't we considered if he may be the heir?"

The heir to the traitor, Lavinia Florence? Ivy had indicated that an heir out there, with some secret clue, was just rumor. Maybe the idea had more backing either than she realized or than she'd wanted Cali to know for some reason.

"I believe you were away when we looked into that," Ivan said. "We dug through his lineage. They didn't arrive in the U.S. until after 1900. We're quite certain he's not the heir."

"Why would he offer himself in exchange for Lebeau?" Deep Voice asked.

"My strongest theory," Ivan said, "is that he was working with her. He found our messages, and she decrypted. I believe he's trying to find the library himself and needs her help."

"She obviously doesn't feel great loyalty to him if she left him and joined us instead."

"Perhaps take him up on the offer to lure him to us

and remove this particular annoyance."

"We may even be able to create a narrative where his death brings Lebeau closer to us—where she asks for our protection," Ivan said.

Walter laughed. "Leave it to Ivan to make everything into a positive."

"Excuse me," Deep Voice said. "I'll be just a moment." Footsteps moved closer.

CHAPTER 30

Something drove Asher not to stop tonight. He'd knocked on countless doors already, but instead of feeling antsy and discouraged, he felt even more driven for some reason. He parked around the corner from the next house on the list and glanced at the clock on the dash. Even with the late hour, he got out of the car and walked toward the house.

After all the colonial-era houses he'd looked at in the last few days, he'd gotten extremely adept at spotting anything unusual. At first glance, this house looked like so many other historically important buildings. Until Asher noticed the hidden security cameras, not the standard cameras one might find on any home nowadays, but professional level and expertly hidden in nooks on the façade. Since the house was on a corner, he could see the backyard fence. Perhaps due to his height—and the fact that he was looking for anything out of the ordinary—he spotted the second fence mostly hidden by the well-maintained, innocuous wooden fence running along the sidewalk. The razor wire just visible along the top of the secondary fence.

This has to be it.

He mentally reviewed the floor plan of the house the Gray Hats had provided and walked casually up to the front door. He felt confident they would not call the police, but he was equally confident they had security measures in place.

He gave a quick *clink, clink* on the antique knocker and waited. The security around the house was excellent—the best way in was the front door. He hoped showing up so late at night would work to his advantage, that perhaps they wouldn't be as on-guard. And perhaps his appearance would delay their recognizing him—he hadn't shaved since Cali had left, which helped to hide his signature scars, and he knew he generally looked disheveled, which he usually strove against. He currently looked like The Beast everyone thought him to be. And perhaps was.

The door opened, and a man in his fifties greeted with, "How may I help you?" He looked the part of a butler—suit and tie, formal demeanor—but Asher could spot the signs of a man wearing a holster under his jacket and the strength with which physically capable men held themselves.

"I'm here for Cali."

The man raised his brows. "There is no Cali here, sir. I'm afraid you have the wrong address." As soon as he started closing the door, Asher grabbed him by the collar of his jacket, pushed him into the house, kicked the door closed, and then swept him to the ground.

The man attempted a ground defense maneuver, confirming Asher's suspicion of being well trained, but Asher was ready for it. He settled his weight on the man's chest and punched him in the face. It took a couple of punches, but the man stopped struggling, knocked out.

Asher knew that was not the last of the security, and he was sure there were cameras, but he didn't have time to research and observe to concoct a stealthier plan of attack. His best option was to barrel through, using surprise to his best advantage.

He started down the center hall, ready for the next attack to come from any side, ready to do whatever was necessary to free Cali. Literally anything.

***

Cali looked up at the sound of a thud from upstairs.

"What was that?" Ivy said.

Cali had barely managed to get back down the hall and avoid being spotted by the men she'd been eavesdropping on, and then she'd run into Ivy in the front sitting room. Ivy had assumed Cali couldn't sleep and had offered to take her back down to the archives, to which Cali had agreed. It was the perfect explanation for her prowling around the house this late. And she'd gotten the impression Ivy wanted to talk some more.

"Could something be wrong?" Cali asked.

"Highly unlikely. Security's really good."

The clang of the lock on the metal door. And then a man came running down the stairs, eyes wild.

Ivy stood from her seat at the table. "Chad, what's wrong?"

"Intruder."

"What do you mean, intruder?"

"Someone forced his way in and is attacking everyone. I came down to make sure you two are secure."

Cali shifted toward the stairs and looked up at the metal door at the landing halfway up.

"Keep back," Chad said. "The guy is crazy. You're safest down here."

When Cali took another step, Chad grabbed her arm and yanked her back forcefully.

"Chad, stop," Ivy said.

Cali looked over at Ivy, reading her.

Then she faced Chad. "Let go."

"I need to make sure you two are protected. That's Ivan's standing orders."

"I know those are not his standing orders. Perhaps for Ivy, but I know the orders for me are a little different."

His expression darkened, and he gripped her arm tighter.

"What's going on?" Ivy asked.

Cali did a wrist release technique and then kicked Chad in the groin. He fell, and Cali ran up the stairs.

Ivy followed. "Cali?"

Cali didn't have time to spare, but she stopped at the door and faced Ivy anyway. "They intend to keep me against my will. I've been playing along to get as much information as possible, but I'm pretty sure I know what— or rather who—is causing that ruckus and the fear in Chad's eyes. I have to go. But I have not been playing *you*. I consider you a friend. I always will. You should stay here where it's safe." She opened the door and continued up the stairs.

As Cali paused at the top of the stairs, Ivy's quiet footsteps followed. She stayed behind Cali. Cali waved for her to get back downstairs and mouthed, "Stay safe."

Ivy shook her head, determination in her eyes.

Cali turned back around and listened. Nothing.

Ivy stepped up to the same stair as Cali and whispered, "I have a guess as to where we should go."

"I don't want you involved in this."

"I'm done doing the easy and expedient thing. I'm doing the right thing. I can make sure the guards don't hurt you." She stepped out of the stairwell and moved slowly down the hall.

Cali followed, racking her brain for a way to get Ivy to go back down to the archives.

Down the hall that Cali had rushed out of earlier, voices came from the same room. But instead of continuing to that door, Ivy took Cali's hand and dragged her into a closet.

"What're we doing?" Cali asked as Ivy closed the door and doused them in darkness. Her logical side said to be cautious. Ivan had seemed to indicate that Ivy was complicit, that she'd befriended Cali in order to help in controlling her. But something in her screamed to trust Ivy. Cali had learned a long time ago to recognize when God was pushing her in a certain direction. She'd always listened, and that was the only reason she was still alive.

Rushed footsteps sounded in the hallway, moving toward the end of the hall. Then the sound of someone rattling a door and then pounding on it.

Ivy slipped past Cali through the hanging coats, and then the quiet sound of a latch. Ivy took Cali's hand, and she followed her through a small opening in the back of the closet into another dark space, this one with shelves, apparently another closet.

The voices were louder. Based on the layout of the house, this closet had to be connected to the room on which she'd eavesdropped earlier. They could now understand the voices in that room.

"Where is she?" Asher. He was here. She'd suspected it was him, but her emotions still made loops through her chest—fear for him, frustration that he hadn't listened to her note, but also something warm… He'd come for her.

A strangled sound, like someone trying to talk while being choked. And then the man spit out, "I told you I don't know." It sounded like Walter.

Cali guessed the other men she'd eavesdropped on may have left by now.

Cali waited a few seconds longer, listening, trying to determine the best course of action to keep Asher safe. She didn't hear anyone else in the room, but that didn't mean no one was. If she stepped out of the closet, could her sudden appearance create enough of a distraction to allow someone to get the upper hand on Asher?

"I guess you're useless, then," Asher growled. A slight metallic sound, perhaps a gun being unholstered.

Cali turned the knob and peeked out into the room.

Asher had Walter in a choke with one arm around his

neck from behind, and with his other hand, he held a gun to Walter's head. Ivan stood in the corner eyeing the door to the hall.

At the movement of the door opening, Asher's attention snapped to Cali. He had blood on his arms and splatted over his shirt and even face. "Cali," he murmured.

Ivan made a move for the door.

"Stop," Asher said and pointed the gun at him.

"Don't shoot him," Cali said.

Ivy stepped forward. "Daddy. I think he just wants to take Cali. Let them go."

"She's not going anywhere," Ivan sneered.

"You don't have a choice," Asher said. "You only have her because she came voluntarily."

"Exactly," Ivan said. "She's ours now."

Ivy's brows drew together, but Ivan obviously didn't notice.

"She does not *belong* to anyone," Asher growled.

"You seem to think she belongs to you. Why else would you have smashed through here like some barbarian?"

Asher turned his attention to Cali. "I can get you out."

Ivan asked Cali, "Would you rather go with this barbarian or stay with cultured people who treat you like an equal? Who feed your desire to investigate riddles. You can focus on nothing else the rest of your life. Completely provided for and protected. Just like you've been these last few days."

Cali turned to Ivan. "Until I'm no longer useful and you dispose of me. Like you plan to do to Matthew. Like you tried to do to Lavinia Florence. Like you have successfully done to who knows how many over the years?"

"What're you…"

"I was listening," she said. "Earlier, to your conversation in this office with Walter and two other gentlemen. You discussed the message Matthew sent you."

"Wait," Ivy said. "People have died?"

"People have been killed. I knew that coming in but played along with the happy family routine." Then she softened her voice, just for Ivy. "I'm sorry."

Ivy's brown eyes were wide. Unfortunately, Cali didn't have time to help her through the realization her father was a monster. In the back of her mind, she prayed for Ivy, but she turned her attention to Asher and nodded toward Walter. "He's passed out." She could see he was still breathing and Asher was using a submission hold, not chokehold, so she felt confident he was just knocked out.

Asher dumped him in an armchair to the side of the room.

"Do we have a couple of minutes?" Cali asked.

"I believe I knocked out all the guards. But we shouldn't take long."

She nodded and turned back to Ivan. "Why did Libervis not share the library with the world once they were safe from threat of persecution from Russian royalty?"

"I may be on in years, but I'm not quite that old, Miss Lebeau."

"But you have records of those decisions—I hadn't gotten quite that far back in your archives. And you've been in charge for quite some time."

"I'm not in charge."

She smirked. "We all know you're the one calling the shots in the end."

The corner of his mouth quirked.

She smirked. "Thought so." She added, "So, what's the answer?"

Ivan lifted his chin.

Asher moved closer to him and aimed the gun again.

"No," Ivy said.

"I prefer not to hurt anyone else," Asher said to Ivy, while keeping his focus on Ivan. "I have not permanently injured anyone in this house, but he does need to answer

Cali."

Ivy turned to her father.

Ivan didn't look at Ivy, but rather at Cali, his mouth curving a little more and wrinkling his cheeks. "Do you really think the unwashed masses could possibly appreciate Homer's Margites, Shakespeare's Cardenio, Jane Austin's Sanditon, Melville's The Isle of the Cross, a Septuagint from the Library at Alexandria?"

Cali's heart skipped a beat at hearing of a Septuagint—Greek translation of the Old Testament—from the Library at Alexandria. "Not everyone, but they should be given the opportunity. Think of the insights that could be gained."

Ivan laughed. "They wouldn't understand the significance." He waved his hand as if indicating the "unwashed masses." "The knowledge—the power—to be gained would overwhelm the simpletons out there. All they can focus on is celebrity gossip and the latest fashion trends."

Cali saw from the corner of her eye the hurt on Ivy's face. She'd noticed Ivy reading about fashion a couple of times.

Ivan continued, "No one else would ever understand. They would never be able to wield the power."

"Except you," Cali said.

He closed his eyes and nodded solemnly. "Yes." He opened his eyes. "I'll decode. I'll find the black magic hidden in the tomes, the magic Ivan the Terrible knew was there. And I'll rule. There will be no war. No hunger."

"Just obedience."

"That is the only way to have a peaceful society. Total acquiescence of power to someone wiser, greater."

"There's truth to that," Cali admitted.

His eyes gleamed.

"But the only one worthy of such power is God."

He burst out laughing.

Cali turned to Asher. "Let's go."

Ivy moved closer to Cali, away from her father. "I'm

coming."

"Are you sure?"

"I'm coming."

"Okay." Cali turned back to Asher, but he hesitated and his gaze flickered to Ivy. "I trust her," Cali added.

He nodded once and moved toward the door.

Ivan trailed behind them down the hall like a child. "You'll never get out of here! This is a fortress."

Cali continued to follow Asher and didn't look back. "Must not be *that* secure. This *barbarian* made it inside."

She could just see the side of Asher's face, his cheek pull up as he smiled or maybe smirked.

As they approached the stairwell to the basement, Cali warned Asher, "We left a man down there. I hurt him, but he was still conscious."

Asher paused at the stairs to stand guard and motioned for Cali and Ivy to continue toward the front door. When no one appeared from the stairwell, he followed behind.

Cali noticed two men sprawled out in the sitting room, bloody and limbs at odd angles, and then the butler near the door. She resisted the urge to check on them.

"Ivana," Ivan demanded. "You stay here, young lady."

Cali paused and looked back as Asher moved to the door, hand on the knob.

Ivy took a quiet breath and turned to face her father.

"You are mine," Ivan said.

Ivy's voice was calm. "I love you, Daddy. I always will. I pray you find your way."

"You're nothing without me. I'm the only reason your life has any purpose. If you walk out that door, you're cut off."

Though Ivy's voice remained calm, Cali could hear how much she was hurting. "Goodbye, Daddy." She turned and moved toward the door.

Asher looked all around and then led them outside and down the sidewalk. They were in his truck a minute later, Ivy in the back seat.

Asher drove for several minutes.

Then he pulled off in a back parking lot, secluded from the road. He parked and turned to Cali. "Are you okay?"

"I'm fine. They pretended to bring me in as an equal." She paused as she looked at him more closely, the blood all over his hands, up his arms, even on his face, mixed with his facial hair that was now longer than usual, more of a beard than just scruff. "Did you... Did you kill anyone?"

His jaw clenched. "No." He paused. "I was close."

She reached over and squeezed his hand.

He took his hand away, put the truck back into gear, and resumed driving.

Cali turned and looked back at Ivy. "Remember what we talked about. Remember what you felt."

Ivy kept her focus out the side window, and her voice came out in a strangled whisper. "That's the only thing keeping me going."

Cali turned back around, gave Ivy as much privacy as they could in these close quarters.

"You can sleep," Asher said. "I'll get us as far from here as I can."

"We can't leave Philadelphia."

CHAPTER 31

Asher gave Cali a hard look.

"Mt Dew is missing, isn't he?" she asked.

"How did you know?"

"I'm sure he's in Philadelphia. We need to find him."

"First, you need a few hours' sleep. I'll find someplace safe to park."

On the other side of the city, he parked behind an office complex.

He looked at Ivy in the rearview mirror. "I realize my introduction to you wasn't inspiring," he said. "But I give you my word you're safe with me."

"Cali trusts you," she said without turning to look at him. Then she added, "Thank you for trusting her enough to let me come."

He nodded once and then reached for the door handle. "I'll keep watch." He stepped out and closed the door.

Inside the truck fell silent.

"That's amazing," Ivy said.

Cali turned and looked at her.

"All you had to do was say you trust me. That's all he needed. No interrogations, no searching me for weapons or demanding my phone. All he does is assure me that I'm

263

safe in his presence."

"He's an amazing person."

"I've never seen anything like that." There was sadness in her voice. She turned back to the side window.

Cali leaned her head back and tried to rest.

But she quickly realized that wasn't going to happen. "I'll be just outside," she said and opened the door.

Asher was leaning against the front of the truck. He glanced over as she shut the door and then turned back to the empty parking lot.

She stood next to him. "Are you all right?"

He didn't look at her. "I'll need to find someplace to wash up before being seen in public."

"I was trying to do the right thing when I left."

"I know."

She paused. "But you're still mad at me."

"No."

She looked at him more closely. "You're not okay."

Silence.

"Will you please talk to me?"

He continued to stare out across the parking lot.

Finally, he said, "I'm not good with emotion. I've been isolated too long."

"That's understandable." She added, "Will you try to talk to me?" There was so much she needed to do, that she'd probably need his help with, but she needed to make sure he was okay first.

He didn't look at her. "You're the first person I've let close since Rose died."

Let close? He considered their relationship close? She was certainly no master of closeness, but he'd actively pushed her away again and again. She considered her words carefully. "I got the feeling you didn't want to be close."

"I realize that." He didn't deny he didn't want to be close. "But you shouldn't have left."

He was hurt—that was the problem. He'd pushed her

away so hard, she'd figured he'd be fine if she left, maybe feel a little guilty since he'd—for whatever reason—taken the burden of her safety upon himself. But she hadn't really believed he might be so hurt. "I'm sorry."

"I understand you were trying to protect me." He finally turned his head and looked at her. "Please don't do that again. Not until this is over. Once it's done, we'll part ways and break contact. We'll continue on our separate paths. But not before then."

She nodded. That tiny hope she'd been harboring that maybe he'd at least want to remain friends died. She swallowed back emotion. "I'm too riled up to sleep. I tried. I'm sure you haven't been sleeping properly. Please get some rest. I'll keep watch and yell if I see anything."

He hesitated but then walked over and sat in the driver's seat.

Cali sat on the front bumper, faced away from Asher to be sure he didn't see any emotion on her face. To distract herself, she plotted out how they might find Matthew aka Mt Dew.

An hour or so later, she heard a car door open and glanced back. Ivy got out and quietly closed the door.

She sat on the bumper next to Cali. "I think he finally fell asleep."

"Good. Did you sleep any?"

Ivy shook her head.

"I'm sorry for everything you have to be going through. And I'm sorry I exposed those things about your dad to you."

"Part of me is glad I know."

"And the other part wishes you could go back to the little girl who thought he was the most amazing man in the world."

"He's legitimately intelligent. And a great leader."

"I agree."

"You do?"

Cali nodded. "Talent and intelligence aren't innately

good or bad. The question is, do we use our talents to gain power or goodness?"

"I think at least a part of him honestly thinks he can make life better for people."

"I think he does truly believe that."

Ivy shook her head. "Everything's so confusing."

"While I think Ivan actually does think he can make others' lives better, he's not coming from a place of kindness. He seems to think most people are simply too stupid to better their lives on their own. Perhaps he doesn't actually hate people, but bigotry of low expectations is what's controlling his actions. To some extent anyway."

"To some extent." Ivy sighed. "You're being kind. I appreciate that. But I have to face the fact that my dad is obsessed with power. He even thinks the library holds the key to black magic."

"Ivan the Terrible thought that too. I assume that's where Ivan got the idea." Cali frowned. "I have something to admit. I lied to you. I said I hadn't had time to research, but I have. Extensively. Asher kept me safe and gave me the means. I'm sorry. I hope you'll forgive me."

"Considering you knew Libervis doesn't have noble intentions and you didn't know me very well, I completely understand. Actually, I'm a little confused why you're trusting me as much as you are."

"I felt a nudge, and I generally follow those nudges."

"Like from God?"

Cali nodded, hoping Ivy didn't think she was nuts. It was sad that so many people in the world believed either God didn't exist or he didn't care.

"That's why I left with you. I just felt like I really needed to. Even though it scares the tar out of me. But it…felt like something outside of me, not from within my own mind. Does that make sense?"

Cali smiled. "Perfect sense."

Ivy took Cali's hand, and they sat there for a while in

silence. Cali squeezed her hand tightly, making sure she knew she wasn't alone.

The sun started to peek out at them from between buildings.

The sound of the car door opening. "You should eat something," Asher said.

Cali nodded, and they all got back in the truck.

A little while later, they were all in the truck eating a light breakfast of grain bars that Asher had grabbed at a grocery store in a suburb not too far away. The stash of food he'd had in his truck was depleted, and he hadn't stopped looking for her long enough to restock. Cali worried he'd barely eaten or slept—he'd had to have been about to collapse last night to have agreed to sleep while she kept watch.

"Who is Matthew?" Ivy asked. "The person you and my father were talking about."

Cali turned in her seat to look at Ivy in the back. She'd reclaimed the front seat to keep an eye on Asher, make sure he ate and that he didn't seem overly exhausted. She quickly explained how she'd suspected and then confirmed who Matthew Dewer from the archives was.

"That's why he went missing," Asher said.

Cali nodded. "Apparently to come offer himself in exchange for me."

"That's why we can't leave yet," Asher said. "You're right—he's probably in Philadelphia."

"Does he have brown hair and a small scar in his eyebrow?" Ivy asked.

"Yes," Cali said. "Do you know him? According to the files I read, he left Libervis about twenty-three years ago. You would've been maybe five. I assumed you wouldn't know who he was."

"He was like ten or eleven. Walter adopted him." She pursed her lips as if contemplating. "At the time, I thought it was so nice that Walter volunteered to be a daddy to Matthew who didn't have his real dad. But now…I think they knew before Walter adopted him that he was a prodigy—that's why he adopted him. I remember my dad telling me all the time how Matthew couldn't play because he was working—at his computer all hours. I didn't understand why he had to work instead of play. He was the only other kid around—I was so excited when Walter brought him home. Maybe I'd finally get to play with another kid. The few times he did play with me he was so nice. I was younger and a girl, but he never teased me. He taught me things and would tell me it was all right when I'd cry when Walter told him to go back to his computer. Then one day he was gone, and Walter was so mad."

"Sounds like his offer to give himself up in exchange for me might be legitimate." Cali turned to Asher. "We have to find him. Quickly, before they catch him."

"Any ideas?"

"Our friends have tried, I assume."

"They were able to figure out Philadelphia, but not because he left a trail online, only from putting together bits of information from over the years. I think it's up to us."

Cali turned to Ivy. "Do you know anything about the buildings around the Libervis house? I assume they have at least some basic information about the area."

"They monitor changes in ownership of all buildings within view of the house and then do a background check on them. I haven't heard of any recent changes."

Cali turned her gaze out the window and murmured to herself, "He'd want to be close enough to be able to watch but not so close that he'd be seen."

Asher took something out of his pocket and handed her the phone she'd left behind.

She smiled at him. "Thanks."

She'd memorized the street address of the Libervis house. She began searching the surrounding buildings on the local Property Appraiser's site, which showed the ownership of each building, which she then did a search for. Asher offered to help, and she gave him the next name to look up. Ivy had left her phone behind, which was probably a good thing anyway. Cali didn't doubt there was some kind of tracking on it. But she offered to write everything down on a notebook Asher had, which helped move it along much more quickly.

Once they were done, Ivy handed Cali the notebook, and Cali analyzed.

"This one," Cali said as she pointed to one of the addresses.

Asher looked at the address and put the truck in drive.

Ivy glanced at Asher and then back to Cali. "How do you know?"

"It's within view but down the road a bit, and it has offices for rent. Their website says they have space available. I'd wager he broke into a vacant office that has a window on the front of the building." She pointed at other addresses. "These are private homes. Matthew wouldn't invade a home or even fake a way to get into someone's house—not his personality. This one's a museum—too much security. This one appears to be vacant, but its owner is a shell corporation—hard to determine the actual owner and therefore the safety of it. He has the skill to dig deep and figure out the actual owner, but he's moving quickly and won't want to risk taking up too much time or making a mistake. He's meticulous."

"Oh." Ivy smiled.

Asher turned onto the road. "There's a back alley, right?"

"Yeah." Cali gave him directions on the best way to get to the back alley while keeping a wide berth of the Libervis house. She brought up the map on his phone so he could see it on the truck's larger screen. At a stop light, he took a good look and nodded.

A little while later, he backed the truck into a spot off the alley. This back entrance to the building looked like it wasn't used much. There wasn't actually a parking space—

Asher had made his own—and it wasn't exactly lovely or fragrant with the dumpster corral, crumbling pavement, and weeds sprouting all over.

Cali and Ivy agreed to wait in the truck while Asher took a quick look around.

"He was a football player, right?" Ivy asked.

"He gave all that up to be a Navy SEAL. I have a feeling he did a lot of black ops stuff." Which was why she deferred to his judgment on checking out the area.

"He doesn't tell you about it?"

"He doesn't tell me a lot of anything. We discuss The Lost Library and what to do next, but he doesn't ever open up."

Ivy looked out the window as Asher checked out a dumpster corral. "But he came to get you. Like, he looked like he'd been awake for days searching for you. I assumed you guys were really close. Like…involved close. Last night I kept wondering if you were going to want a few minutes alone." She paused, still watching Asher. "But you don't touch at all. Like nothing. Like not even friendly touching."

"I don't think he likes to be touched."

Ivy turned back to Cali. "Not even by a pretty girl?"

Cali tried to smile but completely failed. "Not by me, anyway."

"So, why is he so determined to help with this?"

"He happened to be there when I was attacked, or rather about to be attacked, and I think he feels responsible for me now. I think he sees my situation as kind of a surrogate for another situation in his past, one that didn't end well. I wonder if part of him feels like he can make that right—even just a little—by helping me get through this."

Ivy opened her mouth but stopped when Asher opened Cali's door.

"Everything looks fine," Asher said.

"Thank you for protecting us." Ivy opened her door.

Asher stepped back to allow them room to get out.

Cali walked up to the back door of the building and tried the knob. "Regular lock. Not magnetic."

Ivy grinned and stepped forward. "At your service!" She pulled something out of her pocket.

Cali stepped back. "How is it you have lock-picking tools in your pocket but not your phone?"

Ivy knelt in front of the door. "A phone is for talking to other people. If Daddy was home, who was going to message or call me? I had my tools because I'd been practicing—I do that when I can't sleep."

The corner of Asher's mouth twitched. "No wonder you two became quick friends. That sounds like something you would do."

"Probably," Cali admitted. "Although I bet she doesn't read car manuals."

"Nope," Ivy said as she continued working. "I'm not quite *that* weird. To be fair, though, you haven't seen the extent of my weirdness. I won't mention that I have—well, had—a collection of Happy Meal toys. Lined up on shelves in my room. I still get Happy Meals just so I can get the toy. Really dumb, I know. See—weird."

"I can beat that," Cali said.

Ivy looked up at her. "Try me."

"I memorize maps; I speak Latin fluently; make sudoku puzzles in my head; and I play that game, also in my head, where you make words out of the letters of another word, but I also organize them alphabetically and by length of word. When I'm nervous, I replay all the words over and over."

"Okay, you are weird." Ivy grinned and went back to picking the lock. A few seconds later, the door opened. "When we're done here, we should ask Asher what his weirdness looks like."

"My oddities aren't difficult to see." Asher walked in ahead of them, watching all directions.

Ivy whispered, "Everyone is just too scared of him to

271

point out his oddities."

"Probably correct," Cali whispered back.

Then they both fell silent and followed Asher up the stairs. They'd agreed to be cautious in case Libervis had come to the same conclusion about this building as Cali had and had perhaps already set up inside the building in order to catch either Matthew or Cali and Ivy, or all of the above.

Asher paused at the second floor and looked back at Cali.

She glanced around at the doors in the hallway. The office that would have the best view of the street had an umbrella stand outside the door. She pointed up, and Asher continued up to the third floor.

Cali approached the door for the office that should have the best view of the street. There was no peephole, so she put her ear to the door and listened. Silent. There was no indication of occupancy—no umbrella stand, or wreath, or sign, or even dirt from regular foot traffic.

Ivy held up her lock-picking tools and raised her brows.

Cali stepped back and nodded, and Ivy knelt in front of the door, while Asher stood guard watching the hallway, stairwell, as well as the door Ivy was working on.

There was a very quiet click, and Ivy slowly turned the knob.

Asher motioned for her to step back. He opened the door but didn't pull his gun, surely in case the place was occupied by a legitimate tenant. That way, they could claim the door was unlocked and they'd gotten confused on which office they were trying to find, but not if Asher had a gun out and slunk through as if clearing a room.

Cali and Ivy followed and closed the door behind them.

The space was very small, only two rooms—a tiny reception area and an office, which faced the street.

Asher walked into the office. "Good morning."

Cali turned the corner into the office just as Matthew stared at Asher. "Mt Dew," she said. "Or rather, Matthew

272

Dewer."

"Cali. How'd you find me?" Then Ivy walked in, and he stared at her. "Ivy?"

"Hi, Matthew," Ivy said.

Matthew stood from his camp chair at the window. "Is everything okay?" He looked at Cali. "What's going on? Why is Ivy with you? Do you know who she is? When did you all leave? It must have been late last night. I assumed you were all in bed and let myself sleep a little while."

"Sit down," Cali said in a much sterner voice than was usual for her.

Matthew sat.

"Ivy left Libervis with us last night. She's not a spy. That's all the information I'm giving until you explain yourself."

Matthew blew out his breath. He glanced out the window then to Ivy and back to Cali.

Asher moved to stand behind Matthew's chair, which was angled so that he could see down the street, presumably to keep an eye on things and possibly to keep Matthew in his seat if this conversation were to turn aggressive. She wished she could be certain it wouldn't get aggressive, especially knowing he'd apparently come to trade himself for her, but she didn't know him that well. He'd always kept to himself.

"Sit," Asher said.

Matthew obeyed.

"Well?" Cali pressed.

CHAPTER 32

"I have no idea where to start," Matthew said.

"At the beginning," Cali said. "Walter adopted you when you were about ten, and you were a member of Libervis."

"I was not a member of Libervis."

"You're on their rolls. That's how I found your real name."

"How did you get access to the archives?"

Cali crossed her arms over her chest.

"I was not a member of Libervis," he said again. "I was a kid. I had no idea what I was doing. Or at least, I didn't have an understanding of the big picture. Walter adopted me out of foster care, and I just wanted to make him happy so he wouldn't decide to get rid of me."

"That's completely understandable," Cali said. "Ivy said you just disappeared one day." She turned to Ivy. "Sounded like you were still pretty young when that happened?"

Ivy answered, "I think he was there only about a year. In that house anyway. I don't know when exactly he left Libervis."

"I ran away," Matthew said. "I realized things weren't

right, and I left."

"Do you really think I'm going to let you get away with a vague answer like that?"

"I'm here to turn myself over in exchange for you."

"I know. I overheard Ivan and Walter and two other men talking about it. Based on what I know, I think that's the truth about why you came to Philadelphia."

"Then why are you coming at me so hard?"

Asher set a hand on the back of Matthew's chair.

Matthew glanced over his shoulder at Asher, who was still watching out the window, and then turned back to Cali.

"Because," Cali said, "you're not who you presented yourself to be—to me or to your friends. That means you need to answer some questions."

"You weren't exactly forthcoming either."

"I wasn't forthcoming about things that were not related to what we were doing, nothing that should affect any of you. You kept silent about Libervis as we were investigating them. You knew who they were. You knew what their goals are. And you kept quiet. That could have put all of us in danger."

"I was watching everyone's back. That's why I'm here. That's why I abandoned the best friends I've ever had. Every friend I've ever had. All to fight back against Libervis and protect my friends."

Cali took a breath. "I believe you."

"You do?"

"Yes."

"Can I go then? If you're free, we're better off getting away from here."

"Not yet."

"Why not?"

Asher said from behind him, "Because we don't know what to do with you yet."

Matthew looked up at him again, but Asher continued to keep his gaze out the window.

"And as you can see," Cali said, "Asher is keeping watch and will certainly alarm us if there's any movement at the Libervis house."

Matthew huffed and slouched back into his chair.

"Would you like some Mountain Dew?" Cali asked. "I doubt you slept long or well. You might want the caffeine." And maybe it would help him get through this explanation faster.

Matthew shook his head. "Anything but Mountain Dew."

Cali couldn't help but laugh. "If your obsession with that pop is fake, why is that your handle?"

"It wasn't fake when I was eleven. I've had that handle since I left Libervis, and I've spent twenty-three years building up a solid reputation in hacker spheres. That reputation is the reason Floyd and Bl@ze accepted me. I had to keep it up."

Cali was surprised he'd used their handles in front of Ivy. That said something about his opinion of her, though they hadn't seen each other in so long.

Ivy opened a lunchbox-sized cooler that was on the ground, pulled out a Pepsi, and handed it to Matthew.

Matthew smiled at her. "Thanks, Ives."

Ivy smiled back.

Cali asked, "What did you mean when you said you've been watching everyone's back? Do you expect me to believe that with everything that's happened?"

"Why wouldn't you? I thought we were friends."

"I thought so too. But isn't it a bit convenient that you used to be with Libervis, the Gray Hats start dogging their steps online, and then they decided to come after me? Did you send them after me?"

Cali noticed peripherally as Ivy shook her head. Cali's gut agreed with Ivy that Matthew wouldn't do that, but he obviously was holding back details.

"No!" Matthew stood. "I would never."

Asher set a hand on Matthew's shoulder. Matthew

ground his teeth together but sat. "Looks like that idea of mine worked out."

"What idea?" Cali said.

"Nothing."

"Oh, you don't get to give that kind of answer. Out with it."

Matthew closed his eyes and took a breath. Then he opened his eyes again. "I nudged you to apply for the job at Cross Enterprises."

"What? I applied when I found the listing for it online."

"You found it in your email. Remember? You'd signed up for email notifications for that job site. I faked the email that included the Cross Enterprises job at the top."

Cali drew her brows together. "You didn't even know who I was yet."

"I did know who you were. I've known about you for a long time. Twenty-three years to be exact. I sent you that job because the Cross Enterprises building is like Fort Knox—we'd looked into the company when we did several bug bounties for them. And I checked out Cross enough to know he wasn't the beast everyone says he is."

A realization hit Cali. "Twenty-three years. That's when my mom left."

Matthew nodded.

Cali took a step closer to him. "What do you know about my mother?"

"Pretty much everything. That was the first assignment Walter gave me: find the heir."

"The heir is real?" Ivy asked.

Matthew nodded toward Cali. "She's it."

"My mom's dead?" Cali asked. Wouldn't he say her mom was the heir, not her?

For a moment, she thought Matthew's eyes were getting teary. She'd never seen much emotion from him. Floyd, sure. Even Bl@ze on occasion. But never Matthew, other than feigning annoyance at Floyd. "I'm sorry."

"What happened to her?"

"I found her. I didn't tell Walter where I was going and went to where she was living to see for sure. I knew if I was wrong, Walter wouldn't be kind. His patience was thinning—I'd taken over a year to find her."

"Where *she* was living? Had she already left me and my dad?"

"Yes. This was just after. She'd moved to another state, some dumpy extended-stay motel, and found a job. I followed her while she was walking to work."

"But weren't you eleven years old?"

He nodded. "I'd stolen a car and was following her. She obviously didn't see it was only a kid behind the wheel. It was dark—really early morning."

"Did you talk to her? Find out why she left?"

"She started running." He swallowed. "She ran across a street just as a car turned the corner. And…"

"So, you never talked to her?"

"I jumped out of the car and tried to help her. I swear I tried." His expression twisted. "She must have seen that I'd gotten out of the car that'd been following her. She said, 'Don't trust them.' I started to argue, pretending I didn't know what she was talking about, but she said, 'They'll use you. Get away. Get safe.' She gulped in a breath, and added in a strangled whisper, 'Please do one thing for me… Tell Cali I love her.'"

Cali covered her mouth with her hand and looked away.

"She didn't leave you, Cali. She protected you."

Cali swallowed a sob.

Ivy took two steps and clamped Cali in a tight hug.

Cali could barely breathe. She'd always thought her mother had left her, had turned her back on her just like her father had. There had always been a voice in the back of her mind that said she was unlovable. Logically, she knew she was God's creation and he loved her. But she could never eradicate the voice, could never forget what she'd felt like as a little girl waking up and realizing her mommy had left her forever, hadn't even wanted to say goodbye to her. But maybe...maybe she hadn't said goodbye because she couldn't bear to tell her daughter she was leaving her. The daughter she loved.

After a minute, Cali stepped back, whispered, "Thank you," to Ivy, and turned away.

She heard Asher say Ivy's name and then feet shuffling.

Asher came around and stood in front of her. She so wanted for him to hug her, but he didn't touch her. "Whatever you want to happen," he murmured, "I'll make it happen."

She only nodded. She understood he meant anything— leave right this second, intimidate Matthew into divulging everything immediately, storm the Libervis house and haul Ivan and Walter out by force...

He leaned closer and caught her eye. They held eye contact for several seconds. She took a slow breath and felt more in control. "Thanks," she whispered.

She turned back around to find Matthew in his chair but slumped forward. Ivy had taken Asher's spot by the window.

Cali took another breath before she spoke. "How did you and the other Gray Hats end up in the same town as me? Or rather, did you manipulate me into coming to the town you were in?"

He looked up at her and shook his head. "It was your mom's favorite place. I'd researched everything about her. Every tidbit. And she almost always had pictures of Charlotte as her computer wallpaper. Just generic pictures—she never put anything personal. But it was almost always Charlotte or the surrounding areas. At first, I thought that was telling. I even told Walter that's where I thought she was. When that ended up being wrong... Well, he wasn't happy. And I realized it was just a pretty place that she liked."

"Were you hoping to find me there?" Cali had moved

there because her mom had mentioned how pretty it was, and Cali wanted to see it.

He shook his head. "I guess I wanted to... I don't know. Honor her in some way. Maybe it was stupid, but it was the only thing I could think to do that wouldn't put you in danger."

"So, you knew about Cali," Asher said. "You've been watching her."

"I've been watching *over* her. I swear. I listened to her mom and didn't go back to Libervis. I realized what she'd done for her daughter, that she'd put her first no matter how much it hurt." He shook his head. "Walter wasn't like that. He wasn't a real dad. I'd been holding onto the idea that if I was good enough, if I managed to accomplish what he wanted of me, maybe he'd treat me like a real son. Maybe he'd love me."

Ivy set a hand on Matthew's shoulder. A much different touch than Asher's. Her hand was gentle, kind.

"If you've been watching over her," Asher said, "why didn't you do anything about Dinetti?"

"I tried. I swear I did. Dinetti keeps his records in hardcopy only. He communicates in person or sometimes by phone only. No email, no text. He has no online presence. But I watched for indicators that he might be closing in on her. I constantly scanned for his name on flights, and if he was going anywhere near Cali, I'd do whatever I had to do to get the flight canceled or him bumped, something. But sometimes he drove, and I had no idea he was on the move until it was too late."

Asher opened his mouth, surely to push him more on that, but Cali cut him off. "Have you done anything nearer to me? Like add lighting to my jogging path? Get my neighbors to move?"

"Nothing like that. Has that stuff happened? Why didn't you tell us? Us as in the Gray Hats, I mean."

"Why didn't you tell her all of this when you first started working with her?" Asher asked. "You did that background check—you knew exactly who she was. You could've delivered that message from her mother years ago."

"I don't know." Matthew shook his head. "I guess I was scared. If it didn't go well, I would have had to leave. Floyd and Bl@ze are the best friends I've ever had, my only friends other than Ivy. And I'd played the role of socially anxious to the point of being a hermit for so long that I started actually feeling that way. I know—this coming from a guy who traveled across states by himself when he was only a kid. I was finally in a place where I was comfortable, and I was terrified I'd have to leave. I talked myself into thinking you were better off being insulated completely from Libervis. You were already dealing with Dinetti. You didn't need anything else."

"She wasn't insulated from Libervis," Asher said. "You had her decoding their messages."

"Bl@ze came across that. I tried saying we were too busy to dive into it, but he and Floyd were intrigued. I couldn't get them off the scent. I kept trying to find a way to make the trail go cold. But then..." He shook his head. "I never thought they'd come after you because of your decryption skills. I was so focused on hiding the fact that you were the heir, that I didn't anticipate anything else." He paused. "I'm sorry, Cali."

"Why did you get me working with you in the first place?" Cali asked.

"Asher reached out to us about the background check. Floyd realized you were a cryptologist—not just some hobbyist, but a master cryptologist. I tried to nudge him out of the idea, but he was set on it. He pretended to happen to bump into you at the library and struck up a conversation. In the end, I decided maybe it was good— I'd be able to watch over you a lot better than I ever had. Or so I'd hoped."

She'd been bored out of her mind for so many years, it hadn't taken that much convincing from Floyd, once she was sure they weren't connected to Dinetti, to get her to partner with them. And she'd enjoyed using her skills for good. She hadn't felt that in a very long time.

"Hey," Ivy said, standing at the window watching the Libervis house. "We have activity."

CHAPTER 33

"A couple of my dad's personal bodyguards are entering the house," Ivy said. "Doesn't bode well. We should get out of here."

Asher walked over and looked out the window over Ivy's shoulder. Then he moved for the door and checked the hallway. "Clear. Let's go."

Matthew stayed seated and glanced between Asher and Cali.

"You're coming with us," Cali said.

Ivy grabbed Matthew's hand, pulled him from the chair, and followed Asher. It didn't escape Cali's notice that Matthew gripped her hand in return.

Asher led them all out back, and they piled into the truck. Asher took a circuitous route and got them out of the city. Cali suggested a rural highway heading south, and he took that without questioning.

Cali and Asher were both quiet, but Matthew and Ivy started talking as soon as they were out of Philadelphia, surely feeling more secure being out of the city.

"So, the heir is real?" Ivy asked. "I've always thought it was just rumor, like an urban legend, you know? But then I always thought God wasn't real, and turns out I was making assumptions. I'm really, really trying not to do that anymore. Just because someone who's supposed to be smart says something, doesn't mean it's true. And just because someone is smart in one field doesn't mean they know jack about anything else. You know?"

Cali didn't turn to look, but she heard a grin in Matthew's voice. "Still the same chatty Ives."

"I was worse when I was little. I don't know how you put up with me. I had to be so annoying. Little girl chattering constantly at such a serious older boy."

"I liked it when you came around. I was dealing with things that were way out of my depth. I wanted to be a kid, but I wasn't allowed. You were the one bright spot in my day."

"That makes me feel so much better," Ivy said. "I hate thinking all I did was annoy you." Then she said, "Walter knew the heir was real? You said that was the first assignment he gave you? Wait, how did he even come to adopt you, anyway?"

"I was in foster care— Well, actually, at that moment, I was in juvie for hacking. He must have recognized my abilities and decided to see if I could help."

"Exploit a child, you mean." She huffed out a breath. "I'm still dealing with the frustration of realizing most of the people in my life are liars and just bad people."

"That has to be hard."

"Yeah, but this isn't about me. This whole thing is so much bigger."

Matthew's tone softened. "Just don't let yourself get lost in it, okay?"

She paused. "Okay." Ivy's tone regained its usual energy. "But Walter knew the heir was real. That's crazy. Why didn't anyone tell me? Everyone always treated it like some silly story. Around me, anyway."

"I think Walter *suspected* the heir was real."

"Didn't you say he got mad at you for taking so long to find her? If he only suspected, how could he get mad?"

"It didn't take much."

Ivy huffed out another breath. "I'm sorry I didn't realize how bad it was for you."

"You were a five-year-old little girl. How would you know and what could you have possibly done?"

"I could've been more of a friend."

"Trust me, you were a great friend." Matthew paused. "You were the first person I'd ever met who was nice to me just to be nice."

Cali smiled to herself, and she noticed a slight smile in Asher's eyes as he focused on the road.

"I wish I was still like that," Ivy said.

"I don't think you've changed that much."

Cali turned and looked at them in the back seat. "I agree with Matthew."

"Yeah, but I was *assigned* to be nice to you," Ivy said. "Make you feel like you fit in so you wouldn't try to leave. It wasn't real."

"If you were supposed to be fake, you failed."

Ivy pressed her lips together but also smiled a little. Then she admitted, "I was pretty excited to have another girl around, and one close to my age too."

"Have you never gotten to be around people your own age?" Matthew asked Ivy.

Ivy shook her head. "I had a private tutor, and I wasn't allowed to do outside activities."

"Wow," Cali said. "You were basically indoctrinated since birth, and you still have enough strength to have your own mind. That's impressive."

"Really?"

"Extremely," Matthew said. "I've seen plenty of indoctrination, and it's hard to fight against."

Ivy asked what he meant, and he explained what he'd been doing most of his life—uncovering terrorists from the shadows. Ivy seemed intrigued and kept asking question after question.

Asher occasionally glanced at them in the rearview

mirror but didn't add anything. He hadn't said much of anything at all since he'd stormed the fortress to save her.

"There's a little roadside motel in a few miles," Cali said. "It's old but clean. At least it was the last time I was through this way. And they didn't use a computer system, paper records only."

Asher nodded, and when the motel came up, he slowed and pulled into the parking lot. Thankfully, they were still using the same old paper system. Asher gave her cash and Cali got them two rooms, one for Ivy and Cali to share and another for Asher and Matthew.

The first thing Cali and Ivy did was shower. Asher still had the clothes he'd gotten for Cali, and she shared an outfit with Ivy. Then they went next door to chat with the guys.

"So," Cali said to Matthew. "I think you should go home."

Matthew sat down on the end of one of the beds. "I don't even know what that is."

She smiled. "Charlotte. Floyd and Bl@ze."

"I can't even hope that they'd take me back."

"I texted them that we found you," Asher said. "They were upset when you left. I've never heard Floyd that freaked out. They were the reason I found Cali, because they pieced together bits of conversations over the years. They're good friends."

"Friends I probably don't deserve." Matthew turned his head and looked at the bathroom door.

Asher looked at his phone. "Floyd has texted me…" He counted something on the screen. "Twenty-two times. Asking if you're all right, if you'll come home, if I'll ask you to call them."

Matthew looked over at him. But then he said, "I'm responsible for what's going on. At least to some extent. I can't bail."

Cali said, "You're a lot more valuable and useful behind a computer screen."

Matthew paused, but then he nodded. "You're probably right." He turned to Ivy. "I'd like you to come with me. If you'd be all right with that. I'll feel better if I know you're safe."

Ivy smiled, and Cali saw in that smile Ivy wasn't leaving Matthew's side. Cali was thankful they had each other to get through the terrible things they'd both lived through. Ivy appeared to be holding up remarkably well, but she suspected Ivy was struggling to be strong for everyone else, not letting herself feel everything she'd been through in the last twenty-four hours. She was going to need a sympathetic ear and a shoulder to lean on, and Matthew seemed happy to be that for her.

Cali gave one definitive nod. "Okay, you'll head back to Charlotte." She turned to Asher. "Would you mind talking outside? I have an idea of what I think we should do next, but I want your thoughts."

He stood, and they headed outside. The motel was empty other than the four of them, so the only sounds were the cars passing by on the rural freeway and a lonely cricket somewhere nearby.

Asher sat on his truck's bumper, facing the motel, and motioned for her to sit next to him. "I'd rather neither of us be visible from the road."

She sat next to him, a couple of feet between them. He'd made it quite clear he didn't like to be close to her, and she would not make him uncomfortable. "I'd like to take Matthew back ourselves, rather than leaving them at a bus station."

"I figured that was why you had me head south."

"I'm glad Matthew agreed to go back. I think his social anxiety is legitimate."

"Hiding for years will do that."

"I think Ivy could be a big help. She's the jolt of life he needs."

"What do you propose we do after that?"

She took a breath. "We find the library. That's the only

way Matthew, Ivy, or I will be free. And now probably you too after you stormed their fortress."

"Any ideas where to look?"

"The Biltmore. I think it might still be there. My mom—she used to sing a little rhyme to me all the time. It indicates Biltmore, I'm pretty sure anyway. If the location had been changed, wouldn't the current heir have changed the rhyme they hand down to their children?"

"I agree."

A peaceful quiet fell around them, broken only by the sounds of cars passing and that lone cricket.

"I still need to ask Matthew some questions," she said. "But I don't want to push him too hard. I figure I'll let him catch up with Ivy some more."

He kept his gaze on the worn gray siding of the motel. "What questions?"

"It had to have been him."

"What had to have been him?"

"Just a few odd things that happened before Dinetti showed up."

"Such as…"

"There was lighting added to the jogging path I used. My neighbors both moved, and the new people… Something was off."

"The city probably added lighting, and people in apartments come and go."

"I had the Gray Hats check—the city didn't add the lighting, though it was a public area."

"Perhaps a kind gesture from a private citizen. People often take an active interest in their parks."

"Very few people used that jogging trail. No one else would care about it. And something was off about the new neighbors."

"It doesn't sound like anything worth bothering Matthew about, not with his anxiety."

"He's fine with me. I think it's more being out in public and dealing with lots of people that bothers him."

"Might be wiser not to risk it. Not when it doesn't really matter anymore."

Cali looked over at Asher, studied him.

Asher turned to her, expression unreadable.

"What is it?" she asked.

"Excuse me?"

"I've been pretty good about not treating you like an enigma to be solved, and that's because you try hard not to actually lie to me, or even mislead. You prefer to shut down than to do that."

He gave no response.

"But now, you're nudging me. Why?"

He turned back to the worn siding of the motel.

"Asher."

He stood and started toward the door to his room.

She grabbed his arm.

He stopped, and the muscles in his jaw tightened.

She dropped his arm. "I'm sorry. I know you don't like to be touched."

He took another step.

"I don't appreciate being manipulated," she said.

"I'm not manipulating you."

"You're trying to. Why don't you want me to ask Matthew about it?"

No response.

Her tone wasn't demanding, but it wasn't soft either. "Asher."

"Drop it."

"No."

He turned to face her. "I did it. All of it."

"What? Why would you do that?"

"All for the same reason I was in the Gray Hats' neighborhood that night."

When he'd saved her. "Why?"

"Just drop it, all right? We have more important things to worry about."

"No. I gave you an opportunity to let me go. You

refused. You can't keep me tight with one hand and shove me away with the other. We do have important things to do, and I need to know what in the world is going on with you. Why would you do those things?"

He glared past her.

"Asher," she demanded.

His voice rose. "Because I'm in love with you!"

She stepped back as if he'd slapped her.

"I saw the bruise on your face when you came to work that day. You'd tried to hide it with makeup. Maybe I went too far, but I wasn't about to stand by while you got accosted again—perhaps much worse the next time."

"I…" She had no idea how to align that statement with the man in front of her, the man who didn't even like to be in her company most of the time.

His tone was tight with frustration. "I'm sorry. I know this isn't comfortable for you. But it doesn't change anything. I'll help you find the library which will stop Libervis in their attempts to control it and you, and then you'll be free to live wherever you want and finally move on with your life. I'll make sure you're free, and then I promise never to talk to you again." He turned and walked down the sidewalk along the front of the motel, and then disappeared around the corner into the trees at the side of the building.

Cali just stood there.

Asher was gone so long that the chill in the air finally pushed Cali to go back to the room she was sharing with Ivy. She got in bed and turned away from the door in the hopes Ivy would assume she was asleep. She couldn't possibly have any kind of conversation right now.

Ivy came back after a while, turned off the lights, and slipped into the other bed.

Cali barely slept.

Sometimes it took so much energy for her even to understand her own emotions—the more complicated or difficult, the harder it was. "Please God," she whispered.

She heard Ivy get up and forced herself out of bed.

Cali felt she did a pretty good job of pushing her emotions and confusion to the side and focusing on the morning with Ivy. It would take only a few hours to make it to Charlotte, so she didn't have long with Ivy. Depending on how things went finding the library, she could possibly never see Ivy again. Or Matthew.

The sun was still rising when they all piled into the car.

Ivy and Matthew chatted in the back seat, but Asher said not one word. Nothing. He didn't even look at Cali. For some reason, that hurt so much more this morning and served to make her emotions even more scattered. She hated that, hated feeling confused.

She tried to join in with Ivy and Matthew's conversation. She'd never seen Matthew talk so much.

As they neared Charlotte and even more as they approached the Gray Hats' apartment, Asher watched their surroundings, surely making positive they hadn't been followed. Asher parked in front of the building.

Matthew took a breath. "Let's see how furious they are. If they kick me out."

Ivy rested a hand on Matthew's arm.

Matthew gave her a strained smile and then stepped out of the car.

Before Cali could join Matthew and Ivy, Asher said, "Cali."

She turned and looked at him.

"Please check on Willow for me."

She smiled a little and nodded.

Asher waited while Matthew, Ivy, and Cali went into the building. In the basement hallway, they paused. Before Matthew could knock, the door flung open.

"You're all right," Floyd said. "Thank God."

Matthew opened his mouth, but before he could get any words out, Floyd hugged him. Cali had never seen them do anything other than harass each other.

And then Bl@ze was there and hugged Matthew too,

with hard slaps on his back. Then he stepped back. "All right. Get in here and explain yourself."

Matthew took Ivy's hand and brought her inside with him.

Cali stayed in the hallway.

Floyd stood at the door. "Still mad at us?"

"Honestly, there is so much else that I'm dealing with right now, I don't even care anymore."

He flashed his Prince Charming smile, which was more humorous than charming. But then the smile faded. "You're not coming home."

She shook her head. "I have to find it." She didn't want to say more in the hallway.

He pressed his lips together but then nodded. "We're here for anything you need."

"I know. Thanks, Floyd." She turned and walked back up the steps and out the door, half expecting Asher to be gone.

CHAPTER 34

Cali got back in the car, and Asher drove out of Charlotte and then west.

Other than to tell him Willow had been curled up sleeping next to Bl@ze's keyboard, she didn't speak, and he was worried about what he'd admitted last evening. Even contemplating being with her in any real way was out of the question, but he hoped he hadn't made her uncomfortable. Well, he knew she was uncomfortable—how could she not be? And perhaps angry for concealing something like that from her, for overstepping and being overprotective. But he hoped she wouldn't ditch him again. His gut told him things were only going to get more dangerous for her.

Finally, as they approached Asheville, he said, "I figure we should start with taking a tour of Biltmore. Unless you have another plan."

"I agree."

And then they fell into silence again. Until he parked at Biltmore.

***

Cali didn't move to get out of the truck. She needed to focus, so she had to force herself to get this conversation done. She didn't look at him. "I agree we shouldn't be more than friends."

She didn't really trust that she'd ever be safe. Libervis, Dinetti—either of them could decide to keep coming after her, even if they found the library. She would not let Asher be in any more danger than he already was. He deserved some measure of peace after all he'd been through in his life.

He nodded once, barely a movement.

"I won't push you away again because, honestly, I may need your help," she said.

"Thank you."

"We'll part ways after we find the library."

He nodded again.

Some part of her had hoped he might push back in some way. Her heart finished breaking.

The one thing that kept her going was that he did care about her to some degree. She wasn't unlovable.

"I'm concerned Libervis may step up their search for me," she said.

"Matthew's actions insinuated your value. They may put together that you're the heir, since that had been his assignment all those years ago and he offered himself in exchange for you, after having completely disappeared all that time."

She nodded. "But we have to keep going. The only way this will end is if we find the library." She still worried it wouldn't stop them, that they may in the very least seek retribution against her, but it was her only chance of making Asher safe at this point, especially with how he'd stormed in to retrieve her.

She stepped from the car, and he followed.

Although she couldn't fully appreciate it, the walk up to the estate was breathtaking—the trees and then the esplanade and then the house itself. She'd never seen a building more beautiful. She'd expected Asher to be looking at every detail of the architecture, but he kept glancing around, being more of a bodyguard than anything.

With his ball cap low and collar up, he paid for their entrance for a day of self-guided touring.

Asher opened the pamphlet he'd picked up that showed the various areas of the house where they were permitted to go. "Where should we start?"

She looked at the pamphlet and opened her mouth, but before she could say it, he said, "Library."

She grinned.

He folded up the pamphlet, slipped it into his back pocket, and they headed in the direction of the library, the far-left end of the main floor.

Thankfully, there was just one other couple in the room and no security guards or other staff. Cali veered toward the other end of the room. She didn't let herself get distracted by the painting on the ceiling reminiscent of Michelangelo or the fireplace that was so big she'd be able to stand almost straight in it. She started reviewing shelves to get accustomed to the organization system.

Asher kept his voice low. "You look like you're looking for something specific."

"I am. Just a hunch."

She headed to the spiral staircase in the corner and climbed up to the catwalk. Asher stayed close to her as she searched the shelves.

The other couple left the room.

"George Vanderbilt was a huge bibliophile," Cali said as she continued to look through the volumes, "and he also had a strong interest in France, as is pretty obvious by looking at the architecture of this place. He was fluent and read many French novels and history books."

"You think there's a connection to him because we think the library was in France at one point?"

"No, but it would be easy to mix a book into his library

and hide it among his 20,000 volumes, especially one that included French history."

"I assume the library has changed over time."

"But not completely overhauled. Look at these gilded leather bindings. George Vanderbilt had all his books rebound in the highest quality. These are his books."

She moved to the next section.

"Ha!" she said while looking up at the top shelf. "There it is."

Asher must've seen what she was talking about and reached right for the book, which he was tall enough to reach. He handed her a leather-bound copy of *Atlas of Fictional Places*.

"I need a little time to look at this," she said. They weren't supposed to touch the books, so she couldn't just go sit at the table and thumb through it. And then she remembered something she'd seen when studying the floorplan of Biltmore… "Come here." She led him back past the spiral staircase and through a door that led to a passageway behind the chimney. It allowed the second story easier access to the library.

She closed the door behind them, and they fell into darkness. Until Asher turned on the flashlight on his phone.

"Sit and read," he said. "I'll give you light."

"Thanks." She plopped down and started skimming through the book. Thankfully, she knew the book so well now, after studying the copy they'd gotten from the Louisiana State Library, that she was able to move through it much more quickly.

When she got to the inside back cover, something looked off. She tilted the book up and used her fingernail to probe the paper. The old glue gave way fairly easily, without ripping the paper. She slipped what looked like a letter out from behind the paper. Then she carefully closed the book ensuring that the paper on the back cover that she'd disturbed was lying flat.

The letter was in multiple languages all mixed together, and it was written in two different hands and styles of ink—the main body and then a long subscript. She'd likely be able to translate most of it, but she couldn't take the time now. She folded it carefully and tucked it in her pocket.

Asher helped her to her feet. They checked that the library was empty before returning the book to its spot on the shelf. Asher made sure it was perfectly in line with the books on either side.

Then they casually walked out of the library.

"Where to next?" he asked.

"The music room."

They continued at their casual pace back down the gallery, through the main hall, and then left to the music room, where a few other people were looking around.

She took a very close look around the room, lingering at furnishings and instruments but actually looking at the floors and walls.

A little while later, she walked over to Asher and smiled. "Ready?"

They looked through the rest of the house and down to the basement, where the kitchen was, as well as a swimming pool and bowling alley, along with storage rooms and servant's areas. She wanted to be sure she didn't miss anything. The subbasement was off limits, but Asher managed to get her down there. He stayed put while she quickly looked around, this time focused on one area. She was back up in only a few minutes.

"Anything else?" he asked.

She walked toward the stairs to the main floor. "I think I've got some beautiful pictures."

He smiled, but it didn't reach his eyes.

They passed an old woman in the hallway, and she stared at Asher, even though he looked to the side, away from her, as they passed, as he'd been doing the whole time. Was she staring at his scars, or had she recognized him?

When they turned a corner, Cali picked up the pace.

They didn't speak again until they were outside, well away from other people.

"She was older," Asher said. "Less likely to post an Asher Cross sighting on social media."

"True. But she may have grandkids with her whom she tells and who might post it. We should get moving."

A few minutes later, they were driving off Biltmore grounds.

"What did you figure out?" he asked.

For half a second, she wondered how he knew she'd figured something out. "I'd wondered if *Atlas of Fictional Places* had been modified by Jonathan Sikes, a compilation of his research, or if he'd happened upon it. He must've found it somewhere, and I'm guessing he got it added to the Louisiana State Library as a way to protect it."

"You think the one at Biltmore was also modified by the same person?"

"Yes. I actually wonder if it was modified by two people."

Asher raised a brow. "Someone was in league with the heir? Or someone was fighting against her?"

"Yet to be seen. I need to translate this." She carefully took the letter out of her pocket and opened it.

He looked over. "How many languages is that?"

She scanned it. "Latin, French, German, Spanish, Russian, and...I think that's Arabic."

"Can you translate all of that?"

She bared her teeth and frowned. "All except the Arabic. I should be able to get through the Russian pretty well—forced myself to learn it a few years ago, though I haven't had a lot of opportunities to speak it—and the rest I'm fluent. But I have almost no exposure to Arabic."

"Online translator?"

"Those are notoriously bad. Sometimes they spit out literal gibberish, especially languages that don't use the

Phoenician alphabet. And sometimes they get close but miss subtext or colloquialisms. I could try to study it, but we need to move quickly. I'm good with languages, but not good enough to learn something new in a day."

Asher hesitated, as if considering something. "I have a solution." He made a turn. Then he made a call and apparently set up a meeting. His tone wasn't as direct as usual, curiously, as he spoke to whomever was on the phone.

About two hours later, they pulled up to a fast-food restaurant in Knoxville, Tennessee. He parked behind the building, backed into a space hiding his license plate from view.

He hadn't spoken, so she finally asked, "Who are we meeting?"

He paused with his hand on the door. "I told you about how I got my scars."

"You saved a child suicide bomber by ripping the bomb off his chest."

"I managed to get him and his mother to the U.S."

She raised her brows. "And they speak Arabic and live not far from here."

He nodded and stood from the car.

She followed him into the restaurant.

A lanky boy who appeared to be about twelve and a young woman stood when Asher walked in. They both beamed at him, and the boy ran up and threw his arms around Asher.

And Asher hugged him back and smiled. Actually smiled.

The boy had scars on his hand and one side of his face, but not nearly as aggressive as Asher's scars. And he didn't seem to have any physical limitations—no limited movement or apparent problems with his eyesight. Asher had apparently managed to take the brunt of the injuries onto himself.

But this woman couldn't be the boy's mother, could

she? She looked like she could be barely twenty-five. She wore no hijab, let alone a burka, but she was dressed modestly in a long skirt, simple shirt, and coat.

Asher looked at the woman and nodded to the empty play area at the front of the restaurant. They all headed that way. Upon walking in, it was apparent that it was empty because the HVAC system was broken. The day had turned downright cold. But no one said a word when Asher motioned toward a table in the middle of the room. The boy made a beeline for the seat on Asher's good side, and Cali and the woman sat across from them.

"Mama, got her degree," the boy said.

Happiness lit Asher's eyes as he looked at the woman. "Congratulations."

"The credit, at least partially, goes to you."

"It's a lot easier to write checks than do the actual work of earning a college degree."

"And I'm getting straight As," the boy interjected with a proud grin.

"I expect nothing less, as I'm sure Asher does," the woman said in a very motherly voice.

"How about soccer?" Asher asked. "Are you doing the indoor league again this year?"

"Yep. Coach says I'll be starting this year."

"Is everything okay?" the woman asked Asher, probably noticing how he watched their surroundings.

Cali realized he was going out on a limb getting them involved to any degree. They were obviously important to him.

"I can't give you much information," Asher said. "But we need a translation." He nodded toward Cali. "Cali can translate everything but Arabic."

Cali pulled the folded letter out of her pocket and spread it out in front of the woman. "We'll have to work together to make sure we get context and subtext correct." The languages were completely jumbled—not one paragraph, or even one sentence, in a single language and then switching to another language. Each word was a different language.

The woman immediately studied the page. The boy slipped over and pulled a notebook out of the bag the woman had slung over the back of her chair, opened it, and set it and a pencil on the table next to her.

"Thank you." She took the paper and pencil and started writing.

She and Cali discussed each word, translating the different languages and discussing the intended meaning of each sentence. The woman had an excellent understanding of both English and Arabic. She was easy to work with.

While they worked, Asher talked with the boy, whose name she caught was Asad.

About two hours later, both the young woman, whose name Cali learned was Yara, and Cali agreed they had the translation complete. Yara wrote it out in English and handed it to Cali.

Cali held Yara's hand. "Thank you so much."

She smiled and squeezed Cali's hand. "I owe Asher both my son's life and mine. We will do anything to assist him and are forever loyal." She added, "May God protect you."

"You as well."

"We should go." Asher stood. He said to Yara, "Don't tell anyone you've seen me today."

Yara stood and reached for Asad's hand. "We will not say a word." She looked at Asad pointedly.

Asad made a motion of sipping his lips.

Asher led Cali out of the restaurant and to his truck.

When he pulled onto the main road, she asked, "Is Yara Asad's mother?"

He nodded. "She was a child bride. I believe she was thirteen when he was born."

Cali shuddered. She didn't want to imagine what the woman had been through. "She's amazing."

"She is."

The thought came to mind that perhaps Asher had been involved with her at some point romantically, but as soon as the thought entered her head, she dismissed it. There had been zero tension between them, only open friendship. Asher would never even consider approaching her in that way, not after everything she'd been through.

Quietly, Cali said, "Thank you for saving them."

He gave no response. She hadn't expected any.

She busied herself studying the translated letter.

"So, where are we going next?" Asher asked.

"Actually…" She looked over at Asher. "I think we're going back to Biltmore."

"Is the letter written by the heir? Lavinia, you said her name was?"

"Some of it. The postscript appears to have been written by George Vanderbilt."

"So, he knew about the library?"

"This says the architect—William Morris Hunt, though he doesn't state the name but that's who designed Biltmore—had added a secret passage and room unbeknownst to Vanderbilt. But when Vanderbilt found out about it, he went to Hunt and confronted him. Hunt was known for being loyal to his clients, but he told Vanderbilt 'the heir'—he used that term rather than the name Lavinia—had searched him out, explained the situation, and asked him to find a way to help protect the library. Apparently, Lavinia thought a building of that kind of grandeur would survive—wouldn't be overhauled or torn down—and she was right. She showed Hunt some important texts from the library as proof of her claims, and he agreed he had to help her protect it. Hunt died of a heart attack a few days after telling Vanderbilt the situation. Vanderbilt says he was consumed with guilt—he presumably thought he'd caused Hunt's death, but it was several days later, so I'm not so sure. Vanderbilt stopped work on the music room and committed to protecting the library."

"Why the music room? Was that just the last room to be done?"

"I think I know exactly why the music room."

Asher lifted his chin. "That's where the secret passage is accessed."

"He says he put protections into place, so I'm guessing he brought his daughter into the loop and made her swear to continue the protection."

"But the music room was finished. When we toured, it was done."

"It was decorated in the 1970s. The Vanderbilts must have felt confident they'd hidden the entrance effectively. It was probably getting conspicuous that the room had never been finished in eighty years and continued to be blocked off to tourists. In Fact, Cornelia, George Vanderbilt's daughter died the same year the music room was opened to the public. Perhaps it was something she'd felt the need to do before she died, to help ensure suspicion didn't arise or that someone else would finish the room and find the entrance. But…she'd lived abroad for years and died in England. I wonder if she had someone helping her."

"But you saw the entrance? That's what you were looking at so intently."

"I thought it was odd that the music room hadn't been completed in all that time. I think I spotted a trap door. It was expertly hidden. No way any regular tourist would see it, but I was looking for it."

"Where do you think the secret passage goes? A hidden room?"

"I don't think so. Hiding a small passage is doable, but I don't think a hidden room within the house could be missed for so long. Someone would've noticed dimensions being off. There was a tunnel in Biltmore village. It used to be part of the old dairy barn. So, that trade worked on the site during the construction—they had the capabilities. My guess is the passage leads underneath the house to a space large enough to hold the library."

"It has not just a basement but a subbasement. Wouldn't that get pretty deep? They might have hit the water table."

"Maybe. But William Morris Hunt was one of the best architects in the country. He would've figured a way."

"What else does the letter—" Asher stopped speaking, and Cali saw why. Someone was following them.

CHAPTER 35

"Do you think they know we met with Yara?" Cali asked.

"We've driven pretty far away from her. We're back in North Carolina. I'm guessing they're watching this state more closely, specifically all main roads in and out, since this is where you were living. Unfortunately, we had to cross through Great Smoky Mountains National Park, and there are only so many roads that go through it."

"Which means they've most likely come to the conclusion I'm the heir." They probably assumed she was in North Carolina in the first place for a reason, perhaps researching the location of the library or protecting its location.

"I agree." Then he added, "Hold on." He made a tight turn onto a dirt road.

They'd been on a beautiful rural highway and had just gone through what was apparently Cherokee territory—every business was Cherokee something or other. This dirt road was barely a road. Dense trees reached out and scraped the car, and they plowed into standing water that covered the road for a good fifty yards and into the woods.

He turned again, this time into the trees. It reminded

her of that insane drive through the woods back when they'd fled from Asher's house. But he'd known those woods—surely owned them and took runs through them all the time. This time he was almost blind.

He stomped on the brake, the truck skidded to a stop, and he jumped out of the car and ran back the way they'd come.

Cali flung off her seatbelt and raced after him back to the dirt road. She didn't demand to know what he was doing—she trusted whatever his plan, it was smart, and she didn't need to slow him down.

Where he'd entered the woods with the truck, there was a tiny sapling down that he'd had to run over. He pulled it out of the ground, tossed it into the woods, hidden in brush, and stomped at the dirt around it until you could no longer see where it'd been.

Cali understood what he was doing and fluffed up a bush that had been flattened on one side, to make the damage less noticeable.

Asher took her hand and pulled her into the brush as the sound of a car engine came up the dirt road. The car was moving a lot slower than Asher had driven. His truck was designed to handle the terrain, but the sedan ambling up the road was certainly not. They'd fallen enough behind that the water covering the road had settled. It was no longer discernible where they had pulled off the dirt road.

As the sedan moved closer, they ducked down more behind the brush. She could see only tiny slivers of the car through the brush. She heard as the tires sloshed slowly into the water, and then the sloshing stopped.

She heard a car door open, surely the driver stepping out to get a better look around. Someone cursed. "Can't make it through this. I can't see where they could've gone anyway. Are you sure this is the road they turned on?"

"We saw the tire tracks back there."

"Are you sure it's Cross' tire tracks or some random tracks from a local?"

No response.

Another curse, and then the car door slammed closed. She heard tires, again crunching on the rocks and dirt rather than sloshing through the water—they were backing up.

They remained completely still for another couple of minutes.

Then Asher said, "I think we're clear."

He stood, and she followed him back to his truck.

She pulled out her phone and brought up Google Earth to try to find them an alternate way out. They could be waiting for them at the mouth of the dirt road. She showed him what looked like clearer terrain, more grass than trees, to the east. It looked like they could probably get back to a side road from there, take a few more side roads to get a couple of miles away, and then get back on the highway.

He nodded and put the truck in gear. He kept his gaze on the windshield. "Thank you for trusting me."

"We didn't have time for you to stop and explain."

He continued driving. They drove for a while with no signs of the sedan.

Cali's phone buzzed with a text. It was from Floyd's number. *Hey Cali. It's Ivy. We just wanted to check on you and make sure you're ok.*

"Ivy's texting," she said to Asher.

"She's not trying to get involved, is she?"

"I'm actually a little worried about that. I can tell she feels really guilty about being complicit with Libervis."

"She was raised in it. It would be hard for her to know better."

"I don't want to lie to her."

Another text. *The guys say you were researching Biltmore. Is that where you're going?*

Cali typed, *Still just researching. It's a major tourist attraction, so really safe. I think Asher's bored.* She clicked send and told Asher what she'd said to Ivy.

"I'm bored?" he asked.

"I assume you are occasionally. Okay, it was stretching the truth, but I don't want her getting anything into her head about following."

"I haven't been bored since meeting you."

"Back at ya."

He continued driving, and she looked out the side window at the trees flashing by. He so rarely bantered with her. Once they parted, she'd miss it.

They were getting closer to Asheville, when Asher asked, "We never discussed the rest of the letter. You told me about the postscript that Vanderbilt wrote. What about the original part of the letter written by Lavinia? I assume she was your great-grandmother, maybe great-great." He'd been talking with Asad and hadn't paid much attention to her and Yara as they'd translated.

"Probably."

"And obviously where you inherited your propensity for languages and cyphers."

"Looking back, my mom encouraged that kind of thing. She taught me French in tandem with English, and we were always doing puzzles and reading." She pulled the letter out of her pocket but didn't bother unfolding it. She'd read it enough times she didn't need to. "It's a note to whomever finds the library, if she's not able to liberate it before her death. She said she was afraid to liberate it for fear others would be like Libervis and long to possess it. I suspect she understood the tensions that were building around the world. Germany was pushing to rise in power. World War I wasn't yet on anyone's radar, but I wonder if Lavinia had more information than most, or perhaps she was simply more astute.

"She confirms it's The Lost Library from Russia, the Golden Library. The Kremlin servants banded together and saved it one book at a time, at great danger to themselves. At first, the cause was noble, but somewhere they lost their way and thought possession of the library made them better than everyone else. They had access to knowledge, a level of education no one else in the world had. They believed they should be in charge—control all industry, financial markets, even remove children from their parents so they could dictate how they were raised."

"Sounds like Ivan."

"Yeah. Seems they haven't changed much. When they gave themselves the name Libervis—vis means power— she knew she had to take action. She ends it with, 'I pray they see the truth. May God's will be done.'"

"But it doesn't tell us where exactly the library is within Biltmore."

"No. I think she didn't want to be too helpful. If someone deserved to find it, they should be able to find it."

A little while later, they pulled into the Biltmore parking lot. Asher gave her cash to pay for passes again. The clerk reminded them they didn't have long to look around since the house would be closing in an hour or so.

"Back so soon?" came a voice wavery with age.

Cali smiled at the old woman who had come around the corner. Cali had seen her when they were here earlier. She looked ancient, skin even more wrinkled than Ivan's. She had a Biltmore name badge on this time. "There were a couple of little details I wanted to check out again. I'm kind of a nerd when it comes to history."

Asher kept his head turned away, surely pretending to look at something but really trying to make sure he wasn't recognized, and probably watching their surroundings intently.

The woman patted Cali's arm as she walked by. "Me too, dear. Me too." As she walked through the main hall, she seemed to wander and lose track of where she was going. Perhaps a little senile.

A middle-aged woman with a name badge walked by. "Don't mind Ms. Tate. She's been here forever. It just wouldn't be the same around here without her." With a smile, she kept going.

Cali took Asher's hand to keep up the appearance they were a couple to help draw less notice. She was a little surprised he didn't shake her off. They moseyed first through the winter garden, which was basically a greenhouse in the middle of the house off the main hall, and then to the music room. Cali wanted to be sure she didn't appear to be on a mission—though it was killing her to move so slowly.

Thankfully, the music room was empty when they walked in. The room was an elongated octagon with three windows at the far end. It was under the left of those windows where she'd spotted what she was pretty sure was a trap door.

"I don't see anything," Asher said as he looked at the chevron-pattern wood floor.

"Let me borrow your pocketknife."

He handed it to her and then started inspecting a tall candelabra that stood next to a table, though he was obviously really blocking sight of her as best he could.

She knelt on the floor and carefully slid the knife into the tiny seam. The floor didn't budge.

She moved the knife a little farther down. Still no movement. The seam was too small to get any leverage.

She stood and looked around.

Asher glanced at her and then at the several doorways.

A couple of ornate cast iron grates were set into the paneling on the wall to the side of the window. She squatted down to get a better look. She couldn't see much of anything, so she slid her fingers into the grate along the edges.

Her mouth split into a grin.

She looked up at Asher and whispered, "Clear?"

He glanced at all the doorways again and looked down at her and nodded. "Tourists are clearing out."

She pressed on what felt like a latch or a button, and there was a click. The floor panel had popped up about an inch.

She lifted it up. There was a narrow and steep staircase—almost more a ladder than staircase. The space was triangular, so it was very tight. She turned on the flashlight on her phone and stepped down inside the pitch-black space.

Asher followed, though she had no idea how he was able to fit his wide shoulders through.

Holding on to the cold stone wall, she looked up as Asher grabbed a handle affixed to the back of the trap door and closed it. Other than the flashlight on her phone, they were in utter darkness. Asher turned on his phone's flashlight and nodded at her.

She continued down the stairs. The steps were so narrow, she turned a bit so she could tread on them with her feet sideways, careful not to trip. She could hear Asher's shoulders rubbing against the walls as he moved.

The steps seemed to go on forever—probably through both the basement and subbasement. The temperature continued to drop, and she felt moisture on the walls as she held on to them for balance.

She'd been quiet for fear someone inside the house would hear them, but she was pretty sure they were now under the house. "Have you seen anything of interest?"

"Other than a hidden staircase in one of America's most famous landmarks, no." His tone was dry, serious.

She grinned.

"I think I see the bottom," she said, and a few seconds later, she stepped from the stone of the stairs down onto hardened dirt. Asher had to duck his head as they slowly walked into a tunnel with stone walls and ceiling. They'd started at the back of the house in the music room, and now moved under the house toward the front.

They continued on. She heard Asher's shoulders brush the walls with every step, or maybe it was his head brushing the ceiling. "This tunnel definitely wasn't built for a linebacker."

"I wasn't a linebacker. I was the quarterback."

She grinned. He was having fun—she wished she could see his face. Perhaps exploring old buildings was part of why he bought and restored so many of them.

She stopped.

"What's wrong?" he asked.

"The tunnel, it branches off. I'm not sure which way to go."

He lifted his phone and flashed the light over her shoulder at the new branch in the tunnel to the left. She moved forward and tried to light up the new tunnel, but the darkness sucked up the light before it made it a few feet.

"If we choose the wrong way, we'll turn around," he said.

She decided to continue on through the original tunnel, and he followed. But then she stopped again. There was another branch to the right, and when she flashed light down it, she could see yet another tunnel branch off it.

"It's starting to become clear this is a labyrinth," she said. "Since it'd been added in secret, I hadn't anticipated more than one tunnel."

"Perhaps Vanderbilt decided to add more protection for the library and paid for more tunnels."

"That makes sense." She rubbed her finger over the edge of her phone as she thought. Then she closed her eyes as she imagined the layout of the house above them and where she estimated they were in reference to that layout.

"This has to be the load-bearing wall at the side of the main hall." She tapped the wall on her right. Then she pointed up and to the left. "That means the swimming pool is there. I don't think anyone would want to put a tunnel under the swimming pool—that's why this tunnel is so tight. And beyond the pool is the plant storeroom. I doubt they would put the library under there—too much possibility of water or chemical spills."

"So, we were right not to take that tunnel to the left back there."

"Yes." She tapped the right wall of the tunnel branching off to the right. "This should be the load-bearing wall between the main staircase and the gallery." She paused, considering. Then she opened her eyes and pointed down the tunnel on the right. "I think we should take this tunnel but not take that branch off it."

"Okay." He followed her as she made the turn. "You sound like you have a theory as to why we should go this way."

"The plans show structural walls in a few areas of the subbasement, but there's no access. Including under the library. Both Lavinia and George Vanderbilt were major book lovers. I'd think they would love the idea of putting the world's most valuable library underneath another library. Vanderbilt spent a ton of time in his library. I bet he loved sitting there reading, all while knowing what was beneath his feet."

They ignored one more tunnel branching off and came to a stop at a stone wall, tunnels veering both to the left and right.

"The library fireplace is above this. They wouldn't have tunneled under that." She leaned to the left to peer into the darkness. "This way." She stopped at a set of stone stairs leading up and smiled back at Asher. "We're right underneath where the library spiral staircase is, right by where we found the *Atlas of Fictional Places*."

"So, it wasn't just hiding a note but was a clue in and of itself."

She turned back to the steps, and her heart thudded in her chest.

She took the steps and was surprised to see some light. She found a room almost as big as the library above, walls lined with shelves, and a desk with a small lamp in the middle of the room, manned by an old woman.

"Hello there, dearies." Ms. Tate smiled at them.

CHAPTER 36

Cali wasn't sure how to respond upon finding someone in the library. The library that had been lost, as in no one knew where it was.

"Is this…" Cali gestured to the shelves covered in mounds of books and scrolls. "The Golden Library of Moscow?"

"Yes, dearie. I was so certain you'd be the one to find it. I'm so glad I was right."

Asher asked, "And who are you exactly?"

"Everyone calls me Ms. Tate."

"Can we get a little more clarification?" he asked.

"I'm not the one skulking around secret passageways unbeknownst to the owner of the property." She continued smiling, her countenance warm and grandmotherly. Then she winked at Cali.

Despite herself, Cali smiled back at her.

"Oh, I knew I'd like you," Ms. Tate said to Cali.

"How do you know Cali?" Asher asked.

Ms. Tate turned her warm smile on Asher. "And you. Imagine my surprise when she showed up with a legitimate celebrity. You're quite talented at turning away from people at just the right moment so they don't realize who you are. An unusual—but useful—talent."

"How do you know who Cali is?" Asher asked again.

"Didn't take a genius."

Perhaps Ms. Tate was a little senile. But what was she doing here?

Ms. Tate rested her wrinkled hands on her wrinkled cheeks and stood. "Oh, dear. I see I'm not explaining myself very well." She walked around the desk and approached Cali. The only light in the room was the desk lamp and the flashlights on their phones, now pointed at the ground. But Cali's eyes had adjusted well to the low light, and she could still see Ms. Tate's upset expression.

"I've known the heir would be coming. I've been watching over the library most of my life. I pay attention to the guests, you see. And you caught my notice immediately, you and your strapping, and perhaps a bit scary, young man. I wasn't sure what to think of him at first, and so I watched. And then I noticed you looking very closely at things that don't warrant scrutiny—or rather things that most people don't think warrant scrutiny."

"You saw us in the music room?"

"There are several doorways to that room, so it's quite easy to sneak a peek from around the corner. You, my dear, stared awfully hard at that floor earlier. Please tell me how you figured it all out." Her eyes were bright with curiosity.

Cali hesitated. "There was a lot to it."

Ms. Tate gave a wave of her hand. "Of course. But your mother or father did pass on a clue to you?"

"Yes. 'In the house bilt, history doth dwell.' It was part of a rhyme she used to sing to me. But I had no idea it was a clue to anything until recently."

Ms. Tate frowned. "Oh dear, that didn't work out well, did it? Did they not explain?"

"My mother died when I was four."

Ms. Tate's hand shot to her throat. "Oh. How horrible.

Here I was imagining the life of the heir being so sweet and safe."

"I'm sorry to say that's never been my life, not since I was very young. May I ask how you came to know about the library and become its… Is caretaker an apt word?"

"Yes, caretaker works nicely. I was given this honor and responsibility when I was just a girl. My mother worked at the estate, and Mrs. Cecil caught me down in the tunnels. She was quite upset at me. When she caught me a second time, I was terrified. I thought for sure she would let my mother go. But she looked at me with such contemplation and asked if I could keep a secret. Over the years, she trusted me with more of the story."

"That her father, George Vanderbilt, told her?"

Ms. Tate smiled. "She'd said he'd trusted her and only her with the secret. And she decided to trust me. I am honored beyond words to this day."

"That's why you've been here so long." Cali tilted her head and narrowed her eyes. "And that's why you pretend to be senile."

"People do tend to be so relaxed when they think the only ears in hearing distance are attached to an addled mind. But don't let me fool you—I've been noticing my own decline the last few years, I'm sorry to say. I was starting to worry the heir would never show up. I wasn't sure whom I could trust with this secret before my decline goes too far, and I don't really feel like it's mine to share." Ms. Tate started. "Oh, but you don't give a hoot about little old me." She spread her arms to indicate the filled shelves. "This is why you're here."

Cali walked over to the nearest shelf, where Asher had already drifted. Asher pointed to a title without touching the spine.

Cali gasped and spun back around to Ms. Tate. "A Gutenberg Bible." Then she asked, "The Septuagint from the Library at Alexandria?"

"Next shelf over." Ms. Tate pointed to the left.

Cali turned to the shelf and stared. Tears stung the backs of her eyes.

She turned and looked all around the room. It was completely filled—basic wood shelves sagging under the weight. "There have to be 10,000 books in here."

"There are a few repeats and some that weren't actually lost, that do exist in public, but the copies here are, of course, very old and lovingly preserved."

Ms. Tate walked over and stood next to Cali. "The question is, my dearie, what you plan to do with it now."

"I'm guessing the estate technically owns it."

Ms. Tate shook her head. "Mrs. Cecil granted ownership to me. I have the documents, but with the condition that ownership is conveyed to the heir."

Asher asked, "Why are you so sure Cali is the heir?"

Ms. Tate raised a brow.

"The rhyme," Cali said. "You knew at least some of it, and I confirmed I knew it too."

Ms. Tate's eyes twinkled.

"You're not declining as much as you said," Cali accused.

Ms. Tate grinned like an imp.

Cali looked around the room. "So, I own all this."

"Yes, dearie. Now, what do you plan to do with it?"

"Share it," Cali said without hesitation. "Transcribe all the texts and make them available online. And the physical books and scrolls should go to museums."

Asher spoke up. "I'll build a museum. I'll donate the land and building."

Cali smiled at him. "If it's completely available to everyone, that'll stop the desire to possess it. Lavinia didn't have the option of almost instant exposure to the entire world, or else she wouldn't have had to resort to hiding it."

Ms. Tate said, "From what I know of Lavinia, your great-great-great-grandmother, that's what she would have wanted."

After looking around for a while longer, Cali and Asher

left Ms. Tate and headed back up to the main house. Ms. Tate had told them how to get out without sounding any alarms. Asher wanted to make immediate arrangements to bring in people to transcribe the documents. They both agreed getting the documents online was first priority. Ms. Tate said she wanted to stay behind to have one more quiet evening with the library, which Cali completely understood.

They made their way back through the tunnels and up the narrow stairs. But when Asher opened the trap door in the music room, he stopped. He'd requested she let him go first. She stood there looking up, wondering what he was doing, until she heard a voice. A voice she'd hoped never to hear again.

"How gracious of you to find the library for us," Ivan said.

CHAPTER 37

"I'm sure Miss Lebeau is there with you," Ivan said. "Let the poor thing out of that dismal hole."

Cali whispered, hoping Asher would hear but no one else would, "We can't let them down here. Ms. Tate said this is the only way in or out. We can't let them get to the library—and more importantly, to Ms. Tate." Cali assumed Ivan had plenty of muscle with him. Ms. Tate was ancient, possibly even older than Ivan, and appeared to be physically frail.

Asher slowly continued up and out into the music room. Cali closely followed and kicked the trap door closed.

"Cute," Ivan said. As suspected, he had three men with him aiming guns at Asher. Ivan was dressed in another tailored suit, looking at ease in the opulent surroundings. "Do you really think a closed door is going to stop me?"

"Figure out how to open it," she challenged. He surely would eventually, but it gave them at least a few minutes. "How'd you figure it out?" she asked as another way to stall for time.

"All right. I'll give you this, since it is an interesting story. I know who you are, Miss LeBeau. I know you are the traitorous heir."

"I assumed you would figure that out, given a little time. For the record, I didn't know, not until you gave me access to your archives."

Ivan scowled. "Given the knowledge you are the heir, I knew you'd moved to North Carolina for a reason. All main roads in the state are being watched."

"Actually, I didn't move here for any reason other than it was a state I thought at the time I had no ties to. I was on the run from Dinetti, if you'll remember. I've moved numerous times. But it did work out for you that this happened to be the state where Biltmore is. We didn't take a lot of main roads, and we lost your tail a few hours ago. How did you realize we were here?"

"I paid local thugs throughout the state to search for Cross' truck. Cross hid the plates quite well with how he parked, but when the truck remained here past the closing of the estate, things clicked into place."

"So, you got lucky."

"Are you trying to bait me into getting angry?" His wrinkled skin turned blotchy.

She shrugged. "It's working. And if I am purposefully baiting you, it doesn't mean what I'm saying isn't true. You've been searching for the library your entire life. It took me all of a few days."

"You had information we didn't."

"I had already figured out that it was here before I realized the rhyme my mother used to sing to me was a clue."

Ivan's skin went from blotchy to red. He made a motion with his hand, and the men shifted their guns toward her. "And since you are no longer of use, what's stopping me from killing you?"

Asher stepped in front of Cali.

Ivan laughed. "You think I have any problem killing you too?"

Still behind Asher, Cali said, "Now that sounds like a

headache. Little old me—I'm easy to dispose of. Literally no one will miss me. Asher Cross on the other hand—his disappearance would make some serious news." She hated hiding behind him, leaving him in harm's way, but this tactic may be the best way to keep him safe.

"He's already disappeared from his company. No one cares."

"They believe I'm on an extended business trip," Asher said, "which isn't unheard of. I've been in constant contact with my office. I assure you, my team will immediately alert authorities, as well as my private security force, if I go missing. I also have certain contingencies in place."

Cali assumed that meant the Gray Hats, who would certainly move mountains to find Asher if he suddenly disappeared. She peeked out from behind Asher's arm and smiled. At the same time, she drew a line down Asher's back, telling him to get down when the time was right, and rested her hand on the gun he had tucked in the back of his pants. She was a very good and fast shot, and she was no longer feeling any trepidation about doing whatever she needed to do—to protect both Asher and Ms. Tate. "You'll need some ducks in a row before you skip down the lane of killing one of the most powerful people in the country."

"Which I can do with ease."

"I'm sure you can. But you're flying by the seat of your pants right now."

Ivan slowly grinned, and Cali's mind flashed to the sinister slow grin of The Grinch. "Not entirely." Then he called, "Walter."

Walter entered the room from the doorway behind Ivan. He had a blindfolded and bound man by the arm, leading him into the room. Perhaps a Biltmore employee they were holding in case they needed someone for ransom? He wasn't dressed like the other employees, just jeans and a sweater, but perhaps he worked in a back office and wasn't seen by the public. Walter pulled the oversized blindfold off the man.

Cali stepped out from behind Asher, even as Asher grabbed her hand and tried to pull her back behind him. "Dad."

Her father glanced around the room and then to her. His voice shook. "Cali, what's going on?"

Cali glared at Ivan.

Ivan smiled back at her. "Give me the library, and I'll let you, Mr. Cross, and Mr. Lebeau go. You have my word."

"Your word doesn't mean anything."

Her father stepped forward. "You will not use me against my daughter."

"She's stolen something that belongs to me," Ivan said. "I will do whatever is necessary."

"My daughter is not a thief. She's a Godly woman. If she stands against you, then so do I."

Cali stared at her father. He looked like the last time she'd seen him—hadn't shaved in a few days and had bags under his eyes. But she could almost see through the haze the bright energetic man she'd known as a small child, before he'd allowed gambling to consume him.

Her father moved closer to Ivan, and one of his men stepped forward and aimed a gun at him.

"No," Cali said.

Her father's gaze flickered to her but then he focused on Ivan. "If you know anything about me, you'd know you can't scare me. I'm in debt to some of the most brutal people in the country. And now that you've kidnapped me, they'll assume I've tried to run from them. I'm as good as dead. I have no way of getting out of the hole I've doomed myself to." His gaze still on Ivan, he pointed to Cali. "She is the only thing worthwhile I have left. I don't really even have her anymore; I did everything possible to drag her down with me. I gave up any rights as her father a long time ago, but I will literally do anything to protect her, including stopping you from using me against her."

Ivan continued smiling that sinister smile of his. "What a noble speech. Something I've learned about noble speeches is just that—they are nothing but talk. Not action."

Her father lifted his chin. "Try me." Cali could just see the side of his face, the smile. "She's a good person, and even after everything I've done to her, she'd still do anything in her power to protect me."

"This I know." Ivan sounded smug.

"But your failure is that you counted on me letting her." Like a viper, her father grabbed Ivan's throat and choked.

Ivan's men tried to pull her father off Ivan. They pried at his fingers but couldn't get him to let go.

Ivan gasped, obviously trying to talk but unable to.

One of the men aimed his gun at her father. Just as Asher stepped in front of her and pulled her to his chest, shielding her, she heard the gunshot.

"Daddy!" she screamed.

Then a thud, something hitting the floor.

She pulled out of Asher's grip and fell to the floor next to her father.

His lips faltered as he tried to smile. "I've finally done right by you."

She leaned over him and rested her hands on either side of his face. "Get right with God, Daddy. Please. Ask him to forgive you. Ask for his mercy. Please." His blood was pooling around him. He wasn't going to survive. But maybe he could still live, know God's love.

His voice was weak. "Still trying to save me."

"Please, Daddy."

"I don't deserve forgiveness."

"None of us do. But he still loves us. He wants to forgive us."

Tears welled in his eyes. "You think so?"

"I know so. Please."

His voice shook. "God, Jesus, please forgive me. I am

an unworthy…lost soul. Please— Please forgive me."

She whispered, "Please, God."

He met her eyes, and she could see the pain, how much effort it took just to focus on her. His voice barely made a sound. "I love you, Cali." The life drained out of his eyes, and his body went slack.

"Daddy…"

She caught movement out of the corner of her eye and realized Asher stood by her, blocking her from Ivan as best as he could, giving her this last moment with her father. She looked up at his strong back, how he guarded her. She couldn't let him die too. She opened her mouth— to say what, she didn't know.

And then the men started to converge on them.

Asher took his gun from the back of his waist and aimed it at Ivan.

The hammers of several guns clicked as the men aimed their weapons at him.

"No!" She stood and pushed in front of Asher. She stared down Ivan. "This is between you and me."

"That ship sailed when you disappeared from my home and thumbed your nose at my hospitality. Nothing and no one will stand in my way." He growled, "Now show me how to get to the library."

"Cali," Asher warned, a reminder that it wasn't only about them. Ms. Tate was down there, and if she didn't have a heart attack at Ivan's men storming in, if Ivan realized how much she knew about the library, he'd never let her go. She'd die in captivity.

She needed to think.

As she looked at Asher, aiming his gun at Ivan, a solution came to her. Ivan was the central force. She suspected some, maybe all, of his followers thought he was infallible. Walter had the sheen of authority, but that was just an act, obvious by the fact that he now stayed in the back, just watching. If Ivan were gone, she had a chance of breaking Libervis.

But she couldn't murder him.

Please, God, guide me. Help me to do your will.

She turned to the man closest to them, aiming his gun at Asher. "You do realize he'll never share any of the knowledge he gains from the library."

The man's gaze flicked to her but then back to Asher.

Ivan said, "They don't need the knowledge. I'll use it for their good. They know that."

She continued to address the man, whom she noticed was wearing a wedding ring. "Do you really think someone else knows what's best for you? That's what all the dictators in history have said and probably actually believed. But you know what's best for you and your family, not some disconnected ninety-year-old."

"They also know it's best to be under my protection than against me," Ivan said.

"So, you're following him because he's threatening you?" Cali asked the man. "Has he threatened your family too?" She looked at one of the other men. "How about you?" Then she added to all of them, "You are his only power. If you walked away, he'd be nothing."

Ivan lifted his chin. "That's where you're wrong, missy."

"Other than your charisma and, apparently, some money, what do you have?"

"I have the knowledge," Ivan said. "I am wiser than all others." He bored his gaze into her. "I will live forever."

She lowered her brows. "There is only one way to live forever."

Ivan's eyes went wild. "You've found it, then! Where is it? Tell me now how to access the library and in which book is the knowledge."

"It's not some lost text," Cali said. "The way is outlined in the most read and printed Book in the world. It's not a secret."

Ivan laughed. "More Bible talk. Hilarious! Tell me, if it holds the secret of living forever, why is there death all around us?"

"Physical death, yes. But our souls can live on with God." She fought back tears and didn't let herself look down where her father lay. "That's where my father is now."

Ivan laughed louder. "Your father is gone. He was nothing in life, and now he is even less than nothing in death. He's just one more pathetic excuse for a man. His only use was in controlling you, his weak-minded daughter who clings to make-believe to sludge through life."

"Have you never researched the proof of God's existence? I would think someone obsessed with a library would be well-versed on such an important topic. And more than that, have you never opened yourself to feel God's presence?"

"I do not spend time on fairy tales."

Cali's voice lowered, softened. "I'm sorry for you. I pray you find God before you die."

Ivan raised his chin. "I will never die."

Cali turned to the man closest. "Do you really want to risk your life and perhaps soul to protect this man? He is not deity, no matter what he believes. Think to all the cults following men who claim to be divine or somehow powerful? As soon as the man dies, everything falls apart. They were nothing more than charisma."

Ivan spoke up. "Christianity is nothing more than another of those cults."

"All those cults fell apart. Christianity has prospered. People innately feel the truth of it even before they understand any of the logic or historical evidence. Cult members don't continue in service once the leader dies. But Jesus' followers continued on. His disciples almost all were tortured and put to death for their beliefs. But they didn't waver—they knew the truth. They knew the magnitude of it."

"There are other religions around the world. They are nothing more than make-believe for the weak."

"Yes, there are other religions. Many are really just philosophies. Others are mandated by tyrants. Christianity doesn't need to be mandated. People believe in spite of the risk of persecution. Like Jesus' disciples, they know the truth in their heart and are willing to risk physical death in order to save their souls and honor the one true God."

"I'm tired of this," Ivan said. "Kill them."

"How will you find the library?" Asher asked.

"We're close enough. I'll find it from here." Ivan glanced around at his men. "Kill them!"

The two men closest glanced at each other.

"Stop!" Ivy ran into the room, closely followed by Matthew.

Ivan sneered. "The prodigal daughter returns."

"Father, please," she begged.

Ivan glared at her. And then he growled, "Kill her."

Floyd and Bl@ze ran in from the other doorway, behind Ivan and his men. They attacked, and Matthew followed suit, as did Asher. It was instant chaos. Thankfully, Asher must have seen the hesitation in Ivan's men's eyes and didn't kill them, but rather hit the closest upside the head with the butt of his gun. Walter ran out of the room and down the hall.

As Asher defended himself from one of the other men, Ivan took a gun out and lifted to aim it toward Asher. Cali rushed forward and grabbed his gun hand, raising it in the air away from Asher or anyone else.

Ivan's eyes were wild as he struggled with Cali. Curses spit from his mouth. As she fought to keep his gun under control, she prayed—for Asher, for her friends, for Ms. Tate, for Ivan. He was stronger than she would have thought given his age and obvious frailty, but she was able to keep him from shooting anyone.

But then someone knocked her away, and she stumbled to the ground. She immediately jumped back up, but Ivan had fallen as well. In the chaos, one of his men, a huge burly man, stepped on him. The man lost his balance and fell, landing on Ivan.

She knew. Even before the man scrambled back up to standing, she knew.

Ivan was dead.

The man who'd accidentally crushed him stopped and stared. Then Ivy noticed him lying there and screamed.

The chaos stopped, and everyone stared.

Ivy rushed forward and knelt next to him. She felt for a pulse and then for breath. Then she lowered her head, deflating, and a sob bubbled from her mouth.

Matthew was immediately with her, hugging her from behind.

Ivan's men stared.

"No," one of them murmured.

"He was going to live forever," another said.

Another barely whispered to himself, "She was right."

Ivy took a deep shuddering breath and looked around the room at Ivan's men. Perhaps she even knew some of them personally. Her voice was thick with tears. "The Lost Library doesn't offer endless life. There is no black magic." She wiped her eyes and stood. "You need to leave. Go back to your lives." When they hesitated, she added, "We've tracked your locations, your backgrounds, even your finances. You can't hide. But if you leave and live respectable lives, you'll never hear from me or anyone else again."

One man walked quickly from the room. The others glanced at each other and then followed.

Bl@ze motioned to Floyd, and they both trailed behind, surely making certain the men left.

Cali walked up to Ivy and pulled her into a tight hug. "I'm so sorry."

As Ivy cried on Cali's shoulder, Cali prayed—for Ivy and for thanks that Cali's father had somehow been saved. She'd given up hope for her father, but God had made it possible. She closed her eyes, and a tear ran down her cheek.

CHAPTER 38

Cali hadn't seen Asher in months. Though he'd completely funded building the new home for The Lost Library, as well as transcribing all materials, which was progressing well, he hadn't shown up on the job site at all. He'd asked her—via text—to help him oversee the design of the site and building, and then staffing and training. She was thankful for his investment, construction knowledge, and attention to detail, but she missed him.

Today was the opening of the library to the public, and she hoped he'd show up. Though she had no idea what to say to him, what she *should* say. Though she'd taken the risk of staying in Charleston to help with the library, she still wasn't sure how safe she was. Was Libervis totally disbanded? Would someone, like Walter, come after her for Ivan's death? Would Dinetti come after her again? The Gray Hats, which now included Ivy, had kept an eye out for her, but she would never be confident she would ever be truly safe. And she couldn't let Asher be in danger because of her again.

Every time she reminded herself of that, she died inside a little more.

"Hey!" Ivy practically skipped toward her across the

dark-stained concrete floor. Cali had put Ivy's and the rest of the Gray Hats' names down as early entrants, so while a crowd waited outside, along with news crews from all over the world, Ivy and the others had been allowed inside while the library's staff made final preparations to open.

"OMG!" Ivy said. "There's like hordes of people out there. The police had to block off this street and the next one." She looked around at the mahogany paneling, traditional molding, and glass cases displaying the original books. "This is amazing. It looks just like what I imagined the library in *Beauty and the Beast* would look like. All this gorgeous dark wood and trim. And the outside, oh my gosh, it's so beautiful. I can't wait until the crowds die down and I can get a better look—brick and stone and casing everywhere. It looks like a castle. Asher paid for all this? The costs must be crazy."

Cali nodded. "He paid for everything, and he made sure it all happened quickly. And he set up a foundation to ensure it's protected well into the future."

"So, do you technically still own the library? The books, I mean?"

"I donated it all to the foundation."

"That was generous." Matthew walked up and took Ivy's hand. The movement was so natural and easy.

Cali fought back jealousy. And then she caught sight of something on Ivy's hand. She narrowed her eyes at Ivy. "Do you have something to tell me?"

Ivy's smile took over her face. "I was going to wait until after the opening." She thrust her hand out so Cali could see the engagement ring better.

"It's beautiful." Cali pulled Ivy into a hug and then Matthew.

While they toured the shop, the area where they sold copies of the books and anything else related to the library, Ivy gave Cali a rundown of how the engagement had happened. Floyd and Bl@ze caught up with them before they toured the restoration area.

And then it was time for the opening. The Gray Hats took their leave, and Cali retreated to the back office area.

She'd written a long article outlining her experience and how The Lost Library had been found and distributed it to any publication who wanted it, but she didn't do interviews. The last thing she wanted was to become famous. The staff was well-versed in the history of the library—they would handle any questions from the press. And even better, Ms. Tate had agreed to work here and be the face of the library. Cali had worried about the woman, her life's purpose suddenly gone, and when she'd approached Ms. Tate with the idea, she'd seen the excitement in the woman's eyes.

In the security office, Cali watched on the cameras as Ms. Tate stood in front of the main desk and greeted with a bright smile as people flooded in and looked around in awe.

It took hours for the crowd to make it through the building. It made her heart happy to see Ms. Tate smiling as she told stories. To see the excitement in people's eyes as they gazed at the lost texts. To see children sitting on the floor in the store reading.

As the day passed, Cali slowly accepted that Asher wasn't going to show up.

The sun began to fall, and Cali sat alone in the breakroom. She started planning. She hadn't thought about what was next, some part of her still holding on to hope, but she knew it was time to go. She'd go pack her few belongings and catch the next bus out of town. She'd find another job somewhere and disappear.

***

Asher slid by the last of the crowd through the front doors. People stared at him and whispered, but the robust security in the building helped ensure no one approached him. When Ms. Tate saw him, she beamed and held out both hands to him.

He took her hands. "How're you holding up?"

"I'm good. Someone was kind enough to bring me this here stool, and I've been jabbering to anyone who'll listen."

Asher was happy to see that Ms. Tate seemed to be in her glory. It was probably nice not to have to pretend to be senile anymore, though a part of him suspected she enjoyed being crafty.

"Where's Cali?" he asked.

"I haven't seen her since before the doors opened. Been hiding away, I suspect. Probably gone by now."

Panic clawed through his chest. She wouldn't be gone from the city, would she? He'd assumed she'd stick around for a week or so to be sure the library opened without a hitch. But...with Ms. Tate here to oversee everything, maybe she didn't feel that need.

He said goodbye to Ms. Tate and headed to the back office area. He knew his way not only from reviewing the plans of the building but also from coming through at night when he'd check on the building progress. Always at night to ensure he didn't run into Cali.

Room after room, he searched.

The man watching the security cameras said he hadn't seen her in about an hour.

Finally, he came to the last room, the employee breakroom.

As he walked in, Cali was just heading for the door, jacket on and her small purse in hand. She stopped short at the sight of him.

Several seconds of silence.

***

Cali didn't let herself say anything. Everything that came to mind seemed like a bad idea, so she just stood there. This may be the last time she saw him, so she tried

336

to memorize him—how even in jeans and a t-shirt he still exuded strength and power, the stubble always on his face, how his hair was in need of a cut, the intensity in his eyes.

"You're leaving," Asher finally said.

She nodded.

"Will you sit and talk with me for a few minutes first?"

She shrugged. "Okay."

"Outside?"

"Sure."

He led her out the back door, and around to the garden at the side of the building. The crowd on the sidewalk was gone, and this garden was partially obscured from the street by all the trees. The crepe myrtles were blooming white flowers, and she could smell jasmine blooming somewhere nearby. Cali wasn't sure why he'd paid out the extra expense for a garden, but she loved it. It was even more beautiful in the fading light. Shadows ran across the ground, and the white flowers seemed to suck in the fading light and glow among the darkening leaves.

He motioned for her to sit on one of the stone benches along the pea gravel path, and he sat on the one facing her, the path running between them.

"Are you happy with the building?" he asked.

She tried to smile but couldn't hike it up to her eyes. "It's beautiful."

"Good. I wanted it to be more than you could've dreamed."

He paused, and she asked, "Is that it? You just wanted to get my opinion of the building?" She scooted to the edge of the bench, ready to get up. She'd desperately wanted to see him, but now that he was sitting here across from her, it was torture.

"No." He held his hand up, a request for her to stay seated. "I'm just trying to figure out where to start."

"Where to start about what?"

He rested his elbows on his knees and looked down at his hands. Then he looked over at her. "You're safe. I've made sure of it."

"What do you mean?"

"I've been working with Ivy to make sure Libervis is completely disbanded. People will talk to her since she's Ivan's daughter, including their elite contacts—a senator and a supervisor in the NSA. They're done. The library is public. There's no more allure, no promise of some kind of magic in the pages. And she got a hold of Libervis' funds and gave most of it away to charity. She said most of the members seem to want to forget about the whole thing—maybe out of anger at Ivan, maybe out of embarrassment that they believed him so fully. But one way or another, they're done."

"And Ivy's safe?"

He nodded. "Matthew has been scouring the internet to find any hint of any remnants of Libervis. It's done. Ivy is free."

She took a breath and pressed her lips together in a small smile. "Thank you." Though she wondered why Ivy and Matthew hadn't told her all of this.

"And Dinetti is no longer a threat as well. I went to see him."

She sat straighter. "You what? Why would you do that?"

"To make sure he's done with you. To make sure he knows you're under my protection. He made it quite clear he doesn't want anything to do with you. He got his almost two million from Libervis. Your father is gone. He said in not so polite terms he has no wish to see you again."

She paused to process that. But then, she said, "But I'm not under your protection. Or I won't be once I leave and I'm not in this building every day."

"I've also been digging into my own past. I found someone with live contacts over there to verify. That family of the man I killed, they're almost all gone—killed in bombings and skirmishes. The only people left are second cousins who appear to have no emotional connection, no reason to come after me, and may not even realize who I am and what I did. And no one else seems to have realized I was the one who completed any of my other missions. There are no other people wanting to come after me." He paused. "I'm free."

She finally managed a real smile. "I'm so happy." Now she could leave him with the hope that he might finally move on.

He took a slow breath, glanced down at his hands, and back to her. He almost seemed…nervous? Asher Cross did not get nervous.

"What's wrong?"

"Nothing. Or I hope nothing." He paused. "I've been going nuts these past several months."

"Work stress?"

"No."

She waited.

"I've been praying that I could work everything out. I wouldn't let myself see you until I confirmed we're both safe."

"Why?"

"I couldn't… If it turned out that I couldn't make this work, I couldn't bear to spend more time with you."

She had no idea what he was saying.

"I told you how I feel," he said. "But I don't think you really understand. How could you when I basically yelled it at you? You may very well take all of that into account and decide the answer is no."

"The answer to what?"

"I love you, Cali. I've been in love with you for years. But I didn't think there was any way I could ever have you. I'm The Beast—a well-earned name. I've hidden away so long I barely know how to interact with people anymore. And with the way Rose died…I would never risk your life. I love you enough to put you first. You're always first."

She opened her mouth but had no idea what to say.

The pea gravel crunched as he sat down on both knees in front of her. "I know you'd agreed that we shouldn't be more than friends, but I'm here to ask you if you might be willing to give me a chance."

As she stared at him, her eyes filled with tears. She pressed her hand to her mouth.

"I understand if you need to think about it," he said. "I haven't been an easy man for you to deal with. But I want you to know it was all to protect you. I didn't handle everything as well as I should have. I just didn't know how else to keep you safe than to pretend to ignore you—it was all an act. I saw you, everything about you. Every fleck in your eyes, every hair on your head, every endearing unique trait, everything no one else saw. I saw you. I see you."

A tear broke her lash line and slid down her cheek.

She was so overwhelmed she couldn't talk.

He reached his hand out, paused, and then gently swept her tear away. He whispered, "Please."

She still couldn't get her voice to work.

"I'll give you time to think about it." He started to rise.

She grabbed his hand, squeezed hard.

He stopped.

She swallowed and managed to whisper, "I love you."

He watched her, carefully reading.

She moved her hand to the side of his face, his scars. Her voice was raspy from tears. "I see you too, how you risk yourself for others, even people you don't know, who can never repay you, who may not even ever know who you are. Even as the whole world calls you a beast, you are there in the shadows doling out kindness. For no other reason, apparently, than you want to help people. You're amazing, Asher. The most beautiful person I've ever known."

He rested his hand on hers. "Are you sure?"

She pulled him closer and brushed her lips against his. His breathing was instantly ragged, and he kissed her back. He was gentle, but she felt his need.

He abruptly broke the kiss, but stayed close, forehead touching hers.

She curled her fingers into his hair. Her voice shook. "I thought I was going to have to leave. I thought I was never going to get to see you again. I swear I died a little more every day."

He moved back a few inches, just enough so he could meet her eyes. "I'm sorry. I didn't think…"

She cut him off by touching her lips to his again.

Mouth still against hers, he whispered, "Will you marry me?"

"Yes," she said. "Right now." She could feel his smile against her lips.

Then he stood, took her hand, and led her down the path toward the road. She laughed as she jogged to keep up with him.

EPILOGUE

Asher woke with a start, burning up and covered in sweat. He heaved air into his lungs.

It was one of his recurring nightmares. He'd have thought he'd be so used to them by now, that the fear would've worn off. But it hadn't. Every time he saw that woman's terrified face as she was dragged away to be stoned to death by the Taliban, he felt exactly what he'd felt in that moment.

And then Cali was there.

She said nothing, never told him everything was okay. It wasn't for that woman. She'd surely been tortured and killed. Cali simply held his gaze and smoothed her hand over his face, even his scars, and through his hair. It didn't matter how long it took for him to calm down, she continued to soothe him.

While the dreams hurt him as much as they always had, they were becoming less frequent, and she helped him fall back asleep, which he'd never been able to do after one of the dreams before. He could see in her eyes how much she loved him. If someone like her could love him, maybe he was redeemable, even with his failures.

And she'd gotten him to tell her about other times

during his service, all the lives he'd helped save. He'd never thought much about them before. She never said as much, but he suspected she asked about those stories to help him remember, to be thankful he'd been there and was able to help, to make dealing with the failures feel a little more tolerable.

Her gentle caresses lulled him back to sleep, and he slept peacefully the rest of the night.

He woke to Willow standing on his chest and sniffing his face.

He glanced to the side to see Cali was out of bed and turned back to Willow. "Your favorite is unavailable?"

Willow meowed.

Then Asher heard the shower turn off. "Ah," he said to Willow. "You don't love her quite enough to follow her into the shower."

Willow meowed again.

Cali walked into the room wrapped in a towel. "I put the turkey in the oven."

"I meant to be up in time to do that." He sat up and cradled Willow to his chest.

She smiled at him. "You were sleeping so peacefully there was no way I was about to wake you."

"I'll help with the rest." He set Willow down and headed for the shower. On the way, he paused in front of Cali, held her face gently in both hands, and kissed her once softly.

After several hours and a lot of trial and error in the kitchen—neither he nor Cali were very good cooks, but they both wanted to do this themselves, rather than bring in a caterer—they sat at their new dining table for Thanksgiving dinner.

"I still cannot believe my Lovely Lady Lavender spurned me for another," Floyd bemoaned with the back of his hand to his forehead.

Matthew, seated next to Ivy, who was next to Cali, said to Floyd across the table, "A girly that pretty was never going to consider a flea like you."

"Sure, I would have," Cali said.

Floyd and Matthew, and even Bl@ze, looked at her with raised brows.

She addressed Floyd. "You never asked."

Floyd blinked.

"You talked an awful lot, but you never actually asked me to go on a date or anything."

Matthew burst out laughing.

Floyd opened his mouth but said nothing.

Asher said, "Your mistake was my opportunity. I had enough sense to go to her and beg."

"Beg?" Floyd asked.

"On my knees and everything."

Floyd flicked his index finger into the air. "Ah-ha! That is the key. If the mighty Asher Cross resorts to begging, then I shall do the same. The next fair maiden shall be mine!"

"Good luck," Matthew said through laughter.

Ivy turned to Cali and touched the wood tabletop next to her plate. "I love the furniture you picked. The front room is perfect for this house—just a touch formal to match the grandeur of the place but also super cozy. Those chairs by the fireplace eat you up when you sit in them. I could sit there and read for hours." She continued on about the décor Cali had chosen.

Asher had asked her to finish furnishing and decorating the house as a way to help her feel that the place was truly hers. He'd never thought he'd care, but he found himself enjoying the hominess she'd created. And Willow seemed to approve of all the additional soft places to lie down. He'd never felt more at home anywhere in his life. Though that was more to do with the brightness Cali brought. She'd given him more than he could've dreamed—beauty, kindness, friendship, challenge, and she'd even helped him build a relationship with God.

For a while, Asher simply sat there and watched his

wife and their friends and thanked God for his blessings. Cali looked over at Asher and smiled that small, contented smile that he saw on her face so much of the time now. She seemed to glow more every day.

HISTORICAL NOTES

The Golden Library, also known as The Lost Library, is debated to have been real, hidden below the Kremlin in Moscow. Many have searched for it, including Napoleon as mentioned in this story, and many have claimed to have seen it or found some kind of evidence for its existence. Ivan the Great was said to have compiled it, and Ivan the Terrible was said to believe it held black magic.

George Vanderbilt was actually a bibliophile, and I like to think he would have loved to be involved with saving such a library. His library was 20,000 volumes while he was alive. 10,000 of his books currently reside at Biltmore. (Be still my heart.)

William Morris Hunt, Biltmore architect, was known for being loyal to his clients, so it's believable that hiding a secret room and tunnel system from a client would have been hard on him. He did, unfortunately, die shortly before Biltmore was finished.

It's true that the music room was not finished and opened to the public until 1976, the same year that Cornelia, George Vanderbilt's daughter, died. Ms. Tate, however, is entirely fictional (to the best of my knowledge…).

DON'T MISS ANY OF MELISSA KOSLIN'S CHRISTIAN THRILLERS

"Do not start this book until you have the time to read it in one gulp. This is a really fresh twist on a marriage of convenience with the potential for pages of suspense. The hero and heroine are each hugely compelling, and I just wanted to protect them both. It's also a sweet story of the healing power of hope. Highly recommend this novel for those who adore romantic suspense with a fresh twist."

—**Cara Putman**, award-winning author of *Flight Risk* and *Lethal Intent*

Victim is a term that Liliana Vela refuses to call herself—she is a fighter. She fought her way out of the clutches of human traffickers who snatched her from her home in Mexico and has managed to escape to America. But she can't stay unless the man who helped rescue her is serious about his offer to marry her.

When Meric Toledan finds Liliana at a service station, terrified that she will be returned to the awful hands of her captors, he knows he must save her. He has the ability to keep her safe with his wealth and resources and knows he can't just leave her. But is safety truly possible when the mysterious buyer who demanded her capture still wants her—and will stop at nothing to have her?

Can a Former Sniper Stop a Deadly Bioattack Before It's Too Late?

ABOUT THE AUTHOR

Melissa Koslin is a fourth-degree black belt in and certified instructor of Songahm Taekwondo. In her day job as a commercial property manager, she secretly notes personal quirks and funny situations, ready to tweak them into colorful additions for her books. She and Corey, her husband of twenty-five years, and their young daughter live in Yulee, Florida, where they do their best not to melt in the sun. Find more information on her books at MelissaKoslin.com.

www.ingramcontent.com/pod-product-compliance
Lightning Source LLC
Chambersburg PA
CBHW070530260626
47161CB00002B/323